A GRIM AWAKENING

As I rose from the bed, gently removing Sarah's arm draped over my chest, something caught my eye.

Was I seeing things? I blinked and looked once more at the upstairs windows of Rauner Library. There it was again! A flash of light had shone ever so briefly; someone was in there with a torch.

Rauner had been dark when we returned to our room. Had we led whoever else was searching for the Pepys document there? But how had they got past the sophisticated security system?

I checked to make sure that the papers, now stowed in protective envelopes, were still safely taped to the bottom of the large bureau. They were . . . for the time being.

Even if we had led someone else to Rauner, there was nothing left for them to find. A smile spread slowly across my face; I let my eyes close.

Nothing left to find, I thought drowsily . . . unless they found *us*.

My eyes snapped open.

The Booklover's Mysteries
by Julie Kaewert

UNPRINTABLE*

UNBOUND*

UNTITLED*

UNSOLICITED*

UNSIGNED*

UNCATALOGUED*

*Available from Bantam Books

UNCATALOGUED

A BOOKLOVER'S MYSTERY

Julie Kaewert

BANTAM BOOKS

NEW YORK   TORONTO   LONDON   SYDNEY   AUCKLAND

UNCATALOGUED

A Bantam Crime Line Book / January 2002

Crime Line and the portrayal of a boxed "cl" are trademarks of
Bantam Books, a division of Random House, Inc.

ISBN 0-553-58220-8

Published simultaneously in the United States and Canada

Bantam Books are published by Bantam Books, a division of Random
House, Inc. Its trademark, consisting of the words "Bantam Books" and the
portrayal of a rooster, is Registered in U.S. Patent and Trademark Office and
in other countries. Marca Registrada. Bantam Books, 1540 Broadway, New
York, New York 10036.

PRINTED IN THE UNITED STATES OF AMERICA

OPM 10 9 8 7 6 5 4 3 2 1

For Charlie

ACKNOWLEDGMENTS

First and foremost, thanks to Philip Cronenwett, Special Collections Librarian of Rauner Library at Dartmouth College, for making this book a delight to research and write. I am extremely grateful for his sense of humour and generous assistance. Thanks, too to the Friends of the Dartmouth Library for welcoming me into the fold in such a kind way. Warning to all potential biblioklepts: there really are no secret, unsecured entrances to any of the Dartmouth libraries . . . except in Alex Plumtree's world! Also, any temporary hint of suspicion directed at Darmouth College in the plot of this book is purely for fictional fun. My much-loved alma mater and those associated with it have always proved themselves beyond reproach in both Alex's world and my own. While I'm setting the record straight, the Dartmouth Crew is a companionable and relatively civilized bunch. It has never deliberately destroyed a boat or indulged in anything but good-humored rivalry. In addition, the Lord Dartmouth who traveled with Pepys did not misbehave on the Tangier mission (to our knowledge), and had nothing whatsoever to do with the Second Earl of Dartmouth who donated money to found the college.

Thanks to the members of my critique group, Janet Fogg, Jim Hester and Karen Lin for their continuing help at all stages of all manuscripts. Thanks also to Diane Mott

Davidson for her constant encouragement. Barbara Peters of the Poisoned Pen mystery bookstore in Scottsdale generously introduced me to special collections experts Louis Silverstein and Monty Montee, formerly of Yale's Beinecke Library, who allowed me to see their amazing private collection. Although Louis died recently, his love for life and books, and his generosity of spirit, will live on in our memories.

Kathryn and Timothy Beecroft, as ever, deserve huge thanks for their forbearance of my constant questions, their insight into Samuel Pepys, and the stream of books on Pepys and all things English they share so generously.

Finally, things would never come out right for Alex without Kate Miciak's phenomenal editing skills, or Jane Steltenpohl's copyediting. My gratitude knows no bounds.

PROLOGUE #1

Excerpt from *The Plumtree Anthology of Seventeenth-Century Prose,* published by Plumtree Press, London and Boston, Tenth edition, 2002

Introduction to the works of Samuel Pepys
BY PETTIFER BARTLETT, PH.D., PROFESSOR
OF ENGLISH, DARTMOUTH COLLEGE

Samuel Pepys (pronounced PEEPS) was a seventeenth-century Londoner best known for the meticulous diary he kept from 1660 to 1669, between the ages of twenty-seven and thirty-six. He could not have imagined that his diary would one day become the world's most illuminating—and entertaining—chronicle of the events of his time. Providing a valuable record of the nature of daily life in Restoration England, he also recorded the coronation of Charles II (1660), London's Great Plague (1665), and the Great Fire (1666), all in meticulous detail.

Pepys never imagined anyone else would read his diary. Not only is the publication of diaries a relatively recent phenomenon, but Pepys's use of "Shelton's Tachygraphy," or speedwriting, effectively encoded his prose. To further protect the less seemly aspects of his life, including his frequent dalliances with housemaids, he embellished his shorthand with foreign words and phrases. To the modern eye these attempts at subterfuge are charming in their naiveté. Because Pepys seems to have had no fear of his code being broken, we know his innermost thoughts and most private encounters—with his wife, his maids, his friends, and even his monarch. Pepys also had a habit of recording his discussions with the important men of his day, such as King Charles II, the Duke of York (who later became King James II), and Sir Isaac Newton, discussions which provide valuable insight into these public figures. We read his impressions of premiere performances of plays such as *Macbeth,* before Shakespeare was a legend. Pepys took stock of his life at the end of each year, and as he tallies up his finances, silver plate, wigs and clothing, we gain an idea of what was valued in his time.

Pepys was born in London, the son of a tailor, in 1633. He attended prestigious St Paul's School in London, and then Magdalene (pronounced MAUDLIN) College at Cambridge University. Although Pepys was born into a humble branch of the family which his father later relocated to Brampton, near Cambridge, his diary provided him with a far more lasting legacy than that of the aristocratic relative who started him on his career. Edward Mountagu, the first Earl of Sandwich (referred to throughout Pepys's diary as "my lord"), gave young Pepys a job first as his secretary, or domestic steward. From his association with Mountagu, Pepys rose to the lofty position of secretary to the admiralty. Years after discontinuing the diary, he was asked to travel to Tangier with Lord Dartmouth to evaluate England's money-losing establishment there.

Pepys was an avid bibliophile. After his diary, his greatest legacy to mankind is his book collection, which includes the six leatherbound volumes of the diary. The entire collection can be viewed today at the Pepys Library at Magdalene College, Cambridge University.

PROLOGUE #2

And thus ends all that I doubt I shall ever be able to do with my own eyes in the keeping of my Journall, I being not able to do it any longer, having done now so long as to undo my eyes almost every time that I take a pen in my hand; and therefore, whatever comes of it, I must forbear: and therefore resolve, from this time forward to have it kept by my people in longhand, and must be contented to set down no more than is fit for them and all the world to know; or if there be any thing, I must endeavour to keep a margin in my book open, to add here and there a note in short-hand with my own hand. And so I betake myself to that course, which is almost as much as to see myself go into my grave: for which, and all the discomforts that will accompany my being blind, the good God prepare me!

SAMUEL PEPYS
31 MAY 1669

CHAPTER 1

. . . it ravished me . . . that neither then, nor all the evening . . . and at home, I was able to think of any thing, but remained all night transported . . .

Sarah! *Darling.* Say it again—all of it. Please."

Disbelief warred with joy as I struggled to grasp my fiancée's words, the very words I'd wanted to hear.

Rich and exuberant, her laugh reverberated down the line. "I said, my work here is over, Alex. I'm coming home!"

A grin spread across my face. I'd read news reports of the power shift in Iraq, where my American fiancée was involved in something frightfully secret for an international task force. But I hadn't dreamed . . . "And the next bit?"

"I asked you what you would think of a very small, private wedding in Nantucket."

"*When* exactly, did you say?"

"I didn't." A pause. I could see her smile in my mind's eye. "But how soon could you get there?"

It was Sunday noon now. . . . With an incredulous laugh, I said, "How *soon*?! Are you joking?"

I stopped pacing and stared through the French doors into the rose garden. The garden was in all its early glory, the first blooms blazing in every possible shade of pink, red, and yellow. As a shaft of light broke through the blanket of cloud and spotlighted the roses, I decided she was absolutely right. We should do it quickly, make certain nothing got in our way.

"I'll try for the next flight to Boston, my love. I think it's around half-ten in the morning—"

"Hang on, Alex—I can't get to Nantucket until late Tuesday. But could you make it by then? Wedding in the back garden on Wednesday?"

I could hardly believe my ears. "Nothing could *stop* me getting there on Tuesday. I speak for Ian, too, of course. This is *marvellous!* Sarah, this is the best news possible . . . it's . . ."

"Yes?"

"It's *perfect.*" Thoughtlessly I added, "I'll ring the College and cancel my reservations for the reunion."

"The reunion! I'd forgotten all about it—but wait . . . don't cancel. We could always—"

"No. *Absolutely* not. We are not delaying this wedding one instant beyond the very first moment it can take place . . . and certainly not for a college reunion."

"Hey, wait! I'm not suggesting we delay the wedding— only that we *both* go to the reunion. Together, Alex. I've never had the chance to go—it could be part of our honeymoon! We could spend a couple of days somewhere on Nantucket before we drive up to Dartmouth for the weekend. Afterwards, we could go back for some sailing."

"Sounds *stellar*, but darling—are you *sure* that's all right with you?" Sarah and I hailed from the same infamous class of '86 at Dartmouth, and we'd known a lot of the same people. In fact, she'd married my close friend and roommate from Richardson Hall, only to watch him die five years later. She knew that my crew buddies were all coming to relive past glory in the Reunion Row on Saturday, but I didn't want her to feel obliged to go.

"*Yes,* I'm sure! It'll be great fun—I haven't seen everyone in ages. And Alex, I want you to know . . ." Her tone changed; she grew serious. "Everything's going to be all right. It really *is,* this time. I know it."

I grinned at the conviction behind her words. What both of us felt was hope—hope that on our third attempt at being joined in matrimony, we would not be interrupted by ruthless gunmen, international terrorists, or other shocking crises.

Sarah's intuition was right: no crisis struck until after we'd been safely pronounced man and wife. For that I was deeply grateful. But not long afterward, I found myself risking life and limb for nothing more than a handful of loose pages casually scrawled in the seventeenth century. Plumtree Press, my family's small publishing firm, would again publish a volume—obscurely related to those pages—with unforeseen consequences. The combined forces of history and literature would rage against the injustices of mankind until the truth was revealed.

In other words, business as usual.

CHAPTER 2

This put us at the Board into a tosse.

*. . . he giving me caution as to myself, that there are
those that are my enemies as well as his . . . So that he
advises me to stand on my guard; which I shall do . . ."*

*. . . wherein I shall come to be questioned in that busi-
ness myself; which do trouble me.*

SAMUEL PEPYS

The phone was still warm from my talk with Sarah—I'd
tossed it onto the sofa to dance a spirited jig round the library—when it rang again.

"Alex Plumtree," I answered, still grinning.

"Alex! My, don't you sound full of beans. Percival
Urchfont here."

Ah. Chairman of our board of overseers at the Pepys
Library at Magdalene College, Cambridge. My father had
once held Urchfont's lofty position; several months ago
I'd accepted the post of treasurer.

"Hullo, Percy. How are you?"

"I'm afraid I've been better, Alex. We've a serious problem at the Library. I'm calling an extraordinary meeting
of the board for this afternoon . . . and I'm afraid we
really need you there. I'd tell you over the phone, but

given the nature of the difficulty . . . could you possibly make it by three?"

Inwardly I groaned. *I'm off to America to be married, for heaven's sake! I have a tuxedo to pack, a honeymoon to plan . . .*

"If you really need me, I'll be there, Percy. But . . . can't you give us a hint?"

"Sorry, I'll tell all when you get here. Thanks, Plumtree. I know this is inconvenient, but I promise you it's absolutely vital."

We signed off with all the gravity that might be accorded a national emergency. But after an instant of reflection, and five minutes on the computer to book Ian's and my flight to Boston, I continued my dance—this time in the direction of the garage.

As I drove north under increasingly grey skies, the Pepys Library was not uppermost in my mind. Visions of Sarah—her radiant face at our wedding, in my arms alone *after* the wedding, sunbathing on the *Carpe Diem*, the family yacht where we'd spend part of our honeymoon—dominated. More than once I found myself humming like a fool as I sped along. *It was happening. At last!*

But as I turned east off the M1 towards Cambridge a couple of hours later, I saw the road signposted for Huntingdon. Samuel Pepys, the famous diarist whose priceless collection of books was housed in the Pepys Library, had grown up just outside Huntingdon in the village of Brampton. (Coincidentally, part of the Plumtree clan hailed from that same burg.) Pepys had made pilgrimages there all his life to see his father.

What on earth was going on at the Pepys Library that required such an urgent meeting? The most exciting event in recent memory had been a visit by Prince Charles, four years ago.

And then I realised . . . this might be the request for The Donation. I'd never been under any illusion about the reason for my presence on the board of overseers—or my father's. We had an excellent private collection of books, and the Plumtree Collection happened to include several fine items related to Pepys. Although Pepys had been quite specific about his library not containing anything but his books, from time to time people became ambitious for the library and wanted to expand the collection. Rousing speeches along the lines of, "we owe it to the memory of Pepys to acquire so-and-so," and "we are *obliged* to serve as the finest repository of Pepys-related literature on the face of the earth," were not rare. The Board was led at the moment by two such nobly acquisitive men, Percival Urchfont and Charles Mattingley. I knew that one day they would ask me to relinquish our family's private treasures, and I didn't doubt that I would do so. They *belonged* in the world's greatest Pepys repository. It was just that they held particular sentimental value. . . .

And then I was in Cambridge, piloting the Passat through the narrow streets. The nightmare of finding a parking space was cut short by virtue of the hour and day, and it was just ten past three as I strolled through the gate off Magdalene Street into my old postgraduate college.

The porter nodded at me as I passed through the lodge; I smiled back. Even through a veil of misting rain, the manicured courtyard of emerald grass, lined with bright blooms and studded with ornamental fruit trees, was breathtaking after the grey of Magdalene Street. While it is true that Magdalene is far from the most prestigious of Cambridge's colleges—its buildings fewer and less imposing than some of the grander institutions—it is the proud proprietor of the Pepys Library.

The Library had been the draw for me as a postgraduate, as it had for generations of Plumtrees before. Samuel Pepys had written his famous six-volume, nine-year diary in the late seventeenth century and recorded everything from the plague to the Fire of London to the decadent court of King Charles II. As Pepys had once studied within Magdalene's hallowed halls, the College had been fortunate enough to inherit his magnificent collection of books.

I passed from the front courtyard into the rear quadrant and saw the pale stone structure, glowing like a beacon through the damp and drizzle. The Library was positioned as the ultimate destination within the College, tucked protectively within Magdalene's brick walls and lesser buildings. Striding along the gravel footpath, I noted with fondness the slight asymmetry of the building's Georgian facade. The architect, or perhaps the builders (no one quite knew which), may have had one pint too many during the final measurements.

I smiled at the irony: The charming irregularity of the building only served to give it more character . . . to make it more like Pepys himself, not to mention his prose. Part of the wonder of all things Pepysian was their uniform asymmetry. The famous diarist's sinful yet moral life, the prose which should be so stultifying but is unexpectedly vivid and pertinent to life in any era, this Library building in his name, even the "presses" that held his books—all were delightfully, lopsidedly, unconventional.

At last I reached the Library steps and started to climb, my mood darkened by the unavoidable memory that only months ago—in the very same overly eventful week that a murderer had lurked in my back seat not so far from here—one of Plumtree Press's scholarly authors had climbed this staircase for the last time. His demise would forever change this place.

Perhaps that was why I had been summoned to Cambridge, and it had nothing to do with The Donation. Perhaps my author's death in the Library had resulted in an increased premium with the insurance company, or caused some similar ripple in the institution's customary calm.

"Plumtree!" I might have been the prodigal son, so heartily did Urchfont greet me as I entered the main room of the Library. Urchfont resembled nothing so much as a bulldog in country squire's clothing. He was gruff, sturdy and compact, and his close-cropped hair stuck out stiffly from his scalp. When he shook his head in disapproval of some idea, his jowls rippled from side to side with an astounding range of motion.

Now, as he rose from the long table and barrelled towards me with his hand outstretched, I was surprised to notice that there were only three of us in the room. That was odd; I'd expected the entire board. Charles Mattingley, secretary of the board, remained seated, looking very serious indeed.

"Hello, Percival"—Urchfont shook my hand with the relentless grip of a stevedore—"Charles." I nodded and briefly shook hands with Mattingley. Mattingley's hand, as usual, was cold and slack, but his eyes shone with sharp intelligence. Mattingley was as reserved, elegant, and dignified as Urchfont was not. He was older than Urchfont, nearing eighty, and much taller—though slightly stooped. His voice came out in a raspy whisper, which was no doubt caused by a physical disorder but never failed to give the impression that he simply couldn't be bothered to speak up. Impeccably attired as always, he wore a lightweight suit with a pale blue tie that brought out the blue in his eyes—which were magnified to almost frightening proportions by a pair of old-fashioned, wire-rimmed spectacles. Wisps of white hair provided fragile cover for his shiny pink pate.

As usual, we met in the heart of the Library itself—in the very shadow of the famous "presses" (as Pepys had called his custom-made bookcases) brimming with priceless contents. As I sat, I was aware of them behind me.

"Thanks for making the drive up, Alex," Mattingley said in a hoarse whisper.

"Not at all. I'm desperately curious to hear what's happened."

Urchfont glanced at his watch and said, "I've arranged for some tea, but let's get started. To bring you up to date, Plumtree, we are faced with two rather unusual circumstances." He pursed his ample lips. "The first is a financial issue."

Here we go, I thought. *Now, for The Donation speech . . .*

"A shocking sum has gone missing from the Library's Perpetuity Fund. As you know, the Fund was to provide for the future of the Library—the physical building itself, any repairs that might be required over time to the structure, and of course any acquisitions that might come our way."

I frowned. This was a bizarre turn for the staid old institution, and extremely serious indeed. It was a little-known secret that despite its renown, the Pepys Library was far from well-endowed. Perilously close to the edge was a more accurate description. Moreover, since I was treasurer, any financial problems were entirely my responsibility.

"How much is missing?"

"A quarter of a million pounds."

I blinked. "Good heavens. That's—"

Urchfont nodded. "Yes. That's nearly the lot. And as if that isn't bad enough, we've heard a most extraordinary rumour, which we felt you should be informed of privately. The fund manager claims that you extracted the money to an account in your name. Naturally, we told him he must be mistaken . . . but he was adamant. We need you to clear this up as soon as possible."

I bristled at the false accusation, then told myself to calm down. "Some mix-up at the bank must be to blame . . . the manager, Ryan, *knows* that all three of us would have to sign to authorise a withdrawal of that amount. How odd that he didn't ring me immediately! Of course I'll clear it up right away."

Urchfont nodded briskly; Mattingley appeared to study the grain of the wood in the table in front of him.

"I'm afraid there's more, Plumtree," Urchfont continued. "You've gained a reputation for getting to the bottom of the most impenetrable tangles . . . and you're something of an authority on Pepys."

"Oh, I wouldn't say—"

"Mattingley?" Urchfont interrupted my disavowal and nodded to his colleague.

Mattingley cleared his throat and folded his large hands on the table with delicacy. "Some extraordinary papers have come to light." I leaned forward to better catch the nearly inaudible whisper. "It's possible that these papers *might* prove to be a continuation of Pepys's diary."

I nearly toppled off my chair. For both scholarly and popular Pepys-lovers, this rivalled the discovery of fire. "Where? Who has them?"

Mattingley cast a peevish glance at me, then at Urchfont. "If only we knew. This is all the vaguest rumour, Alex. But if by some chance it is true, I think you'll agree that for the sake of its future, the Pepys Library must acquire the papers."

I nodded. It was an issue not only of prestige but obligation. "Yes, I see what you mean. Er, but even if we had the money, we'd need to know where to obtain them. Do you have *any* idea . . . ?"

The old man sighed and closed his eyes briefly. Was he fed up with me, or with the situation?

"Pettifer Bartlett wrote to me," he rasped, "saying he'd seen the find mentioned in one of these Internet chat rooms for collectors."

I felt another frisson of unease; Pettifer Bartlett had been the Dartmouth professor responsible for my interest in Pepys. Bartlett had made numerous pilgrimages to the Pepys Library in Cambridge and we had stayed in touch through the years—he'd been born in England, and had known my father. Plumtree Press had, in fact, published a

seventeenth-century anthology of literature including a
section on Pepys revised by Bartlett some twenty years
ago. It wasn't that I didn't like Bartlett; on the contrary.
But too many Pepys-related personalities cropping up at
once started me worrying.

Mattingley continued. "Of course Bartlett immediately
thought of us here at the Library. Evidently whoever has
the papers wanted to remain anonymous, but was interested in learning how much money he could get for
them—if in fact they are Pepys's."

"Greedy so-and-so," Urchfont muttered as a brisk
knock sounded at the door. "Ah, that'll be the tea." The
door swung open and a uniformed young man entered
with a tray. "Wonderful, thank you."

Mattingley watched until the waiter had left the room.
"Alex, we need you to work out who has these papers—
and then help us acquire them. You've a great deal of experience in antiquarian acquisitions—it's in your blood.
And perhaps, until the insurance money comes through
for our loss, you might help us fund the acquisition. It
won't be long before these papers are snatched up—by
someone."

Ah. There we were at last. At least they hadn't asked for
my Pepys edition . . . yet.

"Mattingley and I have agreed to chip in," Urchfont
added, pouring the tea. "We thought you might like to
help."

"Yes, of course." I accepted a cup from him. "Besides
finding out what's become of our money, I suppose the
most immediate need is for me to get in touch with this
purveyor of the papers. Find out exactly what he's claiming about them."

Mattingley pulled an envelope from the inside pocket of his jacket and passed it to me with a hand that trembled with a mild palsy. "This is the printout from the news page of Pepysiana—the Internet site for Pepys enthusiasts and collectors. You may keep it. As you will see, you may be uniquely qualified to deal with this matter."

Scanning the page, I saw that the work was reputed to be in America, at Dartmouth College. How remarkable. My American mother's family's time-honoured tradition dictated that all males attend the small New Hampshire college. Perhaps Urchfont and Mattingley had recalled this obscure biographical detail.

Further down the page, I spied the words "Shelton's Tachygraphy" and discovered another reason why they'd called upon me.

Few scholarly domains are more obscure than mine. In the pursuit of my master's degree at Magdalene, I'd felt compelled to go back to the raw text of the diarist's papers and translate them for myself from the shorthand he'd used. Shorthand had been something of a fascination in seventeenth-century England, and nothing short of an obsession for Pepys. He used it for practical reasons, too; not only did it save time, but it saved his eyes. Pepys's sight had already begun to fail at the tender age of twenty-seven, when he began the diary. When he discontinued it nine years later, deteriorating eyesight was to blame.

This, too, made me feel something of a kinship with Pepys: my own eyes had started failing at roughly the same age. To make matters worse, now that I was nearly the age Pepys had been when his eyes forced him to cut the diary short, some unsavoury characters had deliberately injured my eyes. As recently as eight months ago, I'd faced the possibility of total blindness. To my never-ending gratitude, the acid had only severely damaged the sight in one eye—but I never forgot that if I wasn't careful I'd be walking with a white stick.

At any rate, I'd learned the shorthand as a sort of homage to the diarist. It would have been a crime, I thought, to study Pepys at his own college and not use the original documents. I'd held the venerable volumes in my own two hands in this very room, at Pepys's own library table—a thrill that made the ordeal of mastering Shelton's strange shorthand pale into insignificance. I was perhaps one of the few alive to possess this privileged—and for all practical purposes useless—knowledge. I felt an unreasonable thrill at the thought that it might be useful now.

"I see," I said, and tucked the letter back into its envelope. "The owner is stymied by the shorthand code, he can't decipher the document to determine whether it's really Pepys's. Is that it?"

Urchfont nodded. "You're with us, then, Plumtree." His gruff question came out sounding more like a declaration.

"Absolutely. The only obstacle will be getting a look at it."

"Do what you must, Plumtree. Mattingley and I will be on hand to help in any way we can. You know our phone numbers. Call any time at all, at any hour."

"I should tell you I'm going on holiday tomorrow," I said, privately enjoying the understatement. These men hadn't come to learn about my private life, and I wouldn't force them to congratulate me while they were mourning the ill fortunes of their beloved library. "But the trip could be to our advantage. I'm going to America, partly for a reunion at Dartmouth College. Pettifer is there, of course, and I know the special collections librarian. Perhaps they can help me track down the owner, speak to him in person—even view the documents."

"How very fortuitous!" Urchfont exclaimed. Normally the fact that I'd attended university in the colonies won me no points, but in this case it would accrue to my credit. "I don't want to say offer the moon, Plumtree, but . . . well, you understand the importance of this."

"Don't worry. This is one business I know well." I gave an encouraging smile, but the two men didn't look particularly cheered.

"Listen to me, Plumtree." Urchfont's sea-green eyes held my gaze with disturbing intensity. "I know you're well acquainted with the world of books, and Pepys in particular. But there are unscrupulous private collectors who would do virtually anything to get their hands on those papers."

As would you, I thought, with fondness for these elderly Pepys fanatics.

"You have, no doubt, heard the rumours about the contents of the lost Tangier diary extension . . . how damaging they might be to the royal family. What I mean to say is—be careful, won't you, Plumtree?"

I had heard the rumours . . . but dismissed them as the fabrications of a few dissatisfied anti-Royalists. Historical gossip held that the royals—in the 1660s, long before Pepys had been asked to travel to Tangier with Lord Dartmouth on an information-gathering trip—had deprived the people of an herb that could have saved them from the plague, while using it to save themselves. Supposedly, English royalty from the Stuarts to the Windsors had struggled to cover up this unconscionable crime—it had become a symbol of royalty's privilege and disregard for the needs of the people. Whenever talk of abolishing the monarchy was resurrected after some royal slip-up, the rumours were dragged out for another go-round, casting the royals in a bad light. Since it seemed doubtful that any such extension of Pepys's diary existed, and since it had nothing to do with the *current* monarch's character anyway, it had always seemed a pointless debate to me.

Still, as the master of one obscure scholarly domain, I should have known better than to be dismissive of another.

CHAPTER 3

Some discourse of the Queene's being very sick if not dead, the Duke and Duchesse of York being sent for betimes this morning. . . .

. . . and it may be that there is some fear of his being . . . heire to the Crown.

But she hath been a handsome woman, and is, it seems, not only a lewd woman, but very high-spirited.

SAMUEL PEPYS

When I arrived back at the Orchard, my childhood home (and soon, I hoped, to be the home of my own children) I found that the affairs of the Pepys Library were child's play compared to what had happened in Windsor that day.

In a lull before the storm, I stood for a moment and relished the quiet calm of the Plumtree family home. The character-filled brick house dated from the seventeenth century, and could only be reached down a long, winding drive lined with ancient hedges. As I grew older, I came to appreciate that path as a sort of cleansing journey between the outside world and home. By the time I'd travelled it, I was usually at peace—and so it was today.

Ian's presence was particularly comforting; I knew he

would be back from his Sunday afternoon run and ramble by now. Ian Higginbotham, Sarah's grandfather and a second father to me, not to mention my partner at Plumtree Press, was living at the Orchard temporarily. I was converting the tenant farmer's house on our property into a proper country bungalow for him. Ian had just turned seventy-seven and had backed off from his former stance of extreme independence. A house within shouting distance of his granddaughter in a nice, quiet village like Chorleywood had begun to appeal, and Sarah and I were thrilled.

Even living in the same house didn't diminish the glow of Ian's halo. Frequent contact only seemed to burnish it. He seemed immune from those casual irritations that often crop up in close quarters, and for my part, the more time I spent around him the better I felt. His gentleness, calm, and wisdom are qualities I struggle to emulate, along with his habit of constantly occupying himself with some productive or healthful activity. Even the man's physical form is impressive. Pushing eighty his muscles are as firm, his heart rate as low during a run as mine. Unlike Mattingley, his six-foot-one form is not at all curved with age, his baby-blue eyes (and handshake) are warm, and his head sports a profusion of white hair that reinforces the illusion of a halo.

I could hardly wait to tell him the news about the wedding; he would certainly want to join me in travelling to the States for the ceremony. But as I left the kitchen to find him, I recognised a most unusual sound intruding on the silence: the squawk of the television in the library. Ian never, *ever* watched TV. . . .

Concerned that Ian of all people would resort to the

spoon-feeding of what he called "intellectual pablum," I walked into the library and said hello. Ian glanced up with troubled eyes, lifted a subdued hand in greeting, and immediately reattached his eyes to the screen. Dropping into one of the big leather chairs, I tried to gauge the seriousness of things, keeping one eye on Ian and one on the telly.

As it happened, the situation was very serious indeed. The instant I saw the topic at hand I knew my news must wait until this had run its course.

To fully comprehend the significance of what I'm about to relate, you must understand that Ian is only slightly older than Queen Elizabeth. He worries about her as if she were his younger sister. He adores the monarch, monitoring her schedule and listening to her radio and television addresses with utter dedication. For him, discussions of abdication and succession carry all the weight of life and death. He worries about her unrelenting work schedule, the rigour of her tours, and how she would cope with any further *anni horribiles.* I love this about Ian, and have often thought that when he lost his wife during the war years he'd transferred some of his devotion to Her Majesty.

A television news reporter who had trouble making her "s" sound was saying, "Once again, late this afternoon, the Queen was injured when her favourite mare reared, apparently spooked, for reasons still unknown. Her Majesty was thrown and struck her head on a fencepost. The Monarch is resting comfortably under her doctor's care at Windsor Castle. Here's the announcement made by Buckingham Palace today."

An elderly gent, his image undergirded by the words

"Aide to Buckingham Palace," appeared and gave voice. "Her Majesty is safe and well. No serious injury was sustained in the fall, and the Queen is in excellent spirits. There is no cause for alarm whatsoever."

"No," Ian said, almost to himself. His tone was uncharacteristically suspicious.

"Sorry?"

He shook his head, still frowning at the television. "There's something they're not telling us. Her Majesty would agree to appear on television herself if she were well, to forestall public worry. Her injuries *must* be worse than they're letting on."

Good heavens. Queen Elizabeth had always been so strong, so steady, so unflappable. I'd never considered what would happen if she were seriously incapacitated. The mind boggled.

"That's not all, Alex." Wearing a grim expression, he nodded at the television.

I turned my gaze back to the lisping, short-skirted TV journalist on camera in front of Windsor Castle. "And so tonight everyone is talking about succession ... and Prince Charles's latest *faux pas*. Our religion correspondent, Tom Darrow, is standing by tonight. ... Hello, Tom."

"Good evening, Cassandra."

"Tom, do you think Prince Charles's comments today at the Foundation for Ecumenical Multiculturalism's festival, labelling the Anglican church an anachronism, will cause the Queen to pass over him in favour of Prince William?"

"That's the question everyone's asking tonight, Cassandra. But the real issue now, of course, is whether the

Queen is *capable* of naming her successor. If she's not *compos mentis*, for whatever reason, I understand there is a document that makes her wishes known in the case of her untimely death. Now as you know, when Prince Charles publicly embraced alternative religions some time ago, there was discussion of Her Majesty leaning towards William instead of Charles, if she were to give up the crown. She's made it quite clear that she has no intention of abdicating, but this head injury is summoning up images of a disabled queen who must be succeeded."

"Oh no," I said.

"Oh yes," Ian answered, turning to really look at me for the first time. His blue eyes shone with startling brilliance. "You see the problem. When, and how, will they decide that she's unable to reign and break the seal on her Statement of Succession? If they do, one or the other heir—and the forces behind them—will claim that it's not valid, because of the circumstances of Her Majesty's injury. The argument could go on for years. It could utterly undermine the monarchy—which is exactly what certain people would like to see happen."

I sat with him in silent commiseration for several minutes while the television droned on. This was a crisis of some magnitude for Ian. Perhaps food would calm him and prepare him for happier news. "Shall I bring you some dinner in here?"

He never took his eyes off the screen. "Yes, thank you, Alex."

I was almost through the door when he added, "Kind of you." This distracted manner was very unlike my adopted father. . . . Deeply concerned, I padded into the kitchen and opened the fridge door. With relief I saw the remains of last night's sesame broccoli tofu (Ian made healthful foods taste like decadent delights) and a large bowl mounded with fluffy, aromatic basmati rice. I prepared two large rice bowls topped with the good stuff, covered them and stuck them in the microwave. I switched on the kettle for Ian's herb tea, and was uncorking a bottle of white burgundy for myself when the telephone rang.

"Alex Plumtree."

There was a slight pause, then a female American voice. "Alex! It's me, Mattie."

"Mattie!" My old girlfriend's voice swept me back fifteen years in an instant. Mattie was a very live wire I'd dated in college on the rebound, after Sarah rejected me for my more marriageable room-mate. I still flushed with shame at the thought of that episode in my life. But at the time, our similarities were too great to ignore: Mattie Harding came from a long line of bibliophiles and was coxswain for our heavyweight eight.

"What a bolt from the blue," I said, recovering my equilibrium. "You sound just the same. It's been years and years . . ."

"Too many. In fact, I'm calling to see if you're coming to the reunion. I assume you've heard that anyone who isn't there will be keel-hauled from the crew launch in future."

I laughed. "I have no choice, then. I'll have to come."

"Seriously—*are* you?"

Her intensity took me by surprise; why was she so concerned about my presence at the reunion? "Yes, actually, I am. I wouldn't miss this for anything—a promise is a promise." I was reluctant to drop the bomb that I would be arriving married . . . to a fellow '86.

"Still the same Alex, I see. Look, I know I've left it a bit late, but I wondered if you could stay at the farmhouse for the reunion. Come a day early—maybe take a hike, have a practice session for the Reunion Row . . ."

Mattie's family had long enjoyed a vacation home they all called "the farmhouse," a rambling stone mansion set in the midst of two hundred acres of Vermont countryside. It had been the site of some of our more . . . well, never mind.

I hesitated. I'd have to tell her.

"Mattie, that's awfully kind of you. But if you can believe it, I'm marrying Sarah Townsend the day after tomorrow. The reunion's going to be part of our honeymoon."

After an unmistakable hesitation, she replied with forced gaiety. "Alex, that's wonderful! Say no more. You've got a suite at the Inn, then, I suppose." The Hanover Inn was the College's own delightful hostelry at the heart of the campus.

"Not exactly . . . more like my old dorm room in Richardson. When in Hanover, etcetera."

I heard a stifled choking sound, and then her bravest voice saying, "God, Alex, that's so like you."

Uh-oh, I thought. Residual feelings of affection, evidently . . . and to my astonishment, I felt a surprisingly strong fondness for her. Shared experience, no doubt. Perfectly natural, I told myself. *Say something, Alex . . .*

"Matt, I'd love to get together, though—how about that hike on Friday?"

"Sounds perfect. Sarah's welcome, too, of course—I always did like her. Tall enough for you, too." She hurried on. "By the way, Alex, I need your advice on something. Didn't you study Pepys in graduate school?"

Pepys again. I cringed.

"Yes," I replied, a bit hesitantly. "Why?"

"I'll tell you when you get here. See you Friday morning, here at the farmhouse. Okay?"

"Great! See you then."

Mattie Harding . . . now *that* was a surprise. I shook my head as I returned from the sudden and not entirely pleasant voyage through time and made Ian's tea. Could her Pepys question have anything to do with the Pepysiana posting? I poured a glass of the wine and pulled chopsticks from the drawer.

When I carried the steaming bowls on trays to the library, Ian looked up for a moment and accepted his dinner with halfhearted thanks. The only other time I'd seen him like this had been after my father's death. Then as now, I thought he was not only mourning his friend but the inevitability of his own demise. I prayed that the Queen would make a speedy and complete recovery not only for her sake, but for Ian's.

I carried my mobile dinner to the far side of the room where the Pepys collection had nearly always been kept. Chewing, I swung open the doors to the garden and let the cool evening air into the library. Then I turned back to the books and regarded the twenty Pepys spines with affection. Pepys, Pepys, Pepys. There were *Pepys, the man,* by Samuel Butler (a signed first edition), half a dozen lesser and two very different sets of six volumes each of the Pepys diary—both quite valuable in their own ways. But by far the most prized was Pepys's own copy of *Shelton's Tachygraphy,* with his notes hand penned in the margins.

I set the bowl down on a desk and reached up to the shelf where the diarist's shorthand book lived. I drew it out with a bit of caution, as though it might spring to life in my hands.

There was no denying the exceptional beauty of the volume. Octavo-sized and handsomely custom bound in dark green calf, the cover had been tooled and gilded with Pepys's own rope-and-birds device. This was the museum piece, and the book with the most sentimental value: my father had reclaimed it from the British Library in 1987, where it had been on loan for roughly a century, and presented it to me in the privacy of this very room. I could still hear the echoes of his words.

"Well done, Alex—you must have this, now you're such an expert on old Pepys. I've no idea what you'll do with your—er—rather *specialised* knowledge . . . but I've no doubt you'll find it useful."

Now, as I blinked tears away, I was grateful for my father—and also for his trust. He'd been too kind to say that he didn't really believe the strange code Pepys had used to write his diaries had been a worthy topic for my thesis. Yet he hadn't hesitated to give me one of the family's greatest treasures. A picture-perfect representation of his entire life, I thought. He had always found ways to encourage me to pursue my dreams, whether he saw purpose in them or not.

What had I done in return? Thanked him, realising the enormity of the gift . . . then informed him over port, just where Ian was sitting now, that I planned to spend the rest of my life sailing in the Mediterranean. My noble father had thought for a moment, raised his glass with a smile, and said, "Then may the wind be always at your back, Alex."

I hoped I'd have the chance to *try* to be the sort of father he'd been to me.

Returning to the leather chair, I cast a glance at Ian. Eating, but spellbound. Some doctor or other was offering his opinion of the Queen's injury. When could I possibly interrupt him, tell him of the other earthshaking event of the day?

I retreated to the book in my lap for the moment. Like many old books, it had extraordinary weight to it—almost felt made of wood. And this had been only a manual for Pepys—the equivalent of a paperback thesaurus in modern times! The patina of the dark leather cover almost shone, a perfect backdrop for Pepys's crest. The tooling was extremely detailed, showing a peacock, a pheasant, and other avian specimens strutting and flying about around the letters of his name: *Samuel Pepys, Esquire,* in a fine italic script. Below the second "P" of Pepys an intricate knot extended from the stem of the letter, fading into peacock feathers at the edges. Even if I hadn't known Pepy's life from my studies, I still would have discerned that the knot represented something nautical: an inscription, "*Secretary to the admiralty for King Charles II & King James II,*" adorned the bottom of the oval crest, lest anyone miss Pepys's elevated position.

The birds, I knew, were meant to reflect his leadership of the Royal Society, the most respected scientific body of Pepys's day. He couldn't have known, but one of the most collectible books (besides his own, of course) in all history had been published under his auspices at the Royal Society: his friend Sir Isaac Newton's *Principia*.

I opened the cover and carefully turned the pages. Pepys's book had been beautifully printed in a Caxton font on thick, soft paper. Because it had been so well cared for, it was in excellent condition—truly a joy to behold. The smell of history added to the enjoyment; the book didn't carry a musty odour, but rather one of indefinable complexity. Perhaps it had recorded its first four hundred and fifty years of existence by osmosis. I tried to imagine Pepys holding the book as he read it in his own library at home, in York's Buildings in Westminster.

I would look back to that peaceful moment with yearning over the next week, as all hell broke loose.

CHAPTER 4

*. . . by the grace of God, I find myself not only in good
health in every thing . . . and also in a fair way of
coming to a better esteem and estate in the world, than
ever I expected. But I pray God give me a heart to fear a
fall, and to prepare for it.*

SAMUEL PEPYS

I an," I said, at ten o'clock.

"Mmm." His eyes stayed glued to the television.

"*Ian.*"

He looked over at last. For two and a half hours I'd
been packing my bags upstairs (throwing in a paperback
edition of Pepys's diary, just in case), coming down inter-
mittently to check on him while he absorbed every nu-
ance of the national drama. From his behaviour, one
might have thought he was personally responsible.

"Hmm?"

His eyes remained clouded with distress. More than
ever, I found myself concerned for him.

"Ian. I know it's a terrible time for you, with this sad-
ness about the Queen. But I have good news. *Very* good
news, in fact, that simply can't wait another moment." I
tried a smile.

His true nobility shone through in the attempt he
made to respond to my obvious delight.

"Sarah rang me today."

He sat up. "She *did*?"

Sarah had been so long occupied with her secret duties that any call from her was extremely unusual. In fact, for two months now, we'd had only coded e-mails.

I nodded. The grin couldn't be contained. "Ian, she's asked us to come as soon as we can—for the wedding."

His eyes lit up. "Nantucket?"

"Absolutely."

He bounded from the sofa and I rose to meet him. "Alex. Thank God!" He embraced me, then grasped me by the upper arms. "When do we leave? For heaven's sake, why didn't you tell me sooner?"

Good, I thought. Ian was going to be all right.

CHAPTER 5

Up, and all the morning at the office; where the Duke of York's long letter was read to their great trouble . . . the Duke of York, I perceive, is earnest in it, and will have good effects of it . . .

The thing is very well writ indeed.

. . . a great fire they saw in the City . . . the City is reduced from a large folio to a decimotertio.

What the meaning of all these sad signs is the Lord only knows, but every day things look worse and worse. God fit us for the worst!

While the business of money hangs in the hedge . . .

SAMUEL PEPYS

I was still on top of the world the next morning when I pulled into the graceful oval of Bedford Square, where the offices of Plumtree Press look out onto the leafy splendour of the private park. A parking space beckoned to me from directly in front of the building, and I decided the day couldn't possibly get any better.

It was an odd, undecided sort of day weather-wise, but what did barometric pressure matter at a time like this?!

Inside, I pressed the brass circle that turned on the lights, and let the heavy door swing shut behind me with a thud. A pile of post waited at my feet; I'd arrived before our receptionist, Dee, or our mail clerk, Derek. I carried it into Reception for Dee to date-stamp and sort. Riffling through the assortment of envelopes, one caught my eye.

It wasn't just the Duke of York's insignia on the front, although that certainly gave me pause. Just last year we'd received an attractive envelope not unlike this and it had been the source of a great deal of trouble. But that unpleasant missive had been one thin letter, which I'd learned was more likely to be bad news than a healthily bulging envelope. The envelope in my hands was straining at its flaps in a most encouraging manner. Besides, Prince Andrew didn't have any sort of relationship to Plumtree Press that I could think of. Telling myself not to worry, I took it upstairs to my office—so full of adrenaline that I took the stairs three at a time.

As I bounded upwards I couldn't help but enjoy the glow of the chandelier that hung in the entryway, and the pleasant softness of the plum-coloured carpeting. The elegant Georgian house that was home to Plumtree Press never ceased to both please and comfort me. I'd spent many a Saturday here with my father, and sometimes even a day or two of school holiday, shadowing him. He'd been wise to teach me the business in such a casual but thorough way; the Press was in my blood. And so, somehow, was this building.

I tossed the envelope on my desk and went through to the caffeine grotto to start the day's first pot of coffee. I'd learned my lesson well, and now made the thick black stew Lisette, my managing director, preferred. Before I'd caught on to her precise brewing method, Lisette would puff her oh-so-French lips into a cheerful pout and say, "'Ow can you drink this—this *dishwater*? No, it is worse—it is swill for my father's *swine*! Out, out, *out*! *I* will make the coffee." Then we'd hear her bashing and slamming about swearing in a jovial melange of languages about "the bloody English." I wondered if she'd noticed that some of the other editorial staff, presumably those without cast-iron stomachs, had brought in their own coffeemakers and brewed their own swill in the privacy of their offices.

Padding back down the hall into my office, I ripped open the envelope and pulled out the thick wadge of paper. A letter on the duke's letterhead, beautifully printed with engraved plates on soft white paper, was paper-clipped to the top of what looked remarkably like a manuscript. *Oh no*, I thought. *Don't tell me the Duke of York has become another would-be Jeffrey Archer. . . .*

Part of my job was rejecting manuscripts by the rich and famous, who seemed to think that they had a right to be published because of their social position. Writing is a craft, and money and fame don't magically result in skill. Of course that wasn't quite how I put it to them . . .

With great curiosity, I read the letter.

Dear Alex Plumtree,

I have learned through considerable research that you are the publisher to approach with my book, now five years in the writing, about Dukes of York throughout history. As the second in line to the throne, at least until heirs are produced, we often lead rather interesting lives before being blessedly bumped out of the limelight.

Occasionally we even make it to the top. I have tried to write a book that treats the subject of being Number Two with humour, while at the same time imparting what I hope will be a valuable history never before presented by one in my position.

I could not resist focussing on James II, who, like me, had the title Duke of York, a brother named Charles first in line for the throne, and a close involvement with the Navy. There are some rather interesting passages in Samuel Pepys's diary about the Duke; I have used them in what I feel is an illuminating chapter on his position, both at court and in the Navy. My staff tell me you are a Pepys man yourself.

Any proceeds from the publication of the proposed book would go to the Pharmaceutical Foundation, of which I am patron. This organisation makes hard-to-find or extremely expensive medicines available to those who would otherwise be unable to obtain them.

I look forward to hearing your thoughts on my book.

Yours sincerely,

Andrew, Duke of York

No question about it; my delight was dimmed by the mention of Pepys. I carried the first chapter with me to the canteen and read it as I poured my coffee, supplementing it with a nice slosh of full cream. Thoroughly impressed with the quality of his prose—paragraph after paragraph was not only skillfully wrought but compelling—I headed back to my office. Whatever the Pepysian involvement meant, at least there was no literary disaster here. The Duke of York was well qualified to write this book.

" 'Ey, you—why don't you watch out where you are going?"

I looked up to see Lisette holding up her palms in a "stop right there!" gesture. My managing director never missed the chance to remind me of the time I'd literally run into her in the hallway, permanently staining her new peach knit suit with coffee.

"Morning, Lisette." Today she wore a bright dress that matched with uncanny precision the coral of the geraniums she'd placed on her office windowsill. "Don't you look lovely! Coffee's ready."

"So I see. Try to keep it in the cup for once, yes?" She paused and frowned at my face. " '*Ow* can you look so 'appy this *bloody* early in the morning? Come on—out with it."

Naturally, I obeyed. One never crossed Lisette, especially in the morning; the consequences, in terms of Gallic wrath, could be dire. I waved the papers in front of her. "Nice proposal from the Duke of York. Oh—and I'm getting married day after tomorrow."

Her face lit up. She wrapped me in an unreserved bear hug that sent my cup wobbling on its saucer just before it spilled its entire load squarely down the back of her dress. No one knew better than I: history inevitably repeats itself.

She didn't even seem to notice.

"Alex! But this is wonderful! 'Ow can you put this in the same sentence with the Duke of York's book—'oo *cares* about York's book? You are getting *married*! Tying the chain at *last*, yes?"

Lisette's Franglais idiom never failed to delight. Still

locked in her embrace, I smiled down the coffee-stained back of my passionate, energetic, devoted friend.

"At last, yes," I agreed.

"Oh, Alex, I am *so 'appy* for you and Sarah!" When at last she detached herself, I saw tears in her eyes. Lisette was always sentimental, even while she swore a blue streak.

"Lisette . . ." I planted a quick kiss on her cheek. Her husband George, my best mate from the rowing club, wouldn't mind under the circumstances. "I don't deserve you." After all, if it weren't for her, I wouldn't be able to leave the Press for a honeymoon and not worry.

In an attempt to divert attention from herself, she said, a sheepish smile on her face, "You idiot . . . you are not marrying *me*!" But as emotion welled up again, she looked down at the manuscript in my hands, a convenient diversion. "Oh—and now *look* what you've done to the Duke's manuscript. Coffee everywhere . . ." Still, she couldn't resist one more exuberant embrace.

Abruptly detaching herself, she exclaimed, " 'Ow will I get myself in order for the editorial meeting? Look at me!" She wiped at her face, and mascara smeared into dark smudges under her eyes. "I'll be right in—I will bring you another coffee."

"Thanks. But don't you want me to work on that stain—"

"You are sweet, Alex. But I think it would be—er—awkward, yes?" She patted her curvaceous derriere and smiled engagingly.

She did have a point. I wandered down the hall to her office for the editorial meeting, which had once again migrated to Monday mornings. This meeting was always a pleasant prospect, with our jovial gaggle of editors.

"Good morning, Shuna." Lisette's assistant, who'd already placed the seven chairs in a rough circle, was setting a tray of croissants on one of them. She returned my greeting with a smile; the geraniums glowed behind her on the windowsill.

The editorial crew came straggling in, right on time. Timothy Haycroft, our brilliant academic acquisitions editor, tried one of his terrifically naughty literary jokes on us and got us all laughing. Even Rachel Sigridsson, head academic and trade copy editor, was caught off guard: I could have sworn I heard a titter escape before she got herself in hand. By the time I looked, Rachel was already checking the structural integrity of the tight knot of grey hair mounted high on her head, her avoidance mechanism.

" Et voila," Lisette said quietly, delivering my coffee and then sitting next to Rachel. Nicola and Ian hurried in together. We were all there; greetings and conversation flew back and forth in happy confusion.

Lisette seized the moment. "All right, you magpies—enough! Alex 'as something to tell you." She couldn't keep the smile off her face; I decided to tease her.

"Well," I began modestly, "it's true. I've received a book proposal from the Duke of York."

Lisette threw her pencil at me and called me a name that only could have sounded affectionate coming from her.

"All right, all right!" I tossed her pencil back. "You're going to have to do without me for a while. I know; don't all cry at once. I'm going to America for a wedding—

Sarah's and mine. It's set for Wednesday. This time I think it might really happen."

Cheers went up amidst congratulations and much conviviality. Ian smiled on the proceedings; congratulations rained down on him, too. In a way, he was father of the groom as *well* as grandfather of the bride . . . perhaps an unprecedented situation.

Lisette brought me back to earth with a cheery, "Just wait and see if you 'ave a job when you come back."

"Yes, well, then. I'd better get down to business. Timothy? Let's start with you."

"Right. You know I've just been to that conference at Plymouth over the weekend on the literature of secondary figures."

I nodded. The Duke of York's manuscript fell into this category.

" 'Literature of secondary figures'? Am I just thick, or is this something new?" Lisette seemed intrigued.

Timothy was glad to oblige. "There's a trend in literature towards featuring someone who might have been a sidekick to a famous person, or even pretending that the sidekick has written the work." He shrugged. "You can see why it's happening; everything's already been done on the big fish, who were usually male. Women want to read about one of their own for a change. Anyway, I've received a manuscript from an American professor who's written a diary of Pepys's maid, for heaven's sake. She's actually done quite a good job. You know about the recent success of the diary written from the viewpoint of Pepys's wife."

Indeed, I had read it and enjoyed it very much. But I felt a twinge of alarm at the old diarist barging right into our editorial meeting like this.

"Now I know it might smack of copy-cat publishing," Timothy went on, "but it does fit perfectly with our editorial profile. And you can't deny that there's a sudden fascination with not only secondary characters, but Pepys himself."

No, I certainly couldn't deny that.

"I'd like to pursue it; here's the proposal." The sheet of paper Timothy passed me was quite different from an author's proposal; it was a cost analysis of publishing the book—how many he thought we would sell, at how much per copy, what it would cost to produce the quantities he was recommending, and finally the projected profit.

I eyed the sheet, trying not to let panic triumph over professionalism. "Looks good, Timothy. Thanks. More?"

He did have more; Plumtree Press was thriving. Everyone had lots to discuss. But the first item of the day had preoccupied me to the extent that everything else was a blur. At the end of the meeting I recalled the Duke's chapter and book proposal; I told the group about it and asked Nicola to call and tell him we'd be honoured to publish the book. I'd have enjoyed calling him myself, but after all, she was head of trade publishing; it wouldn't do for me to swoop in and skim the cream of her authors off the top. I handed her the manuscript and said, "You might want to get going on this right away . . . he won't be used to waiting around. Put Production to work on a design . . . you might even want to have them commission the dust jacket now."

She nodded. "Everything will have to be just right."

It wasn't long after this meeting that Nicola knocked

on my doorframe and came in, looking rueful. "Do you have a minute?"

"Of course."

She came in and sat opposite me. "The Duke's secretary said that they want to work with you, and *only* you, on the Dukes of York project."

"What?!"

This hadn't happened before. Nicola was extremely well qualified, and if anything came from a social stratum that the Duke would prefer to mine.

"They said it's you or they go to another publisher. It's your reputation, Alex, I'm sure. They know you won't turn this into any sort of embarrassment for the royal family. They don't know me from Eve—except that my father was a political disaster for the country."

It had never occurred to me: Nicola's father, a prominent MP, had engaged in some rather dark business and then fled the country. Though in my mind this was all firmly in the past, it could be that the cautious people whose job it was to protect Prince Andrew saw it differently.

"Oh, for heaven's sake. All right. I'll be the contact. But obviously, I can't see it through editing and production— I'm afraid the hard work's still yours. Sorry about this, Nicola."

"I'm not bothered," she replied coolly, and I believed her. For her years, she was remarkably poised and quick on the uptake. "Besides, it's one less thing for me to do, isn't it?" She smiled and made a quick exit, and as I picked up the phone I gave thanks for the hundreth time that I'd hired her. The Duke, ironically, was unavailable. Would I like to leave a message? I left my name, and said that Plumtree Press was indeed most interested in publishing the Duke's book . . . and that I would be delighted to be the one to work with him on it. The secretary told me that the Duke would be most pleased to hear it, and we signed off.

That done, I realised I'd have to deal with the issue of the money missing from the Library, and quickly. My good name was at stake; it wouldn't do to go flitting around the globe after that much money had disappeared into my bank account—or people thought it had. Things were going to be wild right up to the moment I boarded the aeroplane, I had a feeling.

With a sigh, I got to my feet and trotted down the stairs to Reception. "Dee, I'm popping out for a bit."

Our receptionist looked up from her paperback just long enough to give me a perky, "Roger, Mr P."

I had to smile as I pushed open the heavy front door. Dee was reading another World War II romance if she was saying "roger" again. The day was getting hazy, almost smoky, the sky fading to a blue so pale it tended towards grey. Still, it was a pleasant June morning, the perfect day for a walk. A whisper of wind stirred the vivid new leaves on the trees in the Square's park, and there was a hint of something unsettled in the air . . . or was it just me?

Of *course* it was me . . . after all, a man didn't get married every day. My whole world was about to change.

But as I headed eastward towards the city, my thoughts turned to Ryan Hinching, the man I'd hired to manage the funds of the Pepys Library. Nagging irritation with the man was intruding on my premarital bliss. I began to run through what I would say to him when I got there. The *appropriate* words would be, "I understand there's a problem with the Pepys Library account. How did this happen?" But something in me wanted to barge in and demand, *Why didn't you ring me first, you inconsiderate lout?*

I was still pursuing this unproductive line of thought when I arrived at a zebra crossing near the point where Cheapside turned into Threadneedle Street. In the back of my mind, I was aware of tapes blocking off part of the street, and crowds of people standing behind the tapes. Flashing lights on more than one police car signalled that something was up; voices sounded through megaphones, herding people behind the tapes. Perhaps Alan Greenspan was visiting the Stock Exchange.

The next moment would remain frozen in my mind for the rest of my life: an elderly man, meticulously turned out in bowler hat and dark pin-striped suit, stepped into the crosswalk at the Belisha beacon opposite me. The man's knees seemed to buckle; I saw him look down at his legs as if willing them to behave.

Concerned for him, I hurried to his side—or tried to—but found myself no less wobbly. I was literally unable to make my legs cross the pavement. Was I suffering a sudden attack of the flu?

A mighty rumble shook the ground, toppling us all like ten-pins. With an enormous *whoosh*, the building behind the elderly gent—the very financial powerhouse that housed the Pepys Library fund manager—collapsed on itself. For a moment I felt I was in a cinema with rumbling effects, watching a disaster film. But then the old man came back into view. This was indeed reality.

I wobbled across the eight feet between us and enquired whether he was all right. He gave me a distracted nod but seemed intact, confused more than frightened. Once I helped him to his feet, he bravely dusted himself off.

The force of another blast sent us reeling. Fire spewed from the ruins of the demolished building as if from a volcano, sending the rubble flying. I turned away and shielded us both with my arm as bits of debris rained down.

"*Let's get out of here!*" I shouted above screams and the roar of fire engulfing the once-proud structure. I hurried him across the street and got him inside a Barclay's Bank before heading back out to see if I could help an injured woman who'd fallen frighteningly close to the burning remains of the building. By the time I neared her, a small crowd had formed and I saw that she was already receiving attention. Like many others, I stood dumbfounded, hypnotised by the leaping flames.

Then I was on the ground again. Another vast explosion rocked the street, sending us all sprawling. Time had ceased to be predictable or measurable, each explosion was a timeless bubble of confusion and horror. In the wake of each explosion, everything seemed preternaturally quiet. After a small eternity, unearthly noises, horrible in their strangeness, began to erupt from those unfortunate enough to be in harm's way. Men and women cried out; some made unfamiliar keening noises like Middle Eastern women in mourning. It might have been another world, far distant from the City's Square Mile.

The second building, on the far side of the first cataclysm, followed the pattern of the first. It collapsed partially before the fireball erupted, then began to incinerate what remained. I suppose only a few minutes had passed; it felt like hours. Others joined me in helping to move injured and stunned people out of the streets and away from the buildings as the sweeping fire became a roar. The light breeze that had seemed so delightful when I left Plumtree Press had become a deadly enemy; as I helped a rubber-kneed young woman up from the pavement I saw that thick black smoke and dangerous sparks were blowing into neighbouring buildings. What if the City went up in flames?

It was the fire, leaping maniacally from building to building as I watched, that sparked an epiphany. Pepys had cropped up once or twice too often recently to be coincidence: Mattie Harding had rung me up about a supposed Pepys "find," Percival Urchfont had passed on the unpleasant news of Pepys Library finances and asked me to look into the Pepysiana posting, and now I was witnessing a modern-day Fire of London. It all could mean only one thing: I was almost certainly about to embark upon another literature-inspired stand-off with both history and all-too-modern villains. I never got used to these forays into biblioadventure. Eerily, though I lived what was unquestionably my life and not some sort of vision, I lived it (to a surprising extent) according to the dictates of what happened in books.

Pepys! Grimly, I gazed at the disaster surrounding me and thought of what a lot I had yet to endure.

Having got myself back to the office, I stumbled into Ian's office, dazed, and sank onto his guest chair. He was listening to a small transistor radio on his desk. "Have you heard, Alex? The City's—Good heavens. What's happened to you?"

Following his eyes, I saw that my shirt front was stained with something dark—oil or grease, perhaps, from falling in the street.

Ian put a hand on my shoulder. "Alex? Are you all right?"

"Yes—bit of a surprise . . ."

"I'll get you some tea. Stay right here."

The radio played on, issuing a disastrous report I didn't want to hear. A BBC voice said with the perfect touch of urgency, "The City of London was besieged this afternoon in a devastating terrorist attack. Four major banks and the Stock Exchange were the targets of this unprecedented siege on London's financial centre. Fortunately, warnings were given and the buildings were successfully evacuated before the explosions, which were followed by incendiary devices. A fire is now raging out of control at the site of the four buildings, near the Stock Exchange. Although numerous people are being treated for injuries, there have been no fatalities. The organisation responsible has not yet declared itself."

"Here we are." Ian returned with his special brand of herb tea. He had spiked it with honey; I knew his deeply held conviction that hot tea with honey could cure almost anything. "Now. Don't tell me you were anywhere near that mess . . ." He gestured towards the radio.

I nodded and swallowed some tea. "I was going to see someone about the Pepys Library Fund; wanted to get it wrapped up before we leave tomorrow. The first building blew up just as I was crossing Threadneedle Street, and then a sort of firebomb went off. Right in the same building."

"Good gracious! Thank heaven you're safe, Alex. What an utter disaster. It's a wonder more people weren't hurt." He returned to sit behind his desk. "You know what's happening, don't you? I'll wager this is all because of the Queen's injury. You notice she still hasn't come before the nation today, so I know she's in a bad way. The anti-Royalists, the Irish Republicans, anyone who wants radical change—it's a perfect time for spreading doubt and chaos."

"But what could they possibly hope to achieve?"

As he so often did, like the very best teachers, Ian answered my question with a question. "What better way to take advantage of a nation's weakness than to wait until its figurehead is incapacitated? It wouldn't surprise me to learn that Her Majesty's riding accident was planned by sinister elements, while the current situation is conducive to wreaking havoc. William's young and inexperienced—though not when viewed from a historical perspective, of course—and Charles is viewed as weak and unpopular. Anti-Royalists, anyone who wants to see England change, couldn't have chosen a better time to strike."

I didn't know that I believed in an anti-Royalist plot, it sounded like something from the time of—well, *Pepys*.

I promptly choked on my tea. Ian instantly came to my rescue, taking the cup and patting me on the back until I could breathe again.

"What is it, Alex? Perhaps I should take you home . . ."

I shook my head. "It's just that—do you remember the episodes with the works of Dickens, William Morris, and Arnold Bennett? Boccaccio? And *Beowulf* last year?"

Ian froze, sitting abruptly on the edge of the desk. "Oh no," he said. "Not again. You don't mean to say *it's* happening again."

"It" is difficult to explain, but Ian understood. Even after all this time, my best definition of "it" would be: "An adventure having its beginning in books—old, new, or both—involving intrigue, betrayal, and danger." Running the family publishing house didn't seem to bring it on directly—though that's no walk in the park at the best of times, as *anyone* in publishing will tell you. Nor did it seem to result exclusively from my family's fabled collection of antiquarian books, though masked men seek them in my home with surprising frequency.

At least there is some sense of purpose to these ordeals; I've finally arrived at the conclusion that—and only God knows why—it's my destiny to uncover the secrets that lie forgotten in books. The pattern, so far as I can discern it, is that my biblioadventures set history's record straight. I suppose there could be worse legacies to the world, but it might have been nice to have a choice in the matter.

I merely nodded at Ian; yes, *it* was almost certainly happening again.

"Who?" This was a vital question, because my little forays into history and literature usually revolved around the works of a single author.

"Pepys," I peeped.

"*Pepys? Samuel* Pepys?"

In the adolescent humour that so often overcame me when I was with Ian, I nearly asked him if there were another Pepys I'd never heard of. I got hold of myself and answered, "Mmm."

Ian was a quick study. "Fire in the City. The Queen in jeopardy! The book proposed by the Duke of York . . ."

"There's more, I'm afraid."

"And just before your wedding . . ."

I felt it was time for me to take charge, to comfort him if I could. "Ian, both Sarah and I agree that it's going to be all right this time. I almost feel that . . . well, perhaps if we're married, things might be different. With respect to this sort of thing, I mean. You know—the biblioadventures."

Ian looked as though this was very doubtful indeed, but quickly tried to hide it. "Yes . . . oh, yes. I do hope you're right."

We sat for a moment, trying to take it all in. By the greatest misfortune we found ourselves gazing at a certain portrait in Ian's office, the portrait of one Samuel Pepys. Ian, who like Pepys was an avid sailor and amateur scientist, had been responsible for Plumtree Press's outrageously successful *Anthology of Seventeenth-Century Prose*, with contributions from Pettifer Bartlett. This one volume, now in its tenth edition, had singlehandedly funded much of the firm's success, not to mention my public school education. As long as I could remember, the portrait had hung in Ian's office as mute testimony to the great man's gift.

"Oh dear," Ian murmured.

We tore our eyes away from the smug-looking character in the long dark wig and regarded each other with dismay.

It had begun.

CHAPTER 6

*This day, by the blessing of God, my wife and I have
been married . . . bless God for our long lives and loves
and health together, which the same God long continue,
I wish, from my very heart!*

SAMUEL PEPYS

Every detail of our wedding day will be etched in my memory forever: the rumble of the sea, the salt smell, the exuberant warm wind, the brilliant Nantucket sky . . . my profound gratitude for being able to see it all.

On that lovely June Wednesday, my bride walked arm in arm with her father and grandfather, down the path from her parents' house towards the pergola at the edge of the beach. She smiled at me, shining with the strength, confidence, and intelligence I've always adored in her. The timeless drone of bagpipes, courtesy of her brother Rob, hinted at the eternal nature of our union. Bagpipes never failed to give me goose-flesh, today least of all.

My long-awaited bride stood before me at last. I offered my hand; hers was warm and firm as she took mine. "You're gorgeous and I love you," I whispered.

She squeezed my hand and smiled; a single tear escaped from her right eye. I reached up and swiped it away.

"Dearly beloved," the Episcopalian priest intoned, "we

have come together in the presence of God to witness and bless the joining together of this man and this woman in Holy Matrimony . . ." The waves pounded an accompaniment behind him as he recited the timeless words. Turning to Sarah, he asked, "Sarah Lily Townsend, will you have this man to be your husband; to live together in the covenant of marriage? Will you love him, comfort him, honour and keep him, in sickness and in health; and, forsaking all others, be faithful to him as long as you both shall live?"

"I will." Her rich voice was music to me.

"Alexander Christian Lodge Plumtree, will you have this woman . . ."

I watched Sarah's face as she listened to our vows, and wondered whether she was thinking that it was the second time she'd taken them. Would her husband last longer this time?

"I will," I said emphatically, and saw her smile at my enthusiastic response. I took her right hand and began, "In the Name of God, I, Alex, take you Sarah, to be my wife, to have and to hold from this day forward, for better for worse, for richer for poorer, in sickness and in health, to love and to cherish, until we are parted by death. This is my solemn vow."

We exchanged hands as Sarah returned the promise; then it was my turn to place the ring on her finger. "Sarah, I give you this ring as a symbol of my vow, and with all that I am, and all that I have, I honour you, in the Name of the Father, and of the Son, and of the Holy Spirit."

In return, her hand was steady as she slid the ring on my finger and pronounced the same lovely words.

The priest joined our right hands and said with authority, "Now that Alex and Sarah have given themselves to each other by solemn vows, I pronounce that they are husband and wife. Those whom God has joined together let no one put asunder." He smiled.

With a surge of pure joy I grasped Sarah around the waist and lifted her up; her lips met mine. When I set her down again we laughed with glee.

Catching the spirit, Rob and my brother Max gave a whoop and came to join us from where they stood nearby, closely followed by the other five witnesses. This was the wedding that we had all begun to think would never happen, twice thwarted by events decidedly out of our control.

We were married!

Rob recovered himself enough to pipe us all up to the house to the tune of "Marie's Wedding." We enjoyed a superb wedding dinner of lobster interrupted by endless toasts, a *nice* speech by my brother, and much celebration. I couldn't imagine anything better than the intimacy of our complete family around the Townsends' dining room table.

Several hours later I drove my bride to the Wauwinet. This private Nantucket hideaway is the sort of place designed to accommodate people who can't be seen in public: movie stars, presidents, and secret agents—in short, people like my wife. It wasn't until I held Sarah in my arms in utter privacy that I felt a flash of alarm. After a moment I recognised its source: I stood to lose so much now, if anything ever happened to her.

I took that instant to erect one lasting defence against the possible ravages of the future, a once-for-all-time prayer for our life together: *Dear God, please don't let anything come between us . . . ever.*

But even the dread of some distant threat couldn't begin to erode the joy of here and now.

My hands trembled as I struggled to unfasten tiny loops of fabric from the minuscule white, round buttons on the bodice of her dress. Sarah, with considerably less steady hands than before, liberated me from my tie. Neither costume had been designed for easy access . . . their designers had known precisely what they were doing.

And finally, at long last, we knew each other as man and wife.

CHAPTER 7

*For I perceive there are great fears abroad; for all which I
am troubled and full of doubt that things will not go well.*

*But I do perceive by it that there is something in it that
is ready to come out that the world knows not of yet.*

SAMUEL PEPYS

One and a half utterly pampered days later—the details
of which shall remain strictly private—we drove from the
Faraway Island to Vermont to meet Mattie before the reunion. The fires of London and the fear surrounding the
Queen's condition seemed worlds away. We'd talked to
Ian once since he'd returned to England; there'd been no
more bombs, but in a disturbing new trend, isolated fires
were breaking out all over the City. Newscasters spoke of
possible plots against the Queen, and various groups were
marching in the streets—some protesting Prince
Charles's ascension to the throne, and others advocating
the abolition of the Church of England.

Overall, we detected a burgeoning sense of unease
about the country's future . . . but it was less than immediate here in the New England hills. Climbing out of her
convertible in the unpaved driveway of Mattie's "farmhouse," I watched my wife inhale the piney air and stand,
eyes closed, relishing the countryside.

I enjoyed the familiar setting, too, but not as much as I enjoyed watching her. Our time together over the last few days had made her more attractive to me than I'd ever dreamed possible. Every detail was tantalising . . . the classic straightness of her nose, the little crease just above the inside of her elbow. I'd expected marriage to dim some of the delights of Sarah Townsend ever so slightly, but I was beginning to realise that the real thrills had only just begun. She'd come outfitted for the hike with Mattie today, and something about her strong, tanned arms extending tantalisingly out of the tank top and the long, lithe legs with their smooth muscles from the hiking shorts—even her seriously rugged hiking boots—rendered me helpless.

The next thing I knew she had noticed my misty gaze and was giving me her "come hither" look . . . and who could resist that? We were both keenly aware that we were still on our honeymoon, our time for being together. I walked round the car, took her in my arms, and held her close. We might have been ready to leave on a hike with my old flame, but we needed one more embrace. She made a soft luxuriating sound as I moved in for a kiss. Moments later, I reluctantly broke it off. What if Mattie was watching from inside the house?

I kept an arm around her as I steered her towards the front door. I said quietly, "Well. You know all about Mattie, don't you?" Given our preoccupation with other matters, I hadn't spent much time preparing her for this visit with my old girlfriend.

Sarah smiled. "Don't forget: I was watching all the while. It's just possible that I know more than you think I do." I felt a wave of panic at what this might be, but she winked and I saw she was only teasing. "Seriously, this is what I know: she was an exemplary coxswain, sole fellow collegiate bibliophile, all-round stellar student. And I remember her kindness one night during Winter Carnival when I lost my necklace on the Green. She crawled around with me in the snow for half an hour or more until she found it. I was so grateful—it was a gift from Peter."

"She can be a decent sort, our Mattie." Breathing deeply of the damp early summer morning, we trudged up to the elegantly rustic pickled pine door. Mattie, the ultimate intense loner who didn't really seem to need anyone, had painted a sign that said "*The Lone Pine*."

Sarah, upon seeing it, turned and commented, "That seems a little sad."

I shrugged and tightened my arm round her shoulders. "It's just the way she is." I lifted a hand to bang on the door, but saw at the last moment that it was already slightly open.

"Mattie!" I bellowed good-naturedly through the crack, as we might have at the boathouse as undergraduates. When there was no response, I tried again. "Hey, *Matilda!*" The nicknames given by the men's heavyweight crew would never be lived down. "It's Buddy."

No answer. Sarah and I looked at one another.

I nudged open the door and tried again, taken aback by the clutter of fleece jackets, sweatshirts, and shoes on the entryway floor. Mattie had always been tidy to a fault.

"Matt?" There was a very specialised noise for which I'd become notorious—perhaps resembling a bugling moose more than anything else. I tried this noise, once the rallying call of the heavyweight crew, now. It was enough to raise the dead.

Sarah shook with laughter at my regression to the latter part of my childhood. It had been a long time since she'd heard the moose call.

Silence.

Perhaps we'd arrived too early . . . but a glance at my watch told me we were a tactful ten minutes late. Once a friend, always a friend, I decided, and barged in. But after picking my way into the kitchen I stopped short. The beautiful farmhouse kitchen, meticulously fitted with white-painted cupboards, maple worktops, and Shaker table and chairs, was a foul, stinking mess. Careless stacks of plates, pots, glasses, and remnants of food—a bowl of rotting tuna, from the smell of it—looked ready to teeter off the worktop onto the floor.

It was only then that I felt the first ripple of fear. Something had gone badly awry in Mattie's life for her to allow the kitchen to sink to this level of slovenliness. The house instantly took on an air of menace. What if someone had done something to Mattie, and was lying in wait?

One glance at Sarah told me her thoughts mirrored mine. Her stance became cautious, her step light. She put a finger to her lips.

There were, I told myself, advantages to being married to a spook.

I began to move farther into the house, stepping stealthily; Sarah stayed close behind. The kitchen led into a sitting room with sweeping mountain views. Books lined two walls, floor to ceiling, and most of a third. This room was in better order than the kitchen, but was still scattered with an uncharacteristic litter of socks, beer cans, and food wrappers. At least the books were all in place; even as an undergraduate Mattie had never let anyone casually peruse her books.

With creeping dread, Sarah and I moved silently from room to room. I for one fully expected to encounter a hostile squatter. I tried hard *not* to think of what might have become of Mattie. But when, after a thorough search, we stood puzzled in the fifth upstairs bedroom, I knew the house was empty.

"What do you think?" Sarah frowned at the unmade bed. "Judging from your reaction, this is unusual."

"*Very* unusual. She was always one of those fanatically tidy types, couldn't survive otherwise. But what really worries me is that she sounded so normal when she rang, four or five days ago. I doubt that all this could have happened in a few days."

Sarah shook her head. "It doesn't look as though someone's deliberately ransacked it, either. Mattie isn't—well, have you ever known her to be unbalanced?"

The same unpleasant thought had just crept into my mind, too, and unfortunately the answer was yes. But I'd always guarded her secret with my life . . . was it all right to tell a spouse *everything*?

Sarah noticed my hesitation. "She did say something important had happened," I said, "that she'd found something she wanted me to take a look at. She thought it might have been something of Pepys's—and I jumped to the conclusion that it might be something to do with the find Urchfont and Mattingley wanted me to look into. Perhaps she's been held up at work, or is too preoccupied to remember we were coming."

Sarah shrugged and murmured a doubtful, "Maybe." But I could see she believed something was amiss.

Struggling for optimism, I found a scrap of paper in the kitchen and scrawled a note saying that we'd been there but missed her, and reminding her that we'd be staying at Richardson. She could reach us there, I said, or on my cell phone, and I left the number. I vowed to check up on her once we got to Hanover; perhaps she really was just very busy at work.

I took one last look around the revolting kitchen, wondering if I should clean up before leaving. In the end I decided it wasn't part of Sarah's honeymoon, and securely latched the door. Though I tried to tell myself not to be so suspicious, I was certain something had happened to my old friend—and it wasn't good.

No amount of sunshine and cleansing New England scenery could dispel the gloom of that eerie episode as we drove the fifteen minutes or so to Hanover, New Hampshire, home of Dartmouth College. . . . The moment we came upon the Green—the oasis of grass criss-crossed by footpaths and alive with frisbee and ball players that was the heart and soul of the Dartmouth campus—I felt better. Years and worries fell away, and I felt Sarah relax too as happy memories tumbled back.

Surely, I told myself, there had been some misunderstanding with Mattie, and she was fine. The demands of her position as assistant archivist of the new Rauner Special Collections Library—the alumni magazine had announced her appointment a couple of years ago—were probably taking their toll. "Why don't we stop in at the Library, now that we have time to spare?"

"I'd love to," Sarah said promptly. "We can ask about Mattie."

I parked the convertible behind Richardson Hall, not

far from Rauner, and we hiked down the hill. I'd never been back to the College with Sarah before; it was an odd sensation. Almost as if we had reverted to our twenty-year-old selves, except this time we were more like one person than two. I'd always been happy at Dartmouth, but I liked it much better this way.

Rauner Library, a graceful old pillared building of pale stone, had once been known as Webster Hall, à la Daniel Webster. Thousands of Dartmouth students had attended opening convocation there, receiving their official welcome to the college. Less than two years before it had been skillfully transformed into one of America's finest collegiate special collections libraries, and renamed Rauner after a major donor. Inside, the building was cool and dark. Sarah and I stood in the entrance for a moment to let our eyes adjust. Behind me, I heard the door open and saw a shaft of light slice through the darkness.

"Alex Plumtree?!"

I turned to find a smiling, dignified man my own height with wire-rimmed glasses and finely chiselled features. It was Philip Cronenwett, the Librarian at Rauner and Mattie's boss. The Friends of the Library had called me in two years ago to help them search for Rauner's head librarian, and I'd known of Phil from his work at Yale's Beinecke Library. The College had been singing his praises—and mine, for finding him—ever since.

"Phil!" I shook his hand warmly. "Sarah, this is Phil Cronenwett, Librarian at Rauner—he works with Mattie. And this is my wife, Sarah—also a notorious eighty-six."

"Well! This *is* good news. I had no idea—" But even as he greeted Sarah with a smile, I saw that his eyes were bloodshot. Poor Phil; he was a devoted family man with five children under the age of eight.

"We've been married for exactly two days," I explained, beaming.

"I *see!* Congratulations to you both! Very nice to meet you, Sarah."

"And you, Phil."

"The new library looks wonderful." I hadn't been back since they'd completed the building and stocked it with books. "I see you survived the move."

He rolled his eyes. "I sincerely hope *you* never have to move a special collections library. I wouldn't wish it on anyone." He opened his mouth to say something else, then quickly changed his mind. "How are things at the Pepys Library?" I saw the effort it took for him to smile.

"Surprisingly eventful. Who would ever believe that a few stacks of old books could cause so much trouble?" He agreed and launched into a tale of woe over a mysteriously missing volume, and ushered us through the inner doors.

Sarah stopped just inside, taking it all in. She tilted her head back and looked at the massive column of books straight ahead behind a wall of glass, two stories high and perhaps fifty feet across. "This is *magnificent!*"

Though I'd seen the refurbished building before, the inside of Rauner always gave me pause. It was a brilliant design—the precious books were fully on display but at the same time protected, and around the edges of the upper level a gallery dotted with comfortable sofas and chairs welcomed browsers.

"Do you have time for a cup of coffee?" Phil asked us.

"I'm frankly astounded to see you here today . . . I was planning to look up dialling codes and things and call you later. Now we can do it in person. If you like, I can show you our most recent claim to fame, just received last week: the Frost Farm bequest."

"Really?!" Sarah exclaimed.

"That sounds too good to be true—Sarah's something of a Frost fan." I myself felt little but a cloying sentimentalism at the thought of Frost's poetry, but Sarah had taken a freshman seminar from a Frost expert—someone who'd studied with the poet himself—and was deeply attached to the man's work. I thought her fascination with rhymes about woods and snowy evenings might go back to her New England roots.

My wife had the look of someone who had just received a particularly delightful and unexpected birthday present. The roses in her cheeks had just become rosier. "I'll try to control myself," she said with a sideways look at me, knowing my feelings about Frost. She turned to Phil. "What exactly is the bequest?"

"A fellow Frost enthusiast of yours, an alum, lived on Frost's New Hampshire farm for the last forty years. His will stated that all Frost-related memorabilia was to come to us—everything and anything Frost had *touched*, if we wanted it. He died a couple of weeks ago. Believe me, we do have every last thing, too," Phil said confidentially. "We can't offend the donating families by refusing anything, so it becomes an exercise in storage and recordkeeping. We have warehouses of well-meant memorabilia, you know," he told Sarah. "But we've kept a few of the Frost items here at the library for an upcoming display—and all the papers, of course."

Phil led us up the stairs to the carpeted gallery. "Your idea of allowing the students to enjoy the library in this relaxed setting has been very successful, Alex," he whispered, waving a hand at the sofas holding students in varying degrees of repose. "A stroke of brilliance."

I looked around with satisfaction. More than a dozen students lounged in the gallery, absorbed in the precious volumes before them. My personal belief was that if books existed solely to sit untouched on the shelves, there wasn't much point in having them. They should be held, read, and enjoyed. After making an appropriate donation to Rauner as a member of Friends of the Dartmouth Library, I'd quietly made my views known and was delighted to see them come to life.

The door to the staff room closed behind us with a quiet *swoosh*. As Phil poured coffee with an encouragingly strong aroma and invited us to sit, I asked after his next-in-line, Mattie Harding.

"Mattie?" He turned and looked at me with a frown. "I don't quite know what to think. She hasn't shown up for work this week at all. On Monday and Tuesday I tried to call. I thought perhaps she was ill, but she hasn't returned my calls."

Sarah and I exchanged a glance, but she rededicated herself to her Starbucks brew. One of the many things I loved about Sarah was her unassuming way. I had to smile at the thought of the mental and physical powerhouse at my side, cloaked in gentle yet confident femininity. Woe be to the man who underestimates my wife, I thought.

Turning back to Phil, I said, "I'm worried about her. Mattie's an old friend of mine, you know—she called me in London to see if we could come to the reunion early. Evidently she wanted to discuss something important about the world of books. But when I stopped by her house, not only was she not there, but the door was standing open. Things were—well, the farmhouse was in a state."

Phil frowned as he came towards me with a steaming mug, emblazoned—like most things at Dartmouth—with the college crest. He handed me the coffee without offering further information.

"Ah—thanks," I said, intrigued by his reticence. "Was everything all right before she—er—stopped coming to work?"

He shrugged, but my question seemed to give him pause. "Perhaps I should have paid more attention to Mattie. She's been under great pressure with this new bequest. But you know Mattie—always up for a challenge. She'll *create* one if necessary." Phil looked down into his milky coffee too hastily, I decided. He wasn't saying everything he knew. Was there a touch of guilt in his manner?

"She's never disappeared like this before? I mean, since you've worked with her?"

"No. Not in these two years." Phil joined us at the table and sat. "Anyway, on to more cheerful things. The reason I was going to call you, Alex, is that we've had a resignation from the board of the Friends."

Sarah's coffee went down the wrong way and she began to sputter, barely managing to set her mug down on the table. I could almost hear her thoughts: *Not another library board!* Like me, Sarah believed in voluntarism and couldn't imagine life without working for the causes she believed in. But she'd made it known on several occasions that she thought I'd taken on too many charitable duties. For once, I agreed. And in light of my current troubles at the Pepys Library, I couldn't imagine plunging into yet another special collections cesspit.

"Alex, you're our top choice for replacing the resigning member. Obviously you won't be able to attend all of the meetings, but we would value your advice on the collections—and of course your expertise in making certain acquisitions."

I suppose all three of us knew I'd say yes in the end, but he registered my hesitation . . . and I was quite certain he hadn't missed Sarah's sudden coughing attack.

"I'll think about it, Phil—thanks. I'm honoured to be asked."

"Well, if you do decide to join us, your timing's perfect—we're meeting at four this afternoon in the Treasure Room. We'll have drinks and hors d'oeuvres afterwards. I hope you'll both join us if you can."

The three of us settled in for some book gossip; the notable books that had come onto the market, the outrageous price some ordinary volume had fetched the previous week at a Sotheby's auction. I decided to try him out on the supposed Pepys discovery; after all, if the find was rumoured to be at Dartmouth he ought to know about it. "We're hearing wild rumours over in London about a Pepys find at Dartmouth. Is there any truth to it?"

Phil's face shut down; all emotion vanished. Had I put a foot wrong somehow by mentioning it?

"We heard about it," he said, almost coldly. "But whoever posted that message has dropped out of sight. It could well have been a hoax," he said, and sipped his coffee. But I couldn't help wondering what else he knew, and if the real reason for asking me to join the Friends board was my interest in Pepys.

Deftly switching gears, Phil glanced at his watch and announced he had a meeting at eleven-thirty; would we like a quick tour of the library, including a sneak preview of the new collection from the Frost Farm?

Sarah jumped to her feet. "Yes, please!" We both followed him with enthusiasm.

"We'll start with the Realia Room, since it's on this level," Phil said. He led us to a locked, unmarked room where non-book treasures were kept. An ancient-looking wood-and-skin kayak sat beached on the floor, and sturdy metal shelving held a mindboggling assortment of artifacts, including sterling silver punch bowls, lap desks, and carefully wrapped ceremonial robes. Long clay pipes, part of Dartmouth's graduation ceremony to commemorate its close relations with Native Americans, stood in racks next to a giant collection of lovingly carved senior canes, a fad amongst graduates in the late nineteenth and early twentieth centuries.

"The Frost donation is this whole section here," he said, making his way past shelves full of archival boxes bearing the college crest and irregularly shaped items wrapped in heavy cloth, to a far corner of the room. "A butter churn came with the whole assortment, if you can imagine, not to mention a cider press. No doubt you've caught a whiff of the apples."

Sarah bent down and sniffed in the direction of the cider press. "Mmm!" I knew I could count on her to help me prolong our time in this most unusual room, especially given what I'd told her about Mattie's Pepys find. It was possible that it could be right under our noses here somewhere . . .

Phil was saying, "The realia's fascinating, but the papers are the real treasures, of course. Those are mostly in the basement—I'll show you the stacks and the cataloguing area before you go. Mattie's been spending every moment preparing to catalogue it all, going through box after box in the basement. At first glance, there appear to be some unpublished poems of Frost's, but we'll have to call in the scholars first. All this happened just last week—there's hasn't really been time to sort it all out."

"Amazing!" Sarah exclaimed. "A Frost lover's dream."

"It must make your life interesting here at the library," I commented, "with everyone aware that you're sitting on that treasure. Not to mention the Press."

He shot me an ironic look. "Interesting is hardly the word."

Phil generously invited us to look around. Sarah could hardly believe her good fortune when she lifted the cover of the cider press and found a sheaf of papers. With a groan that said, *what a mess,* Phil removed the cover and gingerly lifted out the top of the stack. Meanwhile I inspected the butter churn. Too late I realised that in lifting the lid I'd broken some sort of official-looking Dartmouth College tape that had secured the lid to the body of the churn. Perhaps the churn contained still more memorabilia for Phil to groan over. Wincing at my clumsiness, I glanced at Sarah and Phil. They were fully occupied with a scrap that may or may not have been a newfound Frost opus. *Right,* I thought, *don't call attention to your own act of carelessness,* and peered into the darkness of the churn. No smell assaulted my nostrils, but a jumble of paper slumping haphazardly at the bottom beckoned.

Carefully I lifted out most of the papers and found I was holding a rumpled stack about two inches deep. It was apparent from the sawdust-like quality of the paper that it wasn't older than early twentieth-century. As I rippled through the stack—with great delicacy, of course— my eye and fingers perceived that several sheets in the middle were of a different texture. I went back to them with interest, held the offending sheets of farm records (no doubt of great interest to other scholars) out of the way, and promptly got the shock of my life.

The chicken scratchings I saw, interspersed with foreign words, were undeniably *Shelton's Tachygraphy*. Pepys's chosen code . . . and yet it couldn't be. How could a New Hampshire farm that once belonged to Robert Frost possibly have anything to do with *Samuel Pepys*?

Phil looked up at me just then; I returned a bland smile. For some reason my instinct was to pretend that I'd seen nothing extraordinary, though I certainly had nothing to hide from Phil. I went back to respectfully leafing through the three critical pages, catching glimpses of stunning nuggets of information. Something about Lord Dartmouth, and the mission to Tangier . . . Lord Dartmouth's lackey was evidently a frightful pain in the neck, and many of the men used the English women badly there . . . the natives were mistreated . . . King Charles II gave Lord Dartmouth large grants of land in London in exchange for his service in Tangier . . .

Phil looked at his watch again and gave a small grunt of frustration. "Sorry, I'm afraid I've got to get to that meeting. I'll just take you through the lower level, if you'd like."

Sarah and I took our cue and replaced the newfound treasures.

Phil ushered us out of the room, locking it carefully behind him, and led us down the staircase to the main floor. "The public never sees the stacks, of course—one of the staff retrieves the books upon request." We followed him past the two library tables where librarians looked up from their work and nodded at us. Phil greeted them by name and unlocked a door tucked away behind them.

The metal door snapped shut behind us with finality. We were in the inner sanctum. Here I caught the subtle aroma of the books that rose in their priceless column towards the ceiling. Quickly, Phil led us past a few of the College's most famous collections. "This is the Vilhjalmur Stefansson collection," he said, "the Arctic explorer. It's the most complete in the world. That was his kayak you saw in the realia room. Here is one of eleven known copies of Shakespeare's *Titus Andronicus*, ah, and the Sine collection of British books."

Now at the back of the building, we descended yet another level by a set of industrial-looking stairs. Here there was an almost oppressive feeling; it might have been just the lower ceilings, but there were *so many* books . . . Sarah drew nearer to me.

"No doubt you've seen moveable shelving like this . . . watch." Phil pressed a switch: an entire twenty-foot length of shelving slid along a track in the floor to allow access to the one behind it. "This allows us to store vast quantities." I stepped into the aisle he'd just created, noting with interest more archival boxes bearing the college crest like the ones in the realia room.

"What's in these boxes?"

"Oh, loose papers that don't fit on the shelves, and a few things waiting to be catalogued. Mattie always has plenty of work waiting. By the way, you want to be careful in these shelves. Because it's only staff down here and there are so few of us, we didn't have the emergency shut-off feature installed. You see, if this part of the library were open to the public, someone might wander into harm's way—these shelves are like walls of rock once they get moving. Public shelves have a kickplate at the bottom; one good boot and they stop immediately. Ours, on the other hand, will keep going whether someone's in the way or not."

"Ah," I said, stepping out of the aisle again. I didn't fancy becoming a permanent display.

"I'm afraid I really do have to be on my way—prospective donors don't like to be kept waiting. I'll have to take you back upstairs." We thanked him for his hospitality, and he invited us to come back anytime to see the books. With a brief wave he was gone and striding purposefully across the Green, the very image of the intellectual, diplomatic, elegant academician. Too late I realised that the lack of a proper good-bye meant he fully expected to see me later for the Friends meeting. I was hooked.

CHAPTER 8

He do confess with me that the hearts of our seamen are much saddened . . .

It is a sad sight to see so many good ships there sunk in the River, while we would be thought to be masters of the sea.

. . . we fell to business of the Navy. Among other things, how to pay off this fleet that is now come . . .

SAMUEL PEPYS

Sarah put her hand in mine as we stood in the summer sunlight. "And what, may I ask, was that all about?" The deliberate nonchalance of her tone told me she was on to my find in the Realia Room.

I smiled and gently pulled her along with me across the road towards the path towards Richardson. "I can't tell you how lovely it is to have you notice," I replied. On impulse I pulled her off the path and into the shade of the front entrance to Rollins Chapel, the College's massive Gothic church on the Green, for a kiss.

When we came up for air, her lips brushed mine as she said, "I love to notice things about you."

We studied each other's eyes and were truly content. We were beginning to realise that we were at the beginning of an entire lifetime of moments together. Happily, as if we shared some delightful secret, we carried on up the path to the car to retrieve our things.

"You are quite right, my lovely and very spooky wife. I saw something extraordinary in that butter churn full of papers. And you're not going to believe me when I tell you what it was."

"Just tell me it was completely unrelated to Samuel Pepys, and I'll be happy."

"Darling, you know I love to make you happy, but . . ."

Sarah stopped and looked me in the eye. "In a butter churn from a New Hampshire farm, you found something to do with *Pepys*?? What? Why? How could you tell?"

"Ah, my dear. It's all thanks to Shelton's Tachygraphy, the—"

"I know what it is. Your master's thesis, the code—" She gazed at me as if I might have a screw or two loose.

"Sarah, for heaven's sake, I know it when I see it. I agree that it's totally bizarre, but there's no denying it's his writing. And it's interleaved with smatterings of French and Latin, another of his tricks to disguise those embarrassing secrets. Seriously, it's an authentic example of Pepys's jottings."

"What did it say? And how could it possibly be submerged in a batch of Frost's farm records?"

"I didn't have much time to translate it, but I saw his abbreviation for 'Dartmouth.' That leads me to believe it might have something to do with his Tangier expedition with Lord Dartmouth, but I don't know for certain. I'd love to have another look at it, but something told me to keep mum."

"Yes, I noticed," she said as we lifted our bags out of the

boot. "You're too good at it for my taste. I hope you're not going to start trying to hide things from me."

"Never!" I scooped her up in my arms as we crossed the threshold of Richardson Hall. She gave a satisfying whoop and allowed me to carry her to the reunions desk, where an undergraduate trying to earn a bit of summer money marked us off on his list and gave us a room key.

"Room 303," he said.

"Perfect." I smiled at Sarah. "The most romantic room of my entire college career."

"Yes, I remember it well. But shouldn't you have been studying?" Sarah said, with a backward smile at the reunions worker. The boy grinned and returned to his paperback.

I put her down and raced her up the three flights of stairs to the room. All the while my mind was working away on what Mattie might have found, and how there could be *still* more Pepysiana lying undiscovered in the butter churn. I remembered all too well accidentally breaking the thin but official-looking Dartmouth College tape that sealed the churn. What connection could Pepys possibly have had with rural New Hampshire, for heaven's sake?

I also couldn't help but be increasingly concerned about Mattie. An ominous and unavoidable link was forming in my mind between this supposed Pepys find and her disappearance.

But at the sight of Sarah, who had won the race up the stairs and now stood breathless but triumphant outside the dorm room as she had with my friend Peter so many years ago, those thoughts disappeared without a trace. I unlocked the door, feeling my wife's delicious warmth as she stood close. Then, as the door swung open, I was transported to my collegiate days with dizzying speed and clarity.

The aroma of cleaning products and old building hadn't changed one whiff in fifteen years . . . probably not in half a century. Now that I was halfway between thirty and forty I began to understand the deep craving for an absence of change. There was something almost sacred about this dorm room and its exact replication of my memories.

Sarah had moved to the fireplace and was looking into its grate. It would be impossible for her to visit this room and not have memories of Peter. Sometimes it felt odd, sharing her with my dead friend—but after all, I'd loved him too.

I went to her and put my arms around her. "All right?"

She nodded, and I was relieved to see a smile on her face when she turned to face me. "This was a good room. We used to roast hot dogs and marshmallows in this fireplace . . . but only on the nights you promised Peter you wouldn't be back 'til late. Come to think of it, I suppose you entertained your own dates here on the nights *we* were out."

I gave her a naughty smile and enjoyed my own memories of the fireplace. It had warmed many an evening with various girlfriends, crew buddies, and books. "If you really want to know, I'll tell you what I remember best about this fireplace."

"You're not going to compromise any of my friends' reputations at this point, are you?"

I pretended to consider the matter. "Well . . . I suppose it's more a blemish on *my* reputation. It's reading Pepys's diary here I remember best."

She chuckled.

"I had to damp the fire and sit in a very hard straight chair, drinking strong coffee all the while. Talk about a slog, and in those tender years . . . but at least I knew London. I'll never know how Mattie got through it for that Pepys seminar, never having gone farther from New York than Vermont."

Peering out the front window, I saw that this room had a perfect view of Rauner Library. It might have been designed for a visiting biblio-obsessive.

Well. An entire spare afternoon, complete with Sarah, sun, blue sky, mountains . . . and a bedroom.

Sarah was evidently thinking along the same lines. She gave me that certain look, and I . . .

Several sharp raps sounded on the door.

Blast! Had I forgotten something at the reunions reception desk? I swung open the door.

"Blake!" The son of one of my American copublishing partners, Charlie Goodspeed of Megabooks, stood grinning in the doorway.

"I thought that was you, disappearing into the dorm." He peered into the room behind me and waved at Sarah. "Don't tell me you're here for reunions and didn't even tell me!"

"I remember what it's like. You don't have time for visiting old fogeys. Come in, come in!"

Blake laughed, the very picture of robust youth. He'd obviously just come from crew practice and wore a worn Dartmouth Crew T-shirt and rowing shorts. Charlie had told me his son was on a long-term training regimen, preparing himself for a go at the U.S. Olympic team. Several years ago, I'd spent the better part of a weekend once at the Goodspeed home outside Boston, discussing the benefits of Dartmouth with Blake. I was delighted that it had seemed a good match for him.

"Aren't you going to introduce me?"

I apologised and introduced Sarah. He congratulated us with the awe accorded newlyweds, then glanced around. "Man, you really splashed out on the honeymoon suite!" He grinned. "Just teasing. These places are pretty grim without any stuff in 'em though. Didn't you live in Richardson once?"

"Indeed I did! Well, let's not stand around here . . . have you had lunch yet?"

"No, we just finished practice. Let's get some sandwiches—hey, we could go down to the docks! I'll fill you in on what's happening at the boathouse. Sarah, you used to row too, right?"

We chatted comfortably about the stunning successes of the women's crew as we went back outside, where Blake locked his bike to the rack. Then we set off together on foot for a local sandwich shop. I purchased a vast amount of food, remembering how I'd been famished after crew practice. After a stroll across campus and down the wooded incline to the river, we found ourselves stretched out on the docks, soaking up the sun as we pulled out the components of our immense lunch. I felt as if I'd just come home, there where I'd spent so many hours with the crew; Sarah's nostalgic smile told me she felt it too.

Blake downed the better part of a huge bottle of flavoured iced tea, then spoke. "Notice how dead it is down here? Except for sunworshippers, I mean?"

I had noticed. On a day like this, usually there was

someone taking a boat out. But today there were only kayakers. "I thought perhaps summer term hadn't officially started yet. Why, what's going on?"

"Things aren't too copacetic down here at the boathouse," he said through a bite of sandwich.

"Don't tell me the heavyweight/lightweight rivalry's got out of hand again?" Nearly four years ago, when I heard Blake had signed up for crew, I'd told him about the outrageous forms of torture we'd designed for each other in my day. The lightweights had called us pigweights and we'd called them pests. We threw them in the river, they sabotaged our cars; we stuck fireworks in their back pockets, they threw grapefruits at us in the dining hall.

Blake shook his head. "I wish it were that much fun. No, the powers that be—you know, the alums who raise the money for the rowing club—are fed up with the younger guys wrecking the boats. They cost more than ten thousand dollars now, you know. A freshman eight ran one of the newest shells over the stump just before the end of spring term—ripped the bottom right out. Obviously *that* cox will never be allowed out on the river again. Then some beginners destroyed the Gardner."

"*No!*" The Gardner was the shell my eight had given to the club in honour of our coach in that fateful year politics had prevented us from going to the Olympics. The very thought of it could still make me feel ill; as a team, we had decided to make something positive of it and honour Coach Gardner.

He nodded somberly. "So our two best shells are out for the count. Evidently when they're ripped up that badly, they have to be rebuilt. It'll take months. We still don't have the Somerville-Hull back from the first accident. Henley's only weeks away! And the alums aren't too eager to help out, since they feel everyone's being so reckless with the boats. They've totally suspended fundraising efforts. This could be the end of the glory days of Dartmouth crew. Washed up for lack of funds."

We walked in silence for a moment, contemplating our suspicions. This was serious. It was true that I hadn't received a mailing recently, but quite often there was ebb and flow in volunteer organisations like the Friends of Dartmouth Rowing. I knew the people involved, certainly, as I had often hosted the Dartmouth crew's delegation to Henley, the rowing world's premier regatta on the Thames in Oxfordshire. Every other year the Friends raised the money to get the teams across the pond. Perhaps this was the time to come to the aid of the team.

"What *are* you going to do to train for Henley? Can't you borrow shells from someone?"

Blake shrugged. "We've tried. Doesn't look like there's going to be one for us. You can imagine how eager people are to lend us boats. We're ready, though—training-wise. Did I tell you we won the sprints this year?"

"Wow." This was tragic. For Blake not to get to Henley in his senior year, especially when they'd won the Worcester Sprints, was too awful to contemplate. Henley should be experienced by every serious oarsman—particularly those like Blake who might even be destined for the Olympics. I hated to see him miss it.

"I wonder if I could arrange anything in time," I said. "Is that shell company still across the river in Vermont?"

"Mm-hmm." Lounging on his side, Blake chomped on the second half of a thick chicken salad sandwich and nodded. He hurried to finish the bite. "But wait a minute.

Even if you wanted to be that generous, there's not enough time—"

"Dartmouth and rowing mean a lot to me. I'd like to see what I could do. Maybe I'll pop over there after lunch." Even as I said it, I mourned for Sarah's and my lost afternoon. But my heroic wife said, "Yes, let's." Of course the women's crew would be suffering, too.

I watched as a kayaker deftly manoeuvred his boat through an obstacle course of floating buoys.

Blake shook his head. "I really want to come with you. But I've got a chemistry lab at one-thirty. I can't miss it."

"Good on," I said. "Your father'd have my head if he knew I was tempting you to neglect your studies. Especially with your grade-point average. He's told me, you know."

Blake grabbed a giant chocolate chip-oatmeal cookie and downed it in several bites, rolling his eyes—affectionately—at the mention of his dad. Charlie Goodspeed was justifiably proud of his son, who so effortlessly seemed to be able to achieve perfect grades while being one of the boys and the powerhouse of a winning crew team. In fact, if the truth be known, I felt some vaguely paternal pride myself where Blake was concerned.

We took a leisurely walk back to Richardson, where he picked up his bike. "Thanks again for lunch!" He called over his shoulder as he drifted down the pavement, derailleurs clicking. "Lou's Saturday morning, nine o'clock!" He'd insisted upon taking us out for breakfast at a favourite local diner.

It was a good thing Blake invited us out to breakfast. What I learned nearly killed me, but it also happened to be the key to the Pepys papers paradox.

CHAPTER 9

... nor, as matters are now, can any fleet go out next year.

He tells me his opinion that it is out of possibility for us to escape being undone, there being nothing in our power to do that is necessary for the saving us: a lazy Prince, no Council, no money, no reputation at home or abroad.

This, added to all the rest, do lay us flat in our hopes and courages, every body prophesying destruction to the nation.

SAMUEL PEPYS

I really like Blake," Sarah said. "I hope we can do something about the boat situation. Why don't we call Vermont Shells before we drive over?"

Sarah's constant tendency to be right might have been annoying to another man; it only proved to me how lucky I was. One of the most respected shell-making enterprises was mere miles away, across the river. But when I told the proprietor, a Dartmouth alum and (naturally) fellow oarsman what I was trying to do, he apologised. "I'm sorry, Alex. I'd love to help you—especially since the College is involved. But this is our busiest season; any shell that's within months of being river-worthy is already spoken for."

I thanked him and informed Sarah, who made a little face of commiseration. "What a shame," she said.

Both of us plied the various shell-making firms, from New Jersey to Seattle, with calls . . . to no avail. Perhaps someone in the UK . . . but several calls across the pond were fruitless as well. The Henley Regatta was nearly upon us; shells were in shorter supply in England than in America.

I sighed. "Well. What shall we do with ourselves for the rest of the afternoon?"

She stopped fiddling with her wedding ring and looked me directly in the eye.

All right; it had been a silly question.

"You know," Sarah said later, cradled in my arms, "maybe we could just disappear somewhere for a while."

"Mmm," I said contentedly. "Vanish into thin air." But at the thought, a memory came creeping back . . . one that had asserted itself earlier that day. It was most unpleasant.

"What's wrong?" Sarah asked, twisting to look at me. "You've gone all tense."

"Nothing."

"You know that 'nothing' doesn't work with me, Alex Plumtree. Part of being married is sharing things. Right?"

"Yes, but I don't want to share *horrible* things." I stroked her glossy hair. Could she really be my wife? I gazed at her long, brown legs stretched out on the bed.

Unfortunately, dark thoughts diminished my delight. "I want to bring good things your way and shield you from the rest."

"Sorry. Part of the deal. It's all or nothing." She smiled at me and I felt an unreasonable urge to cry. How could she possibly care so much?

I mastered my tear ducts, but my eyes were moist as I kissed the top of her head and hugged her tightly. Then, with a sigh, I told all.

"Mattie disappeared once before, during our freshman year. I barely knew her, except as our cox. It was right before the Head of the Charles, that ultimate autumnal test of every crew in America. In Boston, too, not her native New York. Besides whatever challenges the Charles River might hold, it was her first term with the pressures of swimming in a big academic pond. Maybe it was just too much pressure. She was missing for three days before they found her in the woods. She was cold, dangerously dehydrated, and catatonic."

Sarah put her hand over mine.

"Her parents took her home, and she came back right as rain for the next term. She never spoke of it, and I never told a soul. Sarah, I'm worried. What if she's—well, gone off the rails again? What if she's languishing in the woods somewhere?"

"Maybe we should call the police."

"I would if she didn't work for the College. Hanover can be a very small town. Mattie might not thank us if she comes back from some sort of self-declared holiday and finds that we've lost her her job."

"I see what you mean . . ."

"What would you think of paying a visit to the *other* Pepys expert in town—Mattie's and my old professor, Pettifer Bartlett? Maybe he'd know something."

"Excellent idea. Maybe they've kept in touch."

Twenty minutes later, after calling the Pet and receiving an enthusiastic invitation to come for a visit, we were flying down the road towards Etna. This idyllic New Hampshire town was one of many like it that housed Dartmouth professors in rustic splendour. Pettifer had a nice little sheep farm on twenty acres or so outside the town; Mattie and I'd been there often in our Pepys seminar days.

Life looked very good indeed, aside from the nagging question of Mattie Harding's whereabouts. *Hang on, Mattie,* I thought, willing her to survive, and drove on. We pulled up to Pettifer's home, a small clapboard colonial that looked as if it had been built in the eighteenth century, and stepped out onto the gravel drive. A magnificent shrub rose of a ripe old age bloomed in pink profusion in the circular drive, and emerald green grass studded with small rocks extended into the distance.

"Look," Sarah breathed. A lamb followed its mother up the incline to the house and stopped not far from our car, making a near-human sound.

I knelt and said a gentle hello, but the lamb beat a hasty retreat to its mother.

"Alex!" The Pet himself appeared, a legendary figure, outside his front door. "And this must be Sarah. Come in, come in!"

As we approached, I could feel Sarah's reticence. Yes, the Pet had angular features that could seem forbidding . . . and a crooked smile that he'd never explained. His height and wide cheekbones gave him a blatantly forceful appearance that could be intimidating to those who didn't know him well. But no one had had a greater impact on my scholarly future than Pettifer Bartlett. Over twenty-seven years he'd won more teaching awards than any other member of the Dartmouth faculty, and was one of the College's favourite "personalities."

"Pettifer," I told him, "wonderful to see you again."

"And *you*." He gripped my hand as if I were a long-lost friend but directed his lopsided smile at Sarah. I was growing used to the attention focussed on her and thoroughly enjoyed it. Couldn't have agreed more.

"This is my wife, Sarah Townsend—er, Plumtree. A fellow eighty-six."

"Delighted to meet you, Sarah." Pettifer spoke in a disconcerting mid-Atlantic dialect, reflecting his British birth.

"And you," Sarah returned. "I've heard a great deal about you."

"How unfortunate," he quipped with humility, making a face as we stepped through his door. The old place, cool and dark and smelling of wood smoke, hadn't changed a bit. We stepped onto the same worn rugs I'd trod as a student, smelled the same musty, woolly, old-house, firesmoke smell.

"Please—sit down. I'm more than eager to hear all your news. Is this a reunion year for you?"

"Indeed it is," I answered. "Fifteenth. It's wonderful to be back—our first reunion in all these years."

Sarah and I settled ourselves on a small sofa in the cosy room that was the body of the house; Pettifer sat across from us in a rocking chair. The kitchen was nothing more than a small nook adjacent to the fireplace.

"Really! But you've been back many times since eighty-six, Alex—I recall your visits well. You're involved with the Friends of the Library, aren't you?"

"Yes—and isn't Rauner a wonder? Well worth all it took."

"Indeed. But if I had to choose, I'd take the Pepys Library any day."

I smiled. "Yes, I suppose you would. Well, please—tell all. Any plans to come over soon? Any new breakthroughs in your research?"

"How I wish, Alex. Sadly, *new* work on Pepys is all but impossible."

I thought fleetingly of Timothy's mention of secondary character work, and the manuscript written from the viewpoint of Pepys's maid.

"Although there's been a fascinating rumour on the Internet lately . . ." he began.

"Yes! I wanted to ask you about that." Suddenly, I was uncomfortable with my old professor. I felt he was behaving differently now Sarah was here, almost putting on an act—as if he were in the classroom. He was . . . well, more *formal*. Ever so subtly, things had changed. It made me wonder. "Do you think it's all a hoax? Or has something new really been found?"

"I'll be honest with you, Alex." He stopped rocking. "I'm in a quandary about this. On the one hand, how likely is it that something new could have been found? On the other hand, how can Pepys scholars like me afford to ignore the possibility?"

It was time to use the shock-approach—softened by a

smile. "Frankly, Pettifer, I'd hoped you were the mysterious author of the posting. Who is more familiar with all things Pepysian—especially around Dartmouth?"

"Ha! You always did have a wild imagination, Alex." He looked me right in the eye, not at all flustered. Nor did he overreact.

Damn.

"It's nice to see you haven't lost your creativity." He seemed amused at the thought.

Ah, well, Alex ... try another tack. "Do you keep in touch with Mattie Harding? Considering her work at Rauner, she *must* know what's going on in the world of acquisitions. And I'm sure Pepys would jump out at her from any list of offerings."

"Alex, to be truthful, I think you're barking up the wrong tree by even crediting this rumour of a find. The fact that nothing more has followed the posting for nearly two weeks—on the Internet or otherwise—tends to make me believe it's a hoax."

I noticed he'd sidestepped my question about Mattie; odd. "But why would someone bother to fabricate such a story?"

He shook his head emphatically. "Alex, the world of academic scholarship can be one of pettiness and deceit. You of all people should know that by now."

I thought, *no, that's not true ... there might be politics and egos in academia, but that was the worst that could be said. Our authors always brought something fascinating to the table.*

"The message might have been the effort of one poor assistant professor at Somewhere University to focus attention on a new book he's bringing out." Pettifer shrugged. "I don't put too much emphasis on it."

"Pettifer," I began, "do you know that Mattie's gone missing?" The moment I'd said it, the angular Bartlett features went rigid as a statue—just like Phil's. What was going on?

"Missing?"

"She asked us to meet her this morning, but she wasn't at home." I decided to minimise the situation, just in case Mattie turned up that night after some sort of spectacular binge. "I'm just a bit concerned," I finished awkwardly.

The scholar turned his head towards the fireplace and grimaced. "It's possible that I've never told you about Mattie's *relationship*"—he pronounced the word as if it were poison—"with my son. Lane works at the equestrian facility here."

"No . . . I didn't know."

"He and Mattie have been seeing each other for some time. Perhaps two years now. Alex, you know I'm fond of Mattie. You were in the same seminar, two of my best students. But she's—unbalanced."

My worst fears had been confirmed.

"You see, she and Lane have a rather mercurial relationship. The fact that she's disappeared now is not particularly unusual. I've tried to help the poor girl, and God knows Lane's put up with a lot." He looked down at the floor as if it might be unkind to say more.

"I'm sorry to hear that. I thought—"

"I know. Mattie puts up a good front, holds down a good job. But have you seen her home lately? I would no sooner advise my son to consider marriage with—But

I've said too much. Forgive me." He rose and tried to smile. Suddenly I felt such sympathy for my old professor that I wanted to help him, do something for him. To my dismay, I couldn't think of anything.

"I've made some scones . . . I do hope you'll have tea," he said. "When I last visited you, Alex, I picked up some Millennium Blend at Fortnum's. Been enjoying it ever since."

"That would be lovely," I assured him. "Let us help you." But the tea ritual was a bleak little occasion, overshadowed by my fears for Mattie's well-being. Moreover, I'm afraid Sarah received a poor impression of my star professor.

As we prepared to leave I asked, "Does Mattie go to a special place when she's—er—off by herself?"

Pettifer shrugged and crossed his arms in front of his chest. "You could try the weather station," he said neutrally.

"The weather station? Something to do with CRREL?" The Cold Regions Research Laboratory was one of Hanover's claims to fame. The area certainly did experience extremes of cold, as Sarah and I could testify.

But Pettifer shook his head. "No. I'm talking about Mount Washington. Mattie has some sort of affinity for that mountain."

"Mount Washington?" I couldn't believe it. It was one of the most challenging peaks in the East. The Dartmouth Crew had trained there regularly, running up and down the trails. Sarah, Peter, Mattie, and I had also run down once when bad weather hit us on the way up, lightning crackling after us all the way.

"The same. I've chased after her a couple of times, Alex, but I'm getting too old for that sort of thing. I try to shield Lane from the worst of it, but there's no escaping the fact that Mattie is a poor marriage risk."

I stood stunned outside my mentor's front door. Sarah finally tugged at my hand. "We'd better go, Alex."

"Call me if you learn anything," Pettifer said.

We said our thanks, waved, and retreated to the car as he disappeared into the house. I got into the driver's seat; it had been understood, since the trouble with my eyes, that I would drive until I could no longer manage it.

"Whew," Sarah said quietly, fastening her seat belt. "That poor man. Something's going on there."

"Yes, I know what you mean. I felt it, too. This issue with Mattie must be very difficult for him—in more than one way."

"Mmm."

Slowly, I turned to look at my wife. "*Mmm?* Now *you're* saying Mmm? What are we coming to? Who will make fun of *whom* in our family?"

I'd succeeded in making her laugh, and that made *me* laugh. There was nothing better than Sarah laughing. It was like the sun shining, the wind rustling the leaves.

"All right, all *right*," she conceded. "But I don't think your professor friend was very forthcoming with us. Moreover, I'm not sure I like him. I know that doesn't sound particularly charitable. Worse yet, I can't explain why."

"No, I understand. The Pet wasn't quite himself today. I thought he seemed rather . . . distant. Less than genuine."

Sarah remained silent, which might have meant that she agreed, or that she had taken my opinion under advisement.

I didn't tell her that this was the first time I'd noticed his hard side, his cold side—if you could even call it that. Was it that I was now married? I shied away from the thought that there was any kind of prejudice on Pettifer's part towards the married. No, probably the dynamics had changed ever so subtly and it was simply a case of bachelor vs nonbachelor. Furthermore, I couldn't ignore the fact that Pettifer had endured two unsuccessful marriages, and it must be difficult for him to see a happy new liaison beginning.

As the car passed along the shaded road that would put us on the highway back to the College, my thoughts turned again to Mattie. *Where was she? Was she all right? Did it make sense for me to go hunting along the trails of . . .*

"I know what you're thinking," Sarah said.

"I don't doubt it."

"You're worried about Mattie. You're wondering if you should head right over to Mount Washington now, and check with the ranger's station. But you're thinking that it's almost three, and we wouldn't even get over there until six . . . and you're planning to attend the Friends of the Library meeting at four."

"Remarkable."

"May I make a suggestion?"

"By all means . . ."

"Call the ranger's station and alert them to the possibility that someone might be missing there. They might not be able to take on a full search, since we don't know for certain that she ever went to the mountain. But maybe the rangers could keep an eye out. It would be better than nothing."

"Sarah. My love. I hope you don't think that I'm too concerned about Mattie for a married man. Please believe me; it's not like that at all."

"I know, Alex. One of the things I love about you is your dedication to your friends. Also your willingness to help someone in trouble."

I reached over and took her hand; she squeezed it. The future looked very bright indeed, Pepys or no Pepys . . . and it had been a refreshingly long time since I'd caught sight of another parallel between Pepys's time and mine. It gave me hope.

The Friends of the Library met in the Treasure Room of Baker Library, an almost ecclesiastical-looking jewel of a room. It had housed part of the College's special collections library before Rauner was built; I could still remember from undergraduate days the huge books of Audubon prints in their glass cases. Brightly coloured stained glass windows featuring the College's founders studded the room with light. Shelves of books covered the space in between, except for the huge fireplace that occupied one entire wall. Pettifer had once showed me a secret about that fireplace: there was a hiding place behind the mantel . . . for what purpose, no one knew.

The meeting came and went with nothing more than a passing, jocular reference to the Pepys find. The College libraries were on a very firm footing in every way, and Rauner had another exciting collection coming its way in addition to the Frost Farm bequest. A quiet word from Phil Cronenwett told me that I was to be on hand in case anything came of this Pepys firecracker. He suspected a hoax, but until then, we'd wait and see, he said.

Once I saw that all was well for Dartmouth's libraries, I allowed myself to enjoy the occasion, hob-nobbing with some frightfully well-read people. The group included one renowned and extremely well-thought-of Boston book publisher, with whom I chatted at length. Fellow collectors abounded, as you might expect, and following the meeting I had a good forty-five minutes animated chat with a whole gaggle of like-minded gentlemen and women.

To my surprise, Phil Cronenwett motioned that I should join him in a corner. He seemed on edge, and steered me farther away from the crowd as a well-meaning waiter came towards us with a tray of canapés. "I must tell you, Alex—it's about our conversation earlier today. I'm worried too, and not just for Mattie's sake. Things have gone crazy around here. First the bequest, which I'm convinced was the start of it all, then Mattie's disappearance, and now . . ."

He broke off.

"Phil—what is it? What's happened?"

His normally sparkling eyes, now at half-mast, met mine. "We had a break-in last night. The first since the library's been open. I didn't want to tell you while Sarah was with us. The security system held, thank God."

On that afternoon's refresher-course tour of the library with the Friends, Phil had shown us the sophisticated system, complete with motion detectors and heat sensors. It certainly seemed impenetrable.

He went on, "I *know* it has something to do with this bequest—but it just doesn't make sense. Mattie hasn't been around for me to ask her about it, but sometimes I wonder if she's found something she's keeping to herself. You know that the anonymous posting on Pepysiana said the find was made at Dartmouth." He looked me in the eye. "There are only two of us here at the College who have much to do with Pepys . . . besides Mattie, who was enamoured of him as a student."

You and Pettifer, I thought. "You've talked to Pettifer Bartlett?"

"Of course. But he's as mystified as I am."

We pondered the strangeness of it all in silence for a moment . . . but then a penetrating, unearthly noise shattered the civilised calm of the Treasure Room. I smiled even as I winced when an older gentleman dropped his glass on the floor.

Only one other person could make that noise: Montgomery "Moose" Musgrave. I looked up to see my old crew buddy beaming at me from the far end of the room. Moose, another member of the class of '86, had been in the so-called engine room of the boat where the real muscles resided. Most oarsmen are tall—anywhere from six feet to six-seven—and have long, sculpted muscles. Moose, on the other hand, is six-six, with giant bulging biceps and quads akin to Arnold Schwarzenegger's. I'd read in the Library newsletter that he'd been appointed to the Friends of the Library board.

Phil hurriedly said, "I must tell you, Alex—my family vacation starts tomorrow. It's the worst possible time, but it's been scheduled for more than a year. The College is making me take it; they think I work too hard." From the look on his face, the idea of going away just then was much harder on him than giving up the holiday. "I'll be in touch when I get back, all right?"

"Of course . . ." I tried to find out where he was going—after all, if I had my way I'd be arranging some family holidays myself—but he pointed at his watch and made an escape through the room's back door.

Moose arrived as Phil disappeared, having made apologies for the noise, helped clean up the broken glass, and greeted everyone along the way. The startled silence resulting from the Moose call had changed into energetic laughter.

"Buddy!"

"Moose!"

We rejoiced in seeing one another again—few relationships can equal those forged during consecutive years of physical torture in a boat—and caught up on my wedding and his divorce. After some good-natured verbal abuse, accompanied by bone-shuddering thumps on the back, he caught me up on the crew news. "Living in Boston, I can drive up for all the meetings," my friend declared, sipping his drink.

Moose hadn't changed one iota. He still looked like someone from the back streets of Bayonne. In fact, he had grown up on Philadelphia's Main Line. The circumstances of his birth caused him to be peculiarly classless and nonjudgemental; he was above all that.

Moose and I shared many secrets. One of the more harmless ones I can recount without damaging his reputation too severely is the pride he took in never changing sheets during term. ("*Whaddaya mean?*" he'd boom, stalking towards me like a cave man. "I take a shower

every day! Why should I have to wash the *!# *sheets?*")
You'll have the full picture if I tell you that he was as
meticulous about his studies as he was carefree about his
bed linens; he graduated Phi Beta Kappa, spoke fluent
Chinese, and volunteered for the campus tutoring pro-
gram.

Ah, I missed my friends like Moose.

"The fact is, some of the guys are getting a little PO'd,"
he said. "About the younger guys not pulling their weight.
In terms of donations, I mean. By the way, thanks for all
you've done." As he snatched an egg roll from the hors
d'oeuvres platter, he raised his eyebrows at me. "It doesn't
help that the students are wrecking all the boats. No
doubt you heard about that."

"Mmm."

He smiled. "A crisis for the crew. Needless to say,
there'll be no trip to Henley *this* year."

"Do you need some help drumming up support
amongst the younger alums? I'd be happy to assist. You
know the oarsmen would be welcome to stay with me, as
usual."

"We *have* been drumming, my friend. It seems everyone thinks that the donation to Friends of Dartmouth
Rowing is the first expenditure to cut, now that the economy's gone south. Or else they're tired of having the boats
ripped apart and sunk." He chomped on a drumstick and
changed the subject. "By the way, I understand you have a
certain crisis of your own over in London." His look said,
man, have you *got problems*.

"I know it. What a mess. And to have the terrorism follow so closely on the Queen's accident . . ."

He gave me a puzzled look. "Pardon me if I haven't understood it properly, but it seems to be the succession crisis that's making people sit up and take notice."

"*Succession* crisis? Last I heard, there were some protests, but—"

"Hey, don't tell me I know more about this than you, Buddy! Yeah, heard it on the way up in the car—everyone figures the Queen's out for the count and they're going to have to put someone else on the throne. On top of that, all the banks are having to close because of the fires and bombings. People are talking about a real economic and social collapse."

I stared at him and realised that Ian's nightmare was coming true. With horrified fascination, I saw that we were sinking deeper into parallels with Pepys's time. There was still a Charles in the picture, too . . . one with religious concerns.

"But that only just edges out the religious crisis for public outcry," Moose commented, as if reading my mind. He plucked another stuffed mushroom off the platter and eyed it, apparently enjoying himself.

I must have boggled.

"Buddy, you'd better find a TV around here somewhere. Wait—don't tell me: you're staying in the dorms! And you've just been married? For the first time?"

By my lack of response, he saw that we were.

"That figures," he said, rolling his eyes. "*You*—"

"Tell me," I interrupted, having finally found my voice. "Exactly what are you calling the *religious* crisis?"

"It's your Bonnie Prince Charlie. He made a statement to the press that he would *not* agree to be head of the church if he were to assume the throne, which looks imminent. People went wild—the churches are full of people holding candles, and the streets are full of others holding placards denouncing a national church. Doesn't look good. Meanwhile, the fires keep erupting—but mostly in the Square Mile."

The City. We might have been discussing the weather, for all the concern Moose showed. For him, this was just an interesting insight into a foreign country, like over-sized insects in Brazil. He chose a shrimp puff, but hesitated long enough to deliver another zinger before popping it into his mouth.

"Then you've got all those people complaining that the kid should be promoted over his father. Oops! I suppose my American capitalist language sounds crass to you. It's 'ascend' . . . and I should say *Prince* William, right? You know, most of the time, Buddy, we just forget you're English." He grinned.

"Moose—" I cleared my throat and started again. It wouldn't do to have the gents surrounding us hear such names now. He smiled.

"Er, *Montgomery*"—we couldn't say each other's real names without laughing—"I can't thank you enough for letting me know. Are you going to the Bema for the cook-out?" The Bema was a large open area where giant college events were held outside.

"That's what I came for. Is it time?" He nearly dropped the fourth shrimp puff trying to catch sight of his watch.

"Past. Want to walk over together?"

In typical Moose style, he didn't answer but instead proceeded to barge towards the exit.

"The truth is, Buddy, I hear Mattie Harding's coming. I've called her a few times, sort of testing the waters. She sounds remotely interested. Thought it might be nice to—you know—re-establish détente. We said we'd try to meet at the Bema tonight."

Ah. I got the picture. Of course it would fall to me to tell Moose what had happened with Mattie—but only just after he'd told me my homeland was going to the dogs.

"Moose, you know—"

"Yeah. She was hot on you. No hard feelings, I trust—especially now that you're married." He regarded me with a touch of worry.

"Good heavens, no," I said. "It's just that—"

"And I know about her and that English prof., Bartlett, isn't it? The one who looks like Frankenstein."

Pettifer Bartlett and Mattie?! Surely not. Moose must be mistaken. And I had to admit, I'd never thought of him as Frankenstein. But there were certain similarities. . . .

"Would you *listen* to me for a moment?" I stopped walking, and he finally sensed that I was serious. "Moose, Mattie has gone missing."

He looked at me askance. "First of all, Buddy, you're sounding real English there. '*Gone missing*?'"

I rolled my eyes.

"Secondly," he lowered his voice, "do you mean to tell me you're *still seeing Mattie*—I mean, even after the wedding—?" He seemed intrigued by the thought, a man after Pepys's own heart.

"For heaven's sake *no*! I only meant"—I felt trapped—"she's gone missing." I winced in the expectation of his mockery.

"Okay. How do you know she's *gone missing*?"

"It's a long story." I sighed. "It all has to do with a potential acquisition for the library that I happened to know something about. Mattie rang—okay, *called*—and asked if I would meet her to discuss it. She never showed up. What's more, her house had either been trashed or she's had some kind of major blowout." My American English was coming right back, I noticed. Nothing like a little peer pressure.

Moose let a particularly ripe epithet fly. "How long ago? Have you heard from her? Have you tried to find her?"

"I haven't heard from her since she asked us to go hiking—I suppose four days ago. That professor you claim she was friendly with told me she sometimes goes to Mount Washington when she's upset."

"Mount Washington! I remember how she used to try to keep up with us monsters, running up there on crew workouts. I was really impressed that she bothered—*and* that she could do it. Maybe the place got into her blood. Geez."

"I was thinking about the time she had a sort of breakdown there. Do you remember that? They found her on some outcropping—wasn't it Dead Man's Ledge? Barely alive."

"You mean *that's* where she went that year? Right before the Head of the Charles? I never knew. You never told us."

"Perhaps I shouldn't have now. But the truth is, I'm worried, Moose. I'm *very* worried."

"Have you called the police?" All thought of racing towards the Bema seemed to have fled his mind.

I shook my head. "Remember, she works for the College. The College doesn't like negative publicity, you know."

"Yeah." He'd been hauled before the College Committee on Student Conduct on several occasions for various forms of outrageous behaviour. It was hard to believe, looking at him now in his pristine khakis, heavily starched Oxford cloth shirt, and tasselled loafers.

Moose stood staring at Dartmouth Hall in the late afternoon, the "gleaming, dreaming" hour according to one of the school songs. Remarkably, the graceful white building with its black shutters and weathervane did summon an emotional response. "I'll tell you one thing, Buddy. If she doesn't surface tonight for the reunion, I'm calling the police in the morning."

CHAPTER 10

*Mighty talk there is of this Comet that is seen a'nights
. . . I will endeavour [to see] it.*

*. . . in all my life I never did see any poor wretch in that
condition.*

I was even afraid myself, though I appeared otherwise.

SAMUEL PEPYS

The next five hours were a wild carnival of reminiscence. Apart from several startling cases of people who seemed to feel they'd been close friends of mine who I didn't recognise, I had a magnificent time. Sarah and I came together occasionally throughout the evening, but always parted again to greet other friends—with the exception of the hour and a half we spent recalling antics with the crew team. We took over a couple of tables and before long had once again become the most exuberant group there.

When most of the gathering broke up around eleven to retrieve children from the Kids' Tent, several hundred of us lingered, reluctant to let the evening end. The band played on. At half-past twelve Sarah announced she was going to her senior society house for a drink—did I want to come? I said no, thanks, and waved good-bye. But the truth was, after she went the party seemed to be over, loud and lively as it was. I decided to visit Shattuck Observatory—it always stayed open late on reunion weekends for viewing. Someone had told me at the Bema that there was some sort of comet visible that night, and I was curious.

I was also tired. Seeing so many old friends at once was a bit like reliving years of life in several hours, and just as exhilarating and exhausting. I followed the trail out of the park, enjoying the incomparable aroma of a cool, moist, leafy summer night in New Hampshire. Bass thumped from the Alpha Delta fraternity house sound equipment, but aside from me, the path was deserted. I looked up at the sky and saw a bright star with what looked like a tail trailing after it. I stopped in my tracks. *The comet!* I'd seen it!

But the joy faded when I recalled that Pepys, too, had seen a comet—and of course written about it in his diary. This was all getting to be too much. Besides, I was so unlike Pepys . . . I would never be unfaithful to Sarah, or—

"Alex!" The intense whisper came from behind the odd, rectangular concrete building known as The Sphinx, one of the secret societies on campus.

I had learned to be cautious about voices whispering from behind looming shapes in the dark. Whoever it was had obviously been waiting, watching for me. Hackles up, I said, "Who's there?"

"*Shhhh!* It's me! Mattie."

I hurried round the side of the building and found her, looking haunted, almost ghostly in the moonlight except for a very human dark blotch encircling her left eye. Of course I would run into *her* just after telling myself how unlike Pepys I was when it came to women. What a sense of humour the Almighty had.

"Mattie! For heaven's sake, what's happened to you?"

She beckoned for me to shut up and follow her, and turned away. Believe it or not, this was not a completely unfamiliar scenario where Mattie was concerned. I thought our chances of being seen there was greater amongst the moss and old leaves by a couple indulging in fantasies of yesteryear, but perhaps she knew what she was doing. Obediently I followed her back out of the woods to a grey Honda Civic with a crumpled bumper. She sat on one broken-down seat and impatiently waved me in, gazing anxiously around us as if the area were fraught with spies.

Inside, the tiny car smelled of mouldy carpets and fast food remnants left too long in wadded-up paper bags. It was all most un-Mattie-like. The last car I'd seen her in had been a white BMW with spotless floor mats.

"Lock your door," she said earnestly, and turned to study me in the darkness. "Alex . . . still just the same."

But married. For just a moment, I remembered how much I'd felt for her . . . and how much fun our times together had been. There was something between us in the car; perhaps just shared memories, or maybe curiosity about what might have happened had things been different. As I studied her face, she looked perhaps a bit more chiselled, but otherwise the Mattie of fifteen years ago. I thought she was probably one of those women who was destined to look like a child all her life, partly because of her size and partly because of an unconscious vulnerability.

With an effort she turned away and started the car. The

spell was broken at the very same moment it occurred to me again that Pepys had been notorious throughout his marriage for his dalliances with everyone from actresses to his own maid. Here I was in the car with my ex-girlfriend, thinking about old times! Had I started down the same slippery road?

But Mattie was talking. "Sorry about all this—I had to get rid of my car and find something undesirable. Something no one would be looking for." Hunched over the wheel, she accelerated out onto the road.

"Mattie, are you going to explain what's going on? Why are we sneaking about?"

She shot me a look. "You're angry. I don't blame you. But Alex, someone's been trying to kill me."

"*Kill* you!" I exclaimed with incredulity. Then I thought of her ravished house, and the violence of it. Perhaps not so very hard to believe after all . . . Stunned, I stared at her as she cast a distracted glance at the rearview mirror. The headlights of a car behind us took on evil proportions.

Or was my old friend just several pages short of a complete signature?

She went on in a shaky voice. "It started after I found the manuscript—the one I asked you to come early to see. *I* didn't post that notice on Pepysiana."

Hmm.

"But somehow, someone found out about my discovery. The day after the posting, the same day Pettifer told me he'd seen it on-line, I noticed some men watching me. They were really creepy, brawny guys, wearing *suits*." She shivered at the thought. "They broke into my house; I barely escaped them. You see what they did to me." She pointed at her eye. "They were going to *kill* me, Alex, I know it. I saw them at Rauner. They've tracked me everywhere; it's eerie, they know where I'm going before *I* do. They even went to Pettifer's house, and must have told him some convincing story. As far as I can tell, he told them all my usual haunts." Her tirade left her out of breath.

"I don't think you realise how worried everyone's been, Mattie. You just *disappeared* . . ."

"Wouldn't you?"

Well, actually, yes, I thought. *I have. More than once.*

She was still driving frantically, the car's tiny, poorly maintained motor churning with all the might of a sewing machine. Did she have a destination, or were we just driving out of desperation—a moving target being harder to catch? She was extremely willful, determined. This I knew all too well. Otherwise I'd have suggested that she pull over so we could gather our wits and calm down a bit. We were nearing the edge of town.

"I'm so sorry, Mattie—I'm going to try to help you out of this. Where are you going, exactly? Do you have a plan?"

"Yes. I'm taking us somewhere safe. It was quite a risk to come meet you, you know. I have to be very careful . . . we're going to circle around, make sure no one's following, then go back to Baker Library. But on the way I can tell you everything."

"May I just ask why you're so convinced it's your Pepys find they're after? And what exactly *is* it?"

"My God, that's right! You still don't know." She shook her head. "I wish I'd never found it, Alex—but it seemed such a boon for my career. Could have finally made my mark. You know the special collections drill: unless you come up with something sensational once in a while, or at least make news for the institution, you'll pass your years in utter obscurity."

A memory of Mattie's bitter catalogue of her father's and brothers' dramatic successes in the financial world, mentioned only once after too many beers, flashed through my mind. She'd always hated the thought of a career dedicated solely to making piles of money, especially because it had always been expected of her. Her ferocious independence had effectively closed the marriage and motherhood route . . . though for a while (mind you, Sarah had just been taken by my best friend) it seemed she was considering joining forces with me. Part of her mother's family was British, it seemed, so I was approved by her mother—the hardest test to pass.

Growing up with her family's collection of books couldn't be ignored as a formative influence, but her lack of interest in commerce and marriage had certainly contributed to her choice of the book world for a career. It was pretty damned difficult to make money from books, no matter what angle you came from, and that was just fine as far as Mattie was concerned. I now saw for the first time her desperation to be selected a Senior Fellow at Dartmouth, her drive for straight As, her fierce independence, for what they were: a driven need to make a name for herself, to be respected in her own right in the world she'd chosen.

"Look, I want you to know, Alex—I've left it in the Treasure Room, at Baker Library, in a hiding place behind the mantel. Perhaps you know it too—the flat white panel." I told her I did, but privately I didn't like the way her revelation implied that she might not be around long enough to retrieve it herself.

She took a ragged breath and unclenched her hands for a second on the wheel before gripping it again, turning her knuckles white. Her hands looked ridiculously small on the wheel, as if a child were driving. "Alex— Pepys *did* write more of the diary. After his eyes went, he taught the Shelton shorthand to his maid, and dictated to her. But the papers somehow passed to her—perhaps he'd asked her to keep them for him." She seemed to calm fractionally as she focussed on her story.

"When Pepys died, the papers remained in the maid's family. Evidently her descendants came over here and farmed, taking with them some of the family's old books. Perhaps they knew of her association with Pepys, knew the papers were important. Well, guess which farm Robert Frost eventually ended up on, and which bequest the Pepys diary was mixed up with?" Her voice was sardonic.

I gazed at her, baffled. "But . . . you said you'd left the diary in the mantel of the Treasure Room. You mean the Realia Room at Rauner, don't you?"

"I ought to know where I put it!" she exploded. With a fierce look of reprimand, she set the car chugging up a steep hill. We were certainly taking the long way round to Baker Library.

"Mattie . . . *I* saw some diary pages. But they were in the Frost Farm butter churn, in the Rauner Realia Room. Just yesterday."

The Civic nearly veered off the road as she fastened her eyes on me. The right front tyre was going over the yellow line when I grabbed the wheel.

She elbowed my hand away with a wiry arm and fixed

her eyes on the road. "In the *butter churn!* You found Pepys diary pages in the *butter churn?*"

"Most definitely. Like you, I left them where they were. Safest place. Even though . . ."

"What?"

"We've a bit of a crisis at the Pepys Library at Magdalene, and I was sorely tempted to hide them away somewhere inconspicuous. Just until I could work out what to do with them."

I feared that Mattie, driving in her erratic frenzy, was going to lose control of the car completely at the thought of a *second* Pepys find. We had come down the other side of the long, steep hill, and were now rocketing round the curves of the winding country road at a frightening speed. It seemed too dark by far out here, and there was no one at all behind us now. It crossed my mind that if we crashed, as we seemed destined to do quite soon, no one would find us for days.

"What to DO with them! Is that Alex Plumtree speaking? The Alex Plumtree I used to know with an unbending moral code? *Stealing* priceless papers from Rauner?!"

"I wasn't going to *steal* them, Mattie. It's just that . . . as they seemed to be undiscovered, I thought I might keep them that way for a day or two longer."

"That's right . . . they were uncatalogued. That's my fault, too. I've been eluding assassins instead of getting my job done! But it does mean that no one, anywhere, knows they exist. Actually, you could have stolen them with impunity."

"Come on, Matt. You don't really believe I was going to steal them! I only wanted a chance to consult with my Pepys Library board."

At long last she pulled off the road, turning in to nothing in particular that I could see. For an instant I was certain we were in the process of becoming statistics; we seemed to be speeding into nothingness. But a second later I'd worked it out: we were bumping down a dirt track of some sort, deep in piney woods. Perhaps she'd changed her mind about Baker Library . . . with Mattie, sometimes you just hung on for the ride.

"Your Pepys Library board," she repeated through clenched teeth.

"Yes—at Magdalene, in Cambridge. You and I haven't been in the closest of touch these last years . . . I suppose I didn't tell you I was asked to carry on in my father's footsteps as treasurer." I paused, unable to pinpoint why the mention of the Pepys Library board should have upset her so.

"My God." There was a frightening emptiness, desolation to her voice. "I understand now. I see *exactly* what's going on."

Was she envious of my position with the board? Did she think I'd come to try to spirit the papers back to their country of origin?

Before I could ask, however, she brought the car to a stop with a jerk, switched off the ignition and headlights, yanked up the hand brake, and buried her face in her hands.

"Mattie, don't. We'll get through this. I'll help you—"

"Don't," came her muffled voice from between the fingers. "You have no idea . . ."

Lord, I thought, *what have I done now?*

Suddenly, she seemed to think of something that gave her hope. Twisting in her seat to face me, she said, "Wait a minute. What exactly was the document *you* found?"

"I assume it was diary pages, like yours—several pages of Pepys's writing in shorthand. I couldn't resist reading the thing—"

Mattie seemed to withdraw again. "I can imagine."

The bitterness in her voice told me part of the problem: she didn't yet know what *her* find said. She had priceless papers with no clue what they meant. That was why she'd wanted me to come a day early.

"Okay," she went on in a voice dripping with resentment. "What did our Samuel record for posterity this time?"

"A lot of ramblings to do with Lord Dartmouth, with specifics of their mission to Tangier. Evidently this section was kept distinct from his Tangier diary for some reason. Perhaps it's an addition. It's only three pages, but it spells out in considerable detail Lord Dartmouth's lackey's character faults, and various antics in Tangier. The most fascinating bit is a confidence his Lordship shared with Pepys one night in the midst of drunken revelling. To minimise their already extensive debts, James II ordered Lord Dartmouth to simply pull up stakes and leave Tangier without keeping promises made to the natives. But tragically, a renegade henchman of Lord Dartmouth's executed hundreds of the natives—without his lordship's knowledge or approval. Lord Dartmouth was given obscenely large holdings in London for dealing with the Tangier problem. When you think about it, it might have been the vast income from those holdings that helped the Earl of Dartmouth finance Dartmouth College, a couple of generations later."

Mattie groaned. "Think how delighted the College would be to hear that! They've only just survived last year's publicity fiasco. . . . Alex! What if the College somehow knows about this diary passage, and is trying to keep it quiet?"

I actually laughed out loud. "Matt, no matter how paranoid you might be, you can't imagine that Dartmouth College would send out hit men to pursue and kill you. They like you. They *need* you. Besides, how could *anyone* know about any of this? I only just saw the papers Friday morning, and the tape around the butter churn was unbroken. If someone had seen them before sealing it with the tape, they'd have removed them! Besides—you said they've been chasing you for days, right?"

"Maybe they suspect the pages about Lord Dartmouth exist and think that I've found them, thanks to the Pepysiana posting." She gave an anguished sigh. "You know, when all this butter churn business comes out it's going to make me look bad—again. I should have been through all that by now. But I focussed on the papers alone, thought the realia could wait . . . you know how wild everyone is about Frost stuff." She made it sound as if she wasn't too enamoured of the great poet; I suppose she'd had enough of him.

"Anyone would have done the same, Mattie. I don't see why you're being so hard on yourself."

"This was going to be my great achievement—at last—finding the lost Pepys diary extension. But you wouldn't understand; you've never lived in your family's shadow. Come to think of it, you *are* in a similar position, given your father's fame and success. But you've never had to *prove* yourself, somehow. Why is that, Alex? How did you manage to change the rules of the game?"

We both heard it at the same instant: a twig cracked

just behind Mattie's car door. I saw her freeze, saw suspicion mingled with terror in her eyes as she looked at me.

"*Go! Start the car!*" I yelled.

She took off the handbrake and fumbled with the key for precious seconds. Just as her miserable excuse for a motor finally coughed to life, a bulky shape loomed outside. At the same instant, something big and dark slammed through her window. Glass exploded into the car with deadly force and Mattie flopped towards me, unconscious.

My tongue-in-cheek musings about a smash-up that wouldn't be found for days had suddenly become all too possible. Only God knew where we were.

I had to get us out of there.

Unjamming my legs from the tiny space on the passenger side, I threw them over the centre console, sitting on the handbrake. My knees were still jammed up against the underside of the steering wheel—I cursed the miniature proportions of the Honda. The hulking shape outside rammed what I now dimly perceived to be a crowbar through the window again, connecting painfully with my left shoulder. I jammed down the clutch, thrust the gear shift into reverse position, and accelerated wildly backwards, the way we'd come.

The man snarled a curse as I plunged the left fender into his thigh in a desperate attempt to escape. I piloted the car over the bumpy track, its tiny motor whining hysterically, and backed onto the main road. Once I'd got a hundred yards down the road I pulled over quickly, half an eye in the rearview mirror, and had a look at Mattie. Instantly my fear mushroomed; there was blood, but that didn't worry me as much as the bump along the side of her head where the crowbar had hit home. It had come up with terrible speed. I needed to get her to the hospital in Hanover. Now that we didn't seem to be in immediate danger, I gently lifted Mattie's inert body—still as easy to lift as when we'd thrown her into the river after a loss—to my seat, trying to arrange her as comfortably as possible. It did cross my mind how I'd explain all of this to Sarah. Then I slid the driver's seat back to relieve my knees and got back on the road.

Two things struck me as I raced my friend to the emergency room: our attacker's curse had been no ordinary American four-letter swear word. It had been "Bollocks!" A decidedly British expression—and a relatively genteel one, at that. Why would Mattie's attacker be *British*? Who in England wanted the Pepys diary extension—or needed to keep its discovery a secret? I had a nasty, creeping awareness that it might be one of my colleagues on the Pepys Library board.

But no, surely not—they weren't violent, unscrupulous men. Who else in England had a reason to care so fanatically about the posting on the Pepysiana web site?

The other was a matter of desperate curiosity: What had been the substance of the Pepys document Mattie had found? I cast an anxious glance at my friend. Would she be safe, even in the hospital? I *had* to get help for her somewhere.

In the fifteen minutes it took to race to Dartmouth Hitchcock Medical Center, the ache in my shoulder became more fierce by the moment. I saw no one following us. Perhaps I'd done enough damage to delay my fellow countryman. When at last Mattie and I pulled up to the emergency room doors, I saw on the car's dimly lit instrument panel that it was nearly two A.M. To their credit, the staff came right out with a gurney and got Mattie inside with all due speed. I was shocked to see how grey she looked; the bump had swollen to frightening proportions, grotesquely distorting the shape of her head. One of the doctors opened her eyes one by one; I caught glimpses of dark red in the whites. It occurred to me that perhaps I had been too optimistic about my friend's injury.

"How long ago did this happen?" the doctor asked, in a hurry.

Fifteen minutes, I said.

"What exactly did happen?"

Crowbar through a car window.

Raised eyebrows. "Was she conscious afterwards?"

No.

I followed doctor, nurse and patient into a small, curtained area, and was told I needed to fill out some forms. They rushed her past as I sat scribbling on papers on a clipboard, the doctor throwing over his shoulder that they were taking her for an MRI. The form called for Mattie's address . . . I didn't know it, exactly, though of course I knew the house. Her purse . . . a driving licence would provide all the necessaries. I wandered back into the room and told the nurse what I needed; she handed me the purse. Back in the hall, I plucked out Mattie's wallet and snapped it open. Her licence was displayed in a plastic window on the inside, but what I saw there was a revelation.

"Mattingley Harding" read the full name on her licence. Surely this was not a coincidence; an unusual name, but *also* that of my fellow Pepys Library Board member, Charles Mattingley? How could I have gone through four years of college with Mattie—even gone home for the parental visit—and not known? Why had she hidden the secret of her full name—joking that Matilda was her cross to bear? So Charles's family was the English relation on her mother's side . . . Charles Mattingley really just happened to hear from Pettifer Bartlett about the posting on the Pepysiana site? For the umpteenth time, I felt an awful conviction that there was far more to this than I knew.

If Mattie was related to *Charles* Mattingley, why hadn't he—or she—simply told me so?

It might have been nearly two in the morning in Hanover, New Hampshire, but that meant it was already a reasonably civilised hour in Cambridge, England. Not that I particularly cared whether I disturbed Charles.

I went to the phone on the wall and used my phone card to place a call to Mattingley, struggling to control feelings of resentment at what I could only feel was his betrayal and manipulation. I couldn't help but wonder if *Mattingley* had somehow let the news out that the Pepys find was at Dartmouth . . . otherwise why were British goons after Mattie?

"Charles Mattingley." His super-smug, I-can't-bother-with-more-than-a-whisper tone rankled.

"Hello, Charles. This is Alex Plumtree."

"Plumtree," he rasped. "I thought you were in America."

"Oh, I am—I am. Can you imagine whom I've run into, Charles?"

Silence.

"I've only just learnt her full first name. Would you like

to know how I found out?" More silence. "I'll tell you . . . someone dispatched an English-speaking thug—a murderer, for all I know—to do her in. He gave her a serious head injury. She's in hospital."

I heard a sharp intake of breath. "Good God. How bad is she?"

"She's still unconscious; they said it could take days for the swelling to go down. Then we might have some indication. So tell me, Charles. Why the secrecy? What exactly is going on here?"

Mattingley drew another long breath with a hint of resignation. The whisper began. "Young Mattie is my niece. I've always had a soft spot for her, Alex. She chose a difficult path, especially with that father of hers. I felt she could use a bit of help. If you don't achieve something substantial by the time you're forty, well . . . She called me as soon as she found the diary pages in some uncatalogued material she was trying to sort through. I thought that perhaps if I stimulated a bit of interest, and you were over there when it all came out . . . well, not only would I help Mattie, but the Pepys Library might benefit. Dartmouth isn't exactly a Pepys centre, after all, and the sale of such an asset would bring a goodly sum to the College for something they *do* want. Good publicity all the way round, and international acclaim for young Mattie before her thirty-sixth birthday."

"Someone's trying very hard to prevent her reaching that birthday."

He must have heard the underlying suspicion in my tone.

"Good heavens, Plumtree! You don't think I've had

anything to do with hiring someone to hurt her. Why, I'd do *anything* for Mattie."

Obviously, I thought. It was the first time I'd heard Mattingley express concern—or was that actually warmth?—for anything but a library. "Exactly how many people have you told that Mattie found the diary?"

"Only two. Neither of them could—*would*—breathe a word."

"I hate to be the one to tell you, but obviously they have. Who, exactly, are these people?"

"I—I can't tell you that, Plumtree. I'm sorry."

Can't or *won't,* I thought. Mattingley was circumspect indeed, but then the man moved in high circles. His secrecy only made me more curious about the identity of his confidantes.

"Good-bye, then, Charles. I'll ring when there's news." I hung up, not caring that I'd been not only abrupt but rude. I didn't appreciate his unwillingness to help me sort through what was becoming a rather nasty puzzle, especially since he'd plunged me into it in the first place.

I had the uncomfortable feeling that Charles had started a runaway chain of events when he threw the first pebble in the Pepysian pond. The ripples were spreading; I envisioned the first few delicate rings widening to monstrous proportions and engulfing not only Mattie but Sarah and me, Dartmouth College, the Pepys Library— and heaven only knew who or what else.

As I sank into a chair to wait for Mattie to return from her tests, I knew that this was only the beginning.

CHAPTER 11

*... by this time it was past two in the morning; and so
to bed, and there lay in some disquiet all night telling of
the clock till it was day-light.*

So to bed mighty sleepy, but with much pleasure.

*I do from this raise an opinion of him, to be one of the
most secret men in the world, which I was not so convinced of before.*

SAMUEL PEPYS

My lovely wife answered her mobile on the second
ring.

"Alex! What happened to you? Where are you?"

"I found Mattie—or rather, she found me—and things
happened from there. She was attacked . . . I've brought
her to the Medical Center."

"Alex, I'm so sorry . . . Are you all right?"

"Fine. But I'm afraid Mattie wasn't so fortunate. I've
rung her parents; they're driving up now. I'm going to
stay until they get here."

"Of course . . ." I fancied I could hear her sizeable
mental wheels turning. "Was she attacked because of
something she might have found?"

She was right to be cagey; mobile phone conversations

could be overheard. "That's my guess. Obviously, I need to find out more."

"We'll talk about it when you get here . . . but there's been a slight change in plan. You know our little love nest at Richardson?"

"Yes . . ." I waited for the inevitable.

"Someone is trying to send us a message. They did everything but set fire to the place. I don't think we should stay where we weren't wanted, so we're now at the other place."

The Hanover Inn.

I felt my face flush. It hadn't escaped my notice that Mattie had been attacked only *after* I came into the picture, and now Sarah was again endangered because of me. *What is it about me that causes these things to take place?*

"Darling, are you all right? Were you there when it happened?" In truth, I'd have felt sorry for anyone who got in my wife's way.

"No . . . they must have come while we were at the party. By the way, it's the usual name."

Good on, Sarah, I thought. We used a code name whenever we thought using the name Plumtree might be to our detriment. "Thanks, Sarah. I'll come as soon as I can."

With a sigh I hung up the telephone. Not exactly what I'd imagined for my honeymoon . . .

And at that thought, a vision of Moose sitting up in his hotel room, worrying, floated before my eyes. He'd wanted to see Mattie. And badly. While I found it remarkable that he'd built up such a concern for her from a distance, I'd seen reunion romances result in marriage before. People had a surprising lot in common if they graduated together from a college like ours . . . an illustrious college president's wife had been quite right to entitle her memoirs, *It's Different at Dartmouth*. I picked up the phone again and called the Inn, asking to be put through to Montgomery Musgrave.

"This is Monk," he growled.

Monk? This was new. I reverted to the familiar.

"Moose—Alex. I know where Mattie is, but it's not good news. She's in hospital—er, *the* hospital."

"Dartmouth Hitchcock?"

"Right."

"I'll be right there."

Seven minutes later he stormed into Emergency, looking as though he might deck anyone in view. But he received the news of Mattie's attack stoically enough.

"Why don't you go back to Sarah?" he asked. "I'm going to be here anyway. I'll keep an eye on things until Mattie's folks arrive. Go on."

His reasoning was irrefutable; there was no reason for me to stay now that he was there and her parents were en route. Certainly I could trust him . . . and Sarah might be waiting.

"One thing, Moose. Don't leave her alone for a minute. You remember I told you about the—er, thingie she asked me to come have a look at?"

He nodded.

"Someone is hell-bent on either terrifying or killing everyone who knows about it."

His eyes widened. "Buddy . . . *you* know about it."

"Exactly. I'm watching my back. Sarah says our room

was ransacked. A word of advice: if you plan to be closely associated with Mattie, you might want to keep your eyes wide open. Don't forget to explain to her parents: she's involved in something extremely important for Rauner. Unscrupulous types are desperate to thwart her."

"Got it," he said, looking as though he itched for a fight.

Mattie would be more than safe with Moose looking out for her.

I walked back to the Inn, keeping an eye out for anything or anyone unusual. But it seemed all the lurking maniacs had finished their work for the night. Taking the staircase instead of the lifts, I found myself plodding like a zombie. The reunion party had sent me through fifteen years in four hours. The little escapade with Mattie had finished me off. I was dead on my feet.

"Darling," Sarah whispered from the doorway, where she must've been keeping watch for me. "Welcome home." She wrapped me in a hug, and I felt all my lost energy returning on a wave of relief and affection.

Ah, the joys of marriage.

Nine o'clock in the morning saw us eyeing each other appreciatively over a Formica-topped booth at Hanover's most revered breakfast spot, indulging in a first cup of coffee.

We'd already been to the hospital; Moose was keeping watch with Mattie's parents. Her condition hadn't changed. I'd quietly told her parents what had happened and why; astounded, they agreed that the less said the better. They did, however, disagree about calling the police, which I could understand. It was their decision to make.

I'd come to peace with it all by resolving to get into Rauner somehow to have a look at Mattie's find as well as the butter-churn papers I'd uncovered. I had to find the secret that someone was ready to kill to silence . . . and my hunch was when I found it, the identity of the killers would be revealed.

"Here's Blake!" I said, and waved to him as he surveyed the restaurant. With a smile he came and parked himself next to me, presumably so he had a better view of Sarah.

"Morning," he said. "How's the reunion so far?"

"Eventful," I replied. "Good, but eventful."

A waitress stopped by to see whether Blake wanted orange juice or coffee. When she'd gone, he leaned over the table. "Tell me more. Dad says things can get pretty exciting with you around."

Sarah and I looked at each other.

"Let's just say that it's not going to be a quiet little reunion," I cautioned.

Blake's young face lit up with curiosity. In a low voice, he urged, "Let me help. No one will notice a student doing *anything* around here."

"You have a point, but your father would never forgive me," I answered. "Besides, I think we've got it in hand."

From there we went into a discussion of his decision to pursue a doctorate in chemical engineering, after having a go at the Olympic team. "I might be a bit older by the time I have a job," he laughed, "but I won't have any regrets."

As we talked about Blake's plans, my mind was working on the knotty problem of getting into Rauner. I already knew it was closed on weekends; already knew that Phil Cronewett was by now off on his famous and well-deserved vacation. He'd have let me in in a minute . . .

Blake was saying, "I hear you're on the Board of the Friends of the Library. I'll bet they can really use you for Rauner."

"I hope I can do more good than harm. Would you believe one of my old crew buddies is on the board? Makes the meetings that much more fun."

"That's great! Hey, speaking of Rauner, I should tell you." He leaned closer. "I might be shooting myself in the foot here, but if you're partly responsible for that library, there's something you should know."

Not Blake, too! Where would it all end?

"You know I've been working on that honours paper. Well, I can get a lot off the web, and also from Fairchild, the physics building. But I still need the main library, and they've let me have a carrel in the stacks." He took a reviving sip of juice. "It gets pretty oppressive in there sometimes—you remember, it's sort of dark, the ceilings are low—to tell the truth, it can get kind of creepy. Especially now, in the summer, I've thought I could stay down there for a week. If it weren't for missing crew practice, no one would ever find me."

I knew just what he meant; I'd had the same feeling in the same place while working on my senior honours thesis. About halfway through the project, I'd rather wished I might magically disappear.

"Well, sometimes I wander a little bit, just to get the circulation going again after a long slog. One Sunday afternoon I was on the very lowest level, sort of aimlessly looking around at the books in the stacks, and I saw a door leading the wrong way."

"The wrong way?" Sarah asked. "What do you mean?"

Blake shrugged. "There is no more of Baker extending to the east. There simply couldn't be anything on the other side of the door."

I felt an inkling of what he was going to reveal: my mother's proper Bostonian grandfather, a staunch Dartmouthian like all the males in her family, used to tell me stories of a rumoured network of tunnels beneath the Dartmouth campus. At first, he would explain, dandling me on his knee, the tunnels were for everyone to use to avoid New Hampshire's hostile weather and mud season. But later they were secured for use only in emergencies—during the Cuban missile crisis era, for instance—and after that they were permanently sealed off.

Still, Dartmouth men loved to invent and pass on myths about mysterious goings-on beneath the Green. There were tales of criminals having been hidden in the subterranean passages and of ghosts lurking there, but I'd always suspected these were the yarns of boys trying to explain away their own troublemaking antics. The only story I heard that had the ring of truth was one set in the 1960s, about administration officials scuttling through the tunnels to safety when threatened by violent anti-war protestors.

"I don't know if you ever did this with the College doors," Blake went on, looking sheepish, "but a credit card goes a long way to opening some of the older locks. You just slide it down to the catch, and *voilà*! You're in."

Sarah and I smiled and nodded. Everyone knew that old trick. It was one of the few advantages to living in a dormitory of very advanced age. That, and not feeling guilty about skiing down the slate staircase after a beer or two.

"Well. Who could resist opening a door that shouldn't *exist*?!" Blake demanded, as if stumbling into a world of wonder. "No one knew I was down there. I pulled out my college ID, fiddled with the catch, and I was in . . . to *something*. It was completely dark. There was a really rank musty smell, too."

He had us hooked into his story. The waitress came and delivered our food, but we only half-noticed. No one picked up a fork.

"I already had the creeps; I wasn't about to go through that door without seeing where I was going. So I trotted back up to my dorm—thought I'd go blind in the sunlight—and got my flashlight." At this point Blake took another sip and shook his head. "Man, I'll never forget it. I felt like a criminal. . . . Anyway, I went back down and went through the door. The flashlight showed that it was a tunnel, but not a long one . . . and guess where it went?"

The story had started with a comment about Rauner, so it wasn't difficult to guess.

"And my ID card worked like a charm again—evidently they didn't update the tunnel door when they turned Webster Hall into Rauner Library. I came out in the basement, behind the end of a long shelf—one of those moveable things. It was a halfhearted attempt to hide the door, and there was just enough room for a person to sneak through if they inhaled. It's almost as if someone intended to leave open the possibility of using the doors—but it could have been chance. Maybe it was more expensive to seal them up than to leave them."

"Right," I said, scarcely able to believe my good luck. It appeared I now had a way into Rauner to go in search of Mattie's find, despite the vacationing Phil Cronenwett.

Sarah gave a little start. "Breakfast!" She forked up a bite of omelet and said, "I think I'd like a tour of that tunnel." I could have kissed her.

"Me too," I said.

"*Seriously*? You want to spend the Saturday of your fifteenth college reunion slinking around the depths beneath Hanover?"

"Absolutely," I said.

But Blake had a full day until four o'clock, he said—so we agreed to meet him later at Baker Library.

We walked to the hospital again to see Mattie, watched over by a mournful Moose. There was no change in her condition, but I was fascinated to see that Moose had become one of the Harding family. He promised to call if there was news, and we went back to the Inn to don traditional rowing gear for the long-awaited Reunion Row.

With high expectations of what had been described as the highlight of the reunion weekend, we pulled out our T-shirts from our senior year. Mine said "SULTANS OF SWING," which was a double-entendre referring to the co-ordinated movement of eight men in a boat and a popular Dire Straits song of the year. Sarah's said "WOMEN OF WING," a classic attempt to go one better than the men. I leave it to you to decide whether the women had succeeded; it was true that that year they flew over the water and beat everyone else handily. Yes, all right, their record was even better than ours.

We set off a few minutes later than we intended. But when we made the trek down the hill to the boathouse, an elegant new building boasting every social and nautical facility available, I could scarcely believe my eyes. I'd have guessed it was a boxing club, from the four groups of men—none of whom I recognised—furiously bloodying one another's noses. The tumult was incredible. Non-rowing spouses watched in horror, trying to keep the children's eyes averted. The younger children howled; older siblings watched in fascination.

Astounded, I leapt into the nearest group and attempted to separate them. "Come on, break it up!" I shouted. "You don't want to—" An enormous fist came at my right jaw and knocked me flat. It didn't look as though I'd be successful in stopping the carnage; I needed reinforcements.

Gingerly checking the operation of my jaw, I ran around to the back of the boathouse, but there I found a sight that was still more shocking. The two remaining Dartmouth College shells lay in pieces on the dock, the bottoms pulverised. *What on earth?*! A forlorn group of oarsmen clustered round them in disbelief, like mourners. I recognised an acquaintance who'd been in the class after mine.

"Tom, what *happened*?" I demanded.

"Alex—great to see you." He gave a half-hearted smile, then turned back to the awful sight. "The boats were out here, smashed, when the first guys arrived at the boathouse this morning." He shook his head. "Who would *do* a thing like this?"

Who indeed? I needed help.

It seemed odd that The Boys, my buddies from our eight, were nowhere to be found. Stalking about in disbelief, I finally found Moose in the locker room, fuming.

"Do you know what's going on?" I asked.

He was seething. I could almost see the mammoth effort he made to control himself as he leaned against a locker. "I have a theory."

I waited, leaning against a locker opposite him.

He turned steely eyes on me. "I think it's the upcoming senior lightweights. They're angry because a lot of them stayed on campus this summer to work out; they thought they had a chance to be a winning boat next year. But the coach has been assigning the boats to the heavyweights—several of whom have a good shot at the Olympics. The lightweights feel neglected. I think they just decided that if coach was going to torpedo them, they'd torpedo the heavyweights. They'll all go down together."

"That's crazy!" But it did explain the fact that the warring groups out front had consisted of a mixture of huge hulks and more reasonably sized men. We'd had fun with a bit of lightweight-heavyweight rivalry in Moose's and my day, but never, ever, had anything like this erupted. "Where is everyone?"

"The Boys got disgusted and took off, just a few minutes ago. They're going to Cave Man's house on Lake Winnepesaukee. I guess he has a boat for waterskiing." As an afterthought he added, "I told him I might come later."

The disappointment of being deprived of my first Reunion Row was unexpectedly immense. I'd been looking forward to this more than any part of the reunion. I talked Moose into going to socialise with some of the older pillars of the Friends of Dartmouth Rowing, who I suspected were upstairs in the boathouse's gathering place. We did find Sarah there, and some of our staunch supporters with her. No one felt much like talking; an aura of shame and despair at the decline of a once-proud organisation overwhelmed us. Together we went down and moved the boats' carcasses into the storage area. When we emerged from the boathouse to go our separate ways, all of the pugilists were gone. Still, the air of disaster and decline lingered.

I vowed that I would not let this organisation that was so worthwhile, and to which I owed so much, fail.

Four hours later, sunburned and hoarse from shouting, Sarah and I returned from Cave Man's spectacular party at Lake Winnepesaukee to make ourselves presentable for our meeting with Blake. We both felt much better; the group of oarsmen had agreed between outings on the lake that something must be done to resurrect Dartmouth Rowing. We'd made some definite plans to improve both the material aspects of the organisation and its esprit de corps. I'd personally volunteered to dedicate myself to rounding up more shells as soon as possible—from overseas if necessary.

At exactly four o'clock Blake came striding across the Green, looking like the Cheshire Cat. He drew close and said, "I've been thinking about this. You *are* letting me in on whatever you're up to, aren't you?"

My pseudo-parental conscience flashed a warning. I couldn't drag Blake into this. The people who'd assaulted Mattie had been far too serious. How could I persuade him we were only curious, so he would just *show* us the door in the Library? Sarah and I would come back later to—er—break in.

"Look, Blake, I hate to disappoint you—but this is just

a holiday for us. I'm afraid there's no great excitement just now—no sinister plot threatening to crush us all—no matter what your father might have told you about me."

"Oh. Yeah." He hid his disappointment with a smile. Ever the good sport, with the gift of the young for allowing bygones to be bygones, he gamely led us into the main library where we started our descent.

The smell of the place was precisely as I remembered it . . . the mustiness of old books mixed with dust and floor cleaner. "Remarkable," I said. "It hasn't changed a bit! Even the buzz of the fluorescent lights is the same. You could go deaf from that endless droning, couldn't you?"

Blake made some quip about the roar of the silence being more disturbing when one had a thesis to write; he had a point. At last we reached the bottom level. "This way," he whispered, then realised he was whispering. He gave an embarrassed smile and led on.

At first it seemed like some sort of joke; we walked endlessly on. I thought I knew the stacks well, but I'd been mistaken. "Good heavens! How did you ever *find* this?" I asked, when at last we reached the door.

"Just shows you how desperate I was for a break that day . . . Okay—here it is." Blake seemed nervous for some reason, and I thought I understood. I looked at Sarah; she winked and shook her head slightly. As Pepys might have said, Lord! but it was good to have someone notice the subtleties of people as I did. I would quickly relieve Blake of any worries about being caught doing something shady for "older" people. It was the summer before his glorious senior year; being brought before all sorts of nasty disciplinary committees before he got to the Olympics really wouldn't be the thing at all.

I felt guilty for putting him in this position. Quickly fingering the Visa card from my wallet, I slid it between door and wall. The skill had been extremely useful in crew highjinks (we were, in truth, an unruly bunch) and came back to me easily. The door popped open; I stared down the dark passageway and pulled out my keychain torch, shining it down the tunnel as far as it would go.

It was, in fact, an extremely creepy black hole. Although I knew where it went, thanks to Blake's bravery, I couldn't say I fancied venturing into it. Glancing back at Sarah, I saw her reticence—masked, of course. My wife didn't show every last feeling on her sleeve, though she never actually misrepresented her feelings. She was merely conservative with her display.

"This is quite a find, Blake." I was impressed. "How on earth did you manage to keep it a secret?"

"For one thing, I only just found it during last term. But you have to understand: I have no desire to bring people here—it's too creepy. And I don't want anyone to think I'm doing anything criminal. *You* understand."

"I do. And I admire you," I said. "Now, we should let you get on with your Saturday night." I moved slightly as if to suggest that we might all go back towards the main stairway. To my excruciating embarrassment, I found that I was whispering, too. A quick look at Sarah told me she'd noticed. Her eyes danced.

"Okay. Let me lead you out of this maze," Blake said. "But I'll just tell you, in case you ever need to know: the tunnel's about fifty feet long. The door at the other end is solid—and I do mean *solid*—wood." He recovered his collegiate sense of humour and commented, "They just don't make things like they used to." People far younger than Blake knew that substantial doors, especially ones through which fire could travel, were now made of metal. He didn't want us to miss the fact—obviously he'd found it strange himself—that for some reason the College had chosen to ignore these doors.

One could only wonder why.

CHAPTER 12

But among all the beauties there, my wife was thought the greatest.

How this should come to passe, God knows, but a most strange thing it is!

SAMUEL PEPYS

I don't quite know what to expect from a class dinner," Sarah said half an hour later. We were back in our room; she was slipping a slinky black dress down over her hips. I couldn't take my eyes off her.

"I don't either," I said, going to zip her dress. Taking my time, I slid the zip up. "But I can tell you that I'm going to enjoy it immensely: I'll be with the most intelligent, capable, talented, beautiful woman there."

She came with me into the bathroom and watched as I shaved. Her hands on my bare summer chest were electrifying.

She breathed a laugh by my right ear. "I'm glad I'll be there to watch over you. You have thought about the danger, haven't you?"

"Me?" I pulled the razor away from my cheek and studied her in the mirror.

Sarah stroked my hair. It was almost enough to make me forsake shaving entirely.

"Mmm. You. Alex Plumtree."

I smiled and gave up, turning towards her. Stubble was still fashionable anyway.

Later, Sarah and I mingled companionably with our fellow '86s down by the boathouse—our site for the reunion dinner. All hint of the earlier unpleasantness was gone; a festive striped tent stretched over the area where my fellow oarsmen had battled that morning. A chorus of voices surged in convivial greeting and conversation. I heard a cry and saw a woman rush at Sarah, shrieking her name. The two women hugged like the long-lost friends they were, and I went to fetch all of us some wine. When I returned, Sarah's friend was asking with abandon, "But how *did* you know you wanted to have children?" I took myself off to find The Boys.

I had no difficulty: they were always the loudest group having the most fun. We sank effortlessly into old patterns, laughing at jokes it would have taken us years to explain to anyone else. When we had finally planted ourselves at tables with our lobster and steak, our illustrious class president went to the microphone. He tapped on it and announced, "Welcome to the Class of 1986 dinner. The good news is that the lobster was here as scheduled— hope you've enjoyed it. And the other news—also wonderful in its own way—is that our speaker for this evening, our comedienne classmate, is having that baby at last!"

A cheer went up for the classmate who'd reached national notoriety as a stand-up comic. We'd miss her, but we'd all seen her waddling through the reunion with the bun obviously extremely ready to burst from the oven. Most of our classmates knew precisely what was involved in the bearing and rearing of children by now. Sarah and I exchanged a look that was discomfort on her side, anticipation on mine. "*I hope they look just like you,*" mine said.

"We are extremely fortunate to have with us in her place a notorious educator many of you scholars will remember for his Shakespeare course. Professor Pettifer Bartlett!"

Sarah and I exchanged another look as a rousing cheer nearly blew the roof off the reunion tent. The Pet had always been a popular professor, and had earned his notoriety by appearing in full Shakespearean garb for each class. He delivered lectures as though he were William himself, accent and all. Although his Pepys course hadn't drawn as many students, he'd performed a similar routine there, enduring significant abuse for wearing Pepys's long dark periwig.

The Pet didn't disappoint us; he appeared in full bard's clothing, tights and all, and threw himself into the role of renegade Shakespearean pundit on love and marriage. With an introduction of, "Here will be an old abusing of God's patience, and the king's English—The Merry Wives of Windsor," he went on to play both man and woman, leaping from one side of the small platform to the other and changing his voice as he switched roles.

Woman: "O Romeo, Romeo! wherefore art thou, Romeo?"

Man, *whispers, aside*: "This is the night, that either makes me, or fordoes me, quite! (Othello.) *Shouts to woman*: "Be not afraid, though you do see me weaponed; Here is my journey'd end, here is my butt. Whip me!"

Woman, *gazing in dismay*. "Do not put me to't, For I am nothing if not critical."

After several minutes the audience was reduced to tearful laughter by the rollicking pace, and apt juxtaposition of great lines from various plays. The Pet kept the riotous act (often raunchy, too, this being Shakespeare) going for more than half an hour, one laugh segueing perfectly into another. Suddenly, during a mockery of drunken revelry, he cried, "Farewell! God knows when we shall meet again!" and tumbled backwards into the darkness with unerring melodrama.

The applause was enthusiastic and sincere—truly it was the most entertaining non-speech I'd ever heard. We continued to applaud, but The Pet did not appear to take his bows. After several minutes, the class president stood up and went to the platform, casting about in the dark for the erstwhile speaker. When Pettifer still didn't turn up, our illustrious leader took over. "Let's have one more round of applause for Pettifer Bartlett, wherever he is," he exclaimed. "Thank you, Professor Bartlett!"

With a quick kiss, Sarah told me she was going to go with some friends from her foreign study group for a drink and a chat. "Would you like to come, Alex? Or are you going with The Boys?" I told her I thought I'd stick with The Boys.

But while everyone was still deciding upon post-party destinations, or dashing to pick up offspring, I wandered out of the tent and around to the area behind the small stage Pettifer had used. It was surprising how quickly the bright rectangle of the tent turned into pitch darkness—mere feet from the edge of the tent. I looked around amidst the litter of plastic cups bearing the college crest, and the bar tables standing empty, smiling as I thought of The Pet's remarkable exit; no wonder he was in such demand as a speaker.

"Hey, Buddy!" Moose sidled up to me, a bit wild-eyed, out of breath. "Just got here . . . had to tell you. She's going to be all right! I thought I'd give her parents some time alone with her. She was really surprised to see me in there, but remembered me right away."

"I can't tell you how relieved I am," I said sincerely.

He beamed. "I think she likes me, Buddy! Her parents are hovering like guard dogs. She'll be all right. The docs are even talking about letting her out tomorrow, things are going so well."

"Excellent!"

"Yeah, I know." We stood gloating on our mutual good fortune, and my gaze drifted over to the old boathouse, farther down the road, hidden in shadow.

"Remember that time Coach's dog took a hunk out of your leg?" I asked.

"I've always kept those sweats, you know," Moose replied, and I could hear the grin in his voice. "Couldn't bear to throw them away. That was the day you started calling me Moose—because of the way I bellowed when I attacked him back—and everyone else followed. Yeah, thanks a lot, Buddy."

"Not at all, not at all."

"What *I* remember," he said as we approached the old wooden building, "is that day we came down here after finals. We were hanging around, watching Warren fix boats."

I chuckled. Warren Binger had cared for Dartmouth's boats as long as anyone could remember. "Yeah, and before he saw us there, he opened that little cabinet he made way at the back in the corner, and took out his whisky bottle. Good old Bing. Did you ever hear what happened to him?"

"Nah." The old boathouse was being allowed to quietly disintegrate, or at least didn't appear to be carefully maintained. I wondered if they still kept some of the old boats here, like a museum. . . .

Moose must have been thinking the same thing. He tried the handle of the wooden sliding door. To my surprise, it glided open with a minimum of fuss. The scent of decaying wood and varnish flooded over us, immediately recalling years of memories. I wondered if I'd been the only one who felt a little wistful when the luxurious new boathouse had been built and this old friend had been left behind.

We stepped inside and looked around; I took out my keychain torch and saw that there were still boats in some of the racks that lined the walls. "Look, Buddy! It's the Lodge." Sure enough, it was the boat my mother's father—Alexander Christian Lodge, class of 1916—had given.

"She doesn't look too bad, but they wouldn't want to use a relic." I walked from bow to stern, running my hand along the smooth underside of the boat. The wood was still as beautiful as it had always been, but the design was antiquated. It looked much finer and more delicate than the modern boats. Moose trailed along to the rear of the boathouse, towards Warren's secret cupboard.

I heard a slight noise, perhaps a raccoon or a fox, near the sliding door. Perhaps Moose heard it too; he asked, "Can I have your flashlight for a minute?"

"Sure." I walked over and handed it to him. But he wasn't interested in the sound. Instead, he put his giant bear paw of a hand over the knob Warren Binger had fashioned for his cabinet. "I wonder if the Bing ever . . ."

We never found out. I felt a whoosh of air, and turned to see who was behind me. But it was a *what* rather than a *who*—a dark something coming very fast. I ducked, and heard an "oof" as Moose crashed into the back of the boathouse. My friend's massive bulk took out part of the rear wall; I heard the Lodge and the other boats on their racks slide and plunge into the woods outside.

Lunging for the attacker, I took him down backwards. We rolled on the floor; I struggled to pin down his arms. He fought back, made it difficult, but wasn't doing me any harm. Not a real fighter, I thought. Something moved where Moose had fallen, and then my friend stood next to me, poised to deliver my opponent a knockout blow.

"I wouldn't do that if I were you," said a cold voice from the doorway. I noticed two things instantly: the middle-class British accent and the unmistakable glint of metal. The voice spoke again, evidently to his colleague. "For God's sake, you berk. Couldn't you get it right just this *once*? Get the big one's hands behind him and tie them with something."

His accent was astonishing; this was no garden-variety thug. My guess was he'd been to one of the better public schools. How on earth had he got into this sort of messy work? I thought I'd have a go.

As he stood watching his friend scramble to his feet and bind Moose's wrists to a wooden support, I said, "Is all this fuss really necessary?" I stood slowly, dusting myself off. I couldn't see his face, only a form. But I'd never forget that accent.

"Be quiet. Don't move. I won't hesitate to shoot."

"I'm assuming you're here because of something to do with Samuel Pepys," I persisted. "If you'll just tell us what you want—"

"You can forget the soft touch. I'm not dense. Now *his* hands," he told his colleague, referring to me. As my hands were being trussed, I tried to work out their intent. Why hadn't they just shot us, if they wanted us out of the way so badly? Perhaps they were going to take us somewhere, and wanted us alive for a bit . . .

"Now give them a drink." The coldness of his tone turned the air of the steamy old boathouse to ice. When I heard the clink of glass as his accomplice grabbed something off of the floor, I finally knew their plan. But I wasn't dense either; I would die trying before I'd let them pour a bottle of drink down our throats, then push us in the river to make it look like we'd drowned after overindulging. They needed to make it look like an accident; that's why they hadn't shot us.

The sound of singing drifted into the boathouse. But these were not just any voices; these were boathouse voices—those of our crewmates. I'd know The Boys anywhere, along with the extremely crude rendition of a popular song we all used to sing on bus rides back from regattas. Never had I been happier to hear that ditty . . . and it sounded as though the lightweights were with them, too. Probably about twenty men in all.

"*Damn.*" The man lowered his public school voice. Eton, perhaps? "Say one word, just one, and you're dead."

I knew we wouldn't have to say a word; The Boys

would see the open door of the old boathouse, and guess that we were there. It took every member of the team to make a party, and they were coming to get us. The gun-toter had said himself he wasn't stupid, and I believed him. He wouldn't shoot an entire crowd.

Now he whispered, "Over here," to his underling and moved near the man-door on the river side of the boat-house. Instantly I prepared to go after them, but remembered his gun. I didn't want to be shot on my honeymoon. "Quiet—or they'll watch you die," he warned us in a soft voice.

The Boys approached in riotous form, holding the last note of their song in extended cacophony. They were only twenty feet or so from the boathouse now.

Our stroke called, "Hey. Buddy! Moose! What're you *doing* in there?" Loud guffaws. The light changed subtly as Eton quietly opened the side door. He would wait, I thought, until The Boys were at the main door, then slip out unseen from the side. He *was* smart. Few things were more to be dreaded than a truly intelligent criminal.

An indefinable sound filled the air—I recognised it as an attempt to imitate my moose call.

Then they were at the door. "What *are* they doing in there—"

I heard the two Englishmen go out the side door; at the same moment our friends stood blinking at us in-credulously in the darkness.

"Make yourselves useful and untie us, won't you?" I said.

"Ohmigod," Alphonse "Cave Man" Baxter said, gaping at our bonds. "You guys are seriously *twisted*."

We did our best to explain, urging them to hurry. Then

Moose and I led the charge out of the boathouse down the path to the river; but even as we hurtled down the bank, the throaty roar of a powerful speedboat told us they were escaping.

"The crew launch!" Cave Man said.

We'd lost them.

"All right, Buddy. You wanna tell us what that was all about?" The jeers and fabrications flew hard and fast, and picked up speed by the moment.

We would never live this down.

Hours later, we were worn out from laughing. The wild inventions of The Boys to explain our bonds and the couple of bottles of liquor in the boathouse were hilarious. It was nearly two in the morning as Moose and I started up the hill again to the Inn, lagging behind the others. I realised I'd have to go back to the Inn and pretend to be going to bed before I could return to the library for my secret inspection. It would be another long night. I yawned.

"I think you should tell me about this 'potential acquisition' for Rauner that's got the goon squad out." Moose sounded truculent. Who could blame him?

"You're right. And you're on the Friends board—you probably *should* know." I sighed. "Last week someone called from our Pepys Library board of overseers. He'd been told about a posting on the Pepysiana web site—by Pettifer Bartlett, no less."

" 'Pepysiana?' "

"I know, but these are true enthusiasts, remember. They

can't help it. Anyway, the anonymous posting said that there'd been a spectacular find. The Secretary of our board at the Pepys Library asked me to check into it, along with the disappearance of a ton of money from the Library coffers. Anyway, soon after the posting a rumour emerged that the find had something to do with Dartmouth College. So it seemed perfect for me to look into it while I was here."

"On your honeymoon."

"Mmm. And then, when I was shown the Realia Room in Rauner, I spotted something that hadn't even been unpacked yet—a new donation to the College. It was unquestionably, and unbelievably, in Pepys's handwriting. Then I started talking to Mattie last night, and she said *she'd* found something in Pepys's coded handwriting in the boxes of papers from the Frost Farm. It turns out that Pepys's *maid's* relatives emigrated from London to New Hampshire, taking trunkloads of papers with them. Eventually Robert Frost moved onto that same farm, and that's how the papers got to the College.

"The papers seem to be the source of all our problems," I told Moose. "Someone, for some reason, must want the papers to remain undiscovered—but who could still be alive to care *what* Pepys wrote? It doesn't make any sense . . . especially because our attackers tonight spoke like members of the royal family."

My own choice of words gave me a flash of insight that I instantly decided not to share with Moose. Surely the current crisis in the royal family could have nothing to do with the writings of Samuel Pepys . . . the Queen had been thrown from her horse after the web-site posting, but how could the appearance of a long-lost journal set off a succession crisis? Perhaps, just perhaps, someone with inside knowledge of the Pepys find might have tipped off a lackey at Buckingham Palace.

But why? What could Pepys have written in the 1600s that was so earth-shattering now?

"Did you hear me?"

"Sorry, what?"

"I said, my friend—and you don't have to be 'sorry' for anything—what are you going to do about it?" Moose had a way of boiling things down.

"I need to get—No, I can't tell you." *Alex, what's wrong with you?* I scolded myself. I'd nearly told him I was going to sneak into Rauner that night.

"You want me to tell Sarah all about you and Mattie in—let's see—what was that, the summer of eighty-five?"

He was threatening me. Well, two could play that game. I stopped chugging up the hill and gave him a thin smile—very civil, no warmth. "Do you want me to tell Mattie about *Abigail*?"

If it weren't so sad, I'd have laughed at my friend's expression. Perhaps I was wrong to bring it up. But just as I was preparing to make my apologies and give in . . .

"You wouldn't! Alex, I—" He looked positively ill.

"All right, then. You go your way, I'll go mine."

"Unless we need each other, all right?"

"Agreed. All right." We'd arrived at the porch of the Inn. "By the way, you handled yourself really well with those characters. You knew just how to play it."

"Thanks. You too." He eyed me as if seeing me in a new light. "Please, let me help if I can."

We said good night and I went up the stairs ("Buddy,

it's after two A.M.! Don't you *ever* take the easy way out?!")
while he took the lift. I mean elevator. Whatever.

But after all that, Sarah wasn't in our room. I let the
door close behind me, feeling let down. All through
the years I'd survived these biblio-ordeals, I'd dreamed of
the day when Sarah would be at my side.

Where was she?

I opened the door again, walked down the stairs,
through the lobby and out into the Hanoverian night.
Scattered noises from revellers at all points of the com-
pass floated through the darkness, but the most notice-
able quality of the night was the absence of traffic noise
and light pollution. I crossed the road in front of the Inn
and stepped onto the plush carpet of the Green. Halfway
across, I stopped and let the darkness hide me, before
moving on toward the Library. I loved this place. I hoped
I would do it no harm, nor it me.

Now that the library was open twenty-four hours a
day—no relaxing as in my time, with eight enforced
hours to provide for that old-fashioned notion of sleep—
it would surely be a breeze to retrace our path of the
morning. I was starting up the steps to the Georgian facade when I heard a noise behind the thick hedge on my
right. With equal measures of anger and fear, I swung
around to see who lurked there.

"Alex! I'm so glad I found you!" Sarah bounded lightly
from behind the shrubbery and gave me a swift hug and
kiss. As I wrapped her in a return embrace, I was surprised
at the wave of relief that washed over me. Though I hadn't
been aware of dreading my Rauner reconnaissance, suddenly the thought of it was much more manageable.

We walked in as if we were merely diligent students, though much too well dressed for the part. As I held the door for her, I had an odd sensation of having gone back in time; no doubt Sarah and I had, at some point, climbed these steps together. I led the way into the Treasure Room and quickly snatched out the panel from the front of the mantel, then reached inside for Mattie's paper. Sarah took it and slid it up the back of her shirt. We were silent as we left the room and made our way down, down, and down; no point in attracting undue attention. Blake's path through the stacks was easily retraceable, and we arrived at the tunnel door with no difficulty.

"I only hope it's all this easy," Sarah said with a wry smile.

"It almost feels *too* easy."

She nodded in response, already sliding her credit card along the edge of the door. The latch clicked; she turned the knob. We were in.

CHAPTER 13

. . . my heart is full of fear.

Why did I feel so nervous? I'd certainly sunk to more dubious things in my time than sneaking around a library in the dark. . . . Perhaps I was just on edge because I sensed the frequency and level of menace escalating hour by hour. I gripped Sarah's arm.

"Darling, do be careful," I warned, before we entered the tunnel. "Earlier tonight Moose and I were mugged in the old boathouse. I'm afraid we're mixed up with some very dark characters."

"Well, if we find what we're looking for, we'll have serious ammunition, won't we?" She smiled and carried on.

We proceeded down the narrow passage, my little pencil of light a pitiful counter to the oppressive darkness. "Do you want to divide and conquer?" she whispered. "I could go up and get the papers out of the butter churn while you're hunting through the uncatalogued boxes."

"Great." Our footsteps echoed in the enclosed, concrete space. "Are you carrying your gun?"

"Yes."

That was my wife. My *wife*! It wasn't that I felt tremendous fondness for firearms, but I did respect Sarah's ability to use them with skill.

At last we reached the Rauner door. Blake had said that the door didn't open more than eight inches because of the placement of the massive moveable shelving. "I'll squeeze through first," Sarah said. I watched her tall, athletic form in its slinky black dress, shod in high-heeled sandals, slide through the narrow opening and wondered if she was going first because she felt better able to protect me with her training. Our relationship definitely lacked certain traditional roles. . . .

Blindingly bright lights flashed on. "Sarah! Come back!" I hissed, grabbing at her arm.

"Wait," she said. I could hear the tension in her voice, feel it in the muscle of her forearm. "I think it's just a motion-sensitive light. All libraries have them."

My heart was beating like a jackhammer. "Darling, sometimes you really are too much. Have you even broken a sweat?"

"Hmm—no." She laughed. "Come on." She held the door for me to squeeze through, and together we gently put the door on the latch without completely closing it.

"Well, this will certainly be easier with light," I whispered, surveying the long aisle we now faced. "I suppose I'll start at the far end of the room and work up. Good luck upstairs!"

She gave a mock salute and moved quickly down the aisle. I followed, but at the end of the shelf turned to go to the far end of the room. The lights gave me the feeling that there was someone watching, but I ordered my imagination to give it a rest. I reached the last shelf and started down the aisle, looking for archival boxes embellished with the college crest. Halfway along, I could see that there were no boxes hiding along the bottom of the two lowest shelves; they were crammed with large, heavy volumes that looked like nineteenth-century dictionaries. No time to investigate now.

I started back across the smooth concrete floor to leave the aisle, but stopped short. What was that sound? In the next second I realised that the shelf on my left was closing in on me fast. In the way that small details loom large in a crisis, I noticed the extreme sturdiness of the shelves and their smooth gunmetal finish as I dashed towards the end of the aisle.

Two feet from the end, it caught me with surprising speed at the shoulders—the widest point. In the next second, the pressure had increased unbearably and the shelves mashed me lengthwise. With horror I realised that one shelf was crushing my nose. At the last possible instant I turned my head to the side, facing the way to freedom, and slid down so my head at least wasn't crushed.

I was trapped. Startled at having been caught so quickly, and with such surprising force, I felt as though I were standing between two giant lorries with mercilessly accelerating drivers. In the next moment, I understood with rising panic that these shelves didn't stop squeezing when something got in their way. An excruciatingly clear memory of having my hand broken in an automatic car window flashed through my mind.

In extremis as I was, the irony of the situation was inescapable: this could be the illustration of my life. Tortured and forced into untenable positions by the infinite weight of books and their deadly truths.

I began to panic, more at the thought of what someone was doing to Sarah than at my captivity. Obviously someone had been waiting for us . . . but no one had fol-

lowed us through the door. I couldn't think clearly. I had
to warn Sarah. But my voice, when I called out to her, was
a poor imitation of itself. She couldn't possibly hear me.

At that moment the lights went out again. I felt another wave of panic. What had they done with Sarah? Was
someone coming to kill me?

Silence. Darkness and silence. *Dear God, please let
Sarah be all right . . .* Unspeakable images ran through my
mind of our demise in Dartmouth's Special Collections
Library—on our honeymoon, in romantic Hanover, New
Hampshire.

And then the lights blazed on again. "Alex! Where are
you?!" Her voice was soft, calm. Her lovely, lovely voice—
thank God!

"Here. Button, end of shelf."

I heard her footsteps race in my direction, then a gasp
of alarm as she realised that my voice had come from between two shelves. She pressed the button; miraculously,
the shelves parted and I sank to the cool concrete floor.

"Alex! Can you walk?" she knelt next to me. "We need
to get out of here."

I felt as though I'd been beaten by a whole mob of
thugs with sledgehammers, but yes, I was mobile. The
bruises, I thought, would be in the evenly spaced stripes
of the shelves; in a day or two I'd look like grilled ham-
burger. I got to my feet and Sarah urged me towards the
door.

"I had to—well, incapacitate someone temporarily,"
she said. "We don't want him raising an alarm."

"Who?" I asked, squeezing painfully through the door
to the tunnel.

"I don't know . . . sort of average, brown hair, medium

height . . . but he was awfully well-dressed. Looked more like an elevated civil servant in London than a thief."

I knew exactly who it was . . . Eton from the boathouse. "We still have to get a look at those papers somehow."

"Oh!" She patted her chest. "I've got them right here."

I gave her a squeeze, and instantly found out the hard way that hugs were going to hurt for a time.

"I'm sorry," she said. "I'll check you over in the room while we take a look at the papers. Did you find anything?"

I'd have told her that I never got the chance, except that the door ahead of us in the Baker stacks opened, revealing quite a crowd. "Come forward slowly, with your hands up." Speechless, we obeyed. A gaggle of Campus Police, a woman I recognised as Patricia Bailey (Phil's second-in-command at Rauner), a man I recognised as the librarian of Baker, and a uniformed Hanover policeman eyed us suspiciously as we reentered the main library.

"I don't think you understand," Sarah began, sounding impressively assertive. I gazed at her with appreciation. "There was an intruder in Rauner. We—"

"Looks to me like *you're* the intruders," Patricia said, her voice dripping with suspicion.

"We can explain," I began, but then footsteps tapped from inside the tunnel. Sarah and I watched in wonder as a medium-brown-haired man of average height emerged. To my immense fascination, it was not Moose's and my attacker from the boathouse. The man was, as Sarah had described him, very well-dressed, in a tan blazer of slubby linen. He was also the Dean of College Affairs, a man I happened to know was trusted implicitly by the President of the College, and who handled the messes that the President couldn't be dirtied by. The Dean, who had an uncanny rapport with the students, had the unfortunate name of Dean Small. This meant that the students called him "Dean-Dean". He'd been a senior when I was a freshman, and I knew him well.

"Lock them up," he said, and rubbed the back of his head—Sarah must have clobbered him with her gun—staring at the floor instead of us. "This is getting old."

"Yes sir," the Hanover policeman said.

At that moment Dean Small lifted his eyes to see what sort of scum he'd unearthed. His eyes widened comically when he saw us. "Alex Plumtree! What on earth?!"

"Good evening, Dean. I'm sorry about all this. You see, Sarah and I stumbled upon some difficulties in the Library. We were only trying to sort them out."

"I'm sorry I hurt you," Sarah said. "People have been trying to kill us, and I couldn't take chances. We thought you were one of them."

"*Kill* you!" Dean exclaimed.

"One of whom?" Patricia asked, bewildered.

"Obviously she means the group that broke in last night," Dean answered. He sighed. "Go home to bed, everyone. I want to have a word with Alex and—?"

"Sarah," she said, offering her hand. "Sarah Townsend Plumtree, eighty-six."

"Ah," he murmured, hesitantly shaking her hand. "I see." He waited until everyone else had trooped over to the lift, with the Campus Police grumbling about all-night libraries, and disappeared behind the doors.

"I won't keep you long—it's terribly late and I'm exhausted. I also have a nasty bump on the head," Dean told us, with a wry look at Sarah. "But I think you may as well know that someone is trying to blackmail the College."

Nastier and nastier, I thought. How many sides *were* there to this mess?

"Supposedly this party has some very damaging information about the College. They've threatened to release it—they claim it's some sort of historical document—if we don't pay. Last night, when we discovered intruders trying to break in to Rauner—the first time ever—we became worried about an all-out attack on the College from these rascals. Someone in possession of a valuable historical document might also be a high-class biblioklept." He shook his head. "At least that was my theory. Now tell me your side of things, Alex."

"The board of the Pepys Library in Cambridge—England—asked me to look into the rumour of a Pepys find here at Dartmouth. They heard the rumour via a Pepys web site and conference." I thought of the papers stuffed into Sarah's dress—front and back—and decided I couldn't tell him about my own Pepys find amongst the butter churn papers. I knew I should, but couldn't.

Onward, Alex, into the breach . . . "Ever since word got out that I was looking for this Pepys find, things have got violent. Moose—I mean, Montgomery Musgrave, a fellow eighty-six, and I were nearly killed earlier tonight. Then we met you in there . . ."

All of a sudden it struck me. "Dean, you pressed that button to crush me in the shelves, didn't you? I must say, I think that was a bit harsh."

He puffed himself up and glared at me with indignation. "How can you accuse me of such a thing? I would *never* . . . Phil Cronenwett told me those shelves could *kill* a man if people weren't careful! I'm almost glad poor Phil's not around to see all this . . . he'd never get over it. He came to me not long ago to discuss the situation. He's quite worried about our liability, thinks we should upgrade to the emergency kickplates. Besides, ask your wife—I was upstairs on the *floor* until just moments ago."

I got goosepimples from head to toe.

Someone *else* had been in the library with us . . . someone who wanted to kill me.

CHAPTER 14

A thing that never was heard of, that so few men should dare and do so much mischief.

We have been lately frighted with a great plot, and many taken up on it, and the fright not quite over.

. . . a fatal day is to be expected shortly, of some great mischief . . . it is observable how every body's fears are busy at this time.

SAMUEL PEPYS

Sarah and I walked slowly back to the Inn, arms round each other's waist. "But who else could it have been?" she asked. "And if they'd wanted to kill you, why didn't they just shoot you while you were trapped?"

"I think the people behind this are eager to make it seem an accident. Maybe it was my two English friends from earlier this evening . . . they were none too eager to shoot. I only wish I could work out why they were so keen to do away with all of us Pepys types—but only through accidental-looking deaths."

"What do you make of the blackmail attempt?"

"I've been racking my brain ever since Dean mentioned it, trying to think of something Pepys might have said that would affect the College." I shook my head.

"Pepys lived a hundred years too early to have written about Dartmouth. The only Dartmouth he could have written about is *Lord* Dartmouth, with whom he went to Tangier."

"Well, maybe there's something there . . ."

"As soon as we can get another glimpse of these papers, we'll know."

We looked at each other. Pilfering priceless papers wasn't anything we were accustomed to. Something gave way in each of us at the same time, and we burst into laughter. My ribs ached, but I couldn't stop. By the time we got up to our room I couldn't have moved another muscle.

Sarah slipped out of her dress. Another bout of hilarity ensued as we thought of the people who would boggle at the sight of her removing stolen papers from beneath her intimate garments.

"Let's do Mattie's lot first," I said, opening the large envelope I'd found behind the mantel. "This has to be what everyone's after, because no one *knew* there was anything else until I opened the churn."

I pulled out the contents as Sarah watched over my shoulder. It was just one sheet of paper, with a sheet of what appeared to be archival cardboard to keep it from being damaged. But what a sheet of paper it was!

I gaped. It was unquestionably of Pepys's era, a nice, thick, folio-sized cream-coloured sheet. It was written in Pepys's favoured shorthand, Shelton's Tachygraphy. So the fact that it wasn't actually in Pepys's own hand did little to diminish my interest in the piece, especially because I could see that it was signed, albeit in the code, by none other than the King of England.

"What? What does it say?" Sarah asked. My motionless, wordless awe would have told her exactly how remarkable this discovery was.

"It says, 'On this day I have successfully completed my friend Samuel Pepys, Esquire's, lessons in Shelton's Tachygraphy. In gratitude to him I present the accompanying gift, and express my thanks in my new language. The value of this secret language for conveying information at court is inestimable, and I shall be in Mr. Pepys's debt always.

Signed this day of 15 June, 1688,

James II'"

"So it wasn't by Pepys after all!" Sarah exclaimed.

"Actually, darling, this is a much more valuable document. Mattie needed a discovery to make her name, to take her from cataloguing gifts in the basement up to the Librarian's suite. A personal letter from the King himself—any king—is a far greater coup than a letter from Pepys."

"So Mattie is well placed for the future. She'll be delighted to know! We'll visit her again in the morning and tell her so. But Alex . . . there was nothing in there that would cause all of this intrigue."

"No . . . you're right. But remember: Mattie couldn't read the shorthand. That's why she asked me to come out before Reunions, to translate it for her. Someone must be terrified that Pepys wrote something damaging about them, but they don't know for a fact that it exists. So they went after *any* Pepys find."

Sarah sank down onto the bed. "So we now have two unknown Englishmen of good background trying to kill you and Moose—you haven't really told me about that yet—someone with a crowbar trying to render Mattie incapable of publicising her find, if not kill her, and yet another unknown party blackmailing the College using an historical document—which may or may not be a Pepys diary extension."

"The blackmail part bothers me . . . obviously, no one else *has* the Pepys papers. We do."

"The motivations bother me, too," Sarah said, flopping over and resting her chin on her hands. "Maybe the butter churn papers will tell all."

I looked through the papers as I had during our Rauner tour with Phil. Since they did not seem to be organised in any way, I had no qualms about setting the pulpy twentieth-century paper to one side and winnowing out the lovely creamy sheets. In the end, there were five. They'd suffered remarkably little damage from resting against the acidic, discoloured leaves. There was no way to tell what their proper order was—the sheets were unnumbered—so I started with the one on top. ". . . *and my lord has vexed me exceedingly with his wanton acts of destruction in the name of the King. I wonder if I dare reveal the full extent of his misconduct in Tangier. I must wait to see the lie of the land . . . and if his behaviour improves. But as of this very moment, I want no further contact with him. And Lord! to see how he carries on with the ladies marooned here in Tangier.*"

I stopped and glanced at Sarah. She was once again looking over my shoulder. "The rumoured Tangier diary extension!" I told her. "But it's in his own hand . . . he swore at the end of the diary—years before—that he wouldn't damage his eyes further by writing any more of his diary. He must have felt very strongly indeed about it . . . perhaps it was too secret to dictate to anyone else."

"That makes sense," Sarah said.

"I remember something about that at the end of his diary . . . let's see." I pulled my paperback Pepys out of my bag. "Here it is, on the very last page: '*I . . . must be contented to set down no more than is fit for them and all the world to know; or if there be any thing, I must endeavour to keep a margin in my book open, to add here and there a note in short-hand with my own hand.*' But he certainly wrote more than a few notes . . . he probably couldn't resist writing any more than he could reading, no matter how much it hurt his eyes."

I placed the paper gently back on the table. "If I know anything about Samuel Pepys, these were the pages of his diary that he had to write himself because they were so secret. Why did he tear them out of the original book? And how did they get mixed up in this lot? Obviously they used to be bound in to a diary . . . Of course! The Tangier Diary extension! These could be wayward pages!"

"It's a good thing I'm a strong Dartmouth woman with—as the old song puts it—the granite of New Hampshire in my muscles and my brains. Because if I weren't, life with you might be just a little too exciting," my wife teased me, her eyes glowing with the excitement of our find.

"Ready for more?"

She told me she was with a loose-lipped kiss that sent me reeling. When I opened my eyes she was smiling, a sparkle dancing in her green eyes. "Aren't you going to read on?"

I wasn't sure if she was too much for me, or I too much for her. Perhaps we would carry on in this lovely balance forever. I certainly looked forward to trying.

"Right. Just let me toddle back to the desk here . . ." As each moment passed, my bruised body was becoming that much more sore. I doubted if I'd be able to move for days if I ever actually laid down for a few hours' rest . . . or recreation.

But at the sound of her musical laugh I felt on top of the world, aches or no aches. "Okay. Page three. *'It saddens my heart more than I could have believed to learn from His Majesty, by way of a joke when he'd drunk too much wine, the crime his father committed against all Londoners. It makes me marvel that I could ever have walked with him at court, supped with him, served him . . . and his father. Perhaps my tendencies to Roundheadedness were well-founded, and I should never have . . . but no. This suits no purpose. I must, however, record for posterity'* "—I broke off to share a bit of Pepys lore with Sarah—"Pepys was always doing things 'for posterity,' in case you haven't noticed. He claimed it was the reason for penning the diary."

I looked for approval from my wife for this scholarly insight, but she merely gave me a bemused look and made her hand revolve in a sort of exaggerated royal wave, a "let's-get-on-with-it" gesture. Chastised, I returned to the paper and tried to focus on the tiny symbols again.

" *'How great was my surprise, and bitterness, to discover the depth of the royal family's treachery towards their own people . . . the very people who served them so loyally. His Majesty told me most jocularly that at the time of the Plague, certain herbalists had told them of a potion that could forestall disease and death. But the herbs were in exceedingly short supply, and came only from Tangier. The royal family, scarce can I believe that I am relating this, even in my most secret code, purchased as much of this herb as they were able. They took it in large doses, not sharing it with the people, nor obtaining more as they ought, while Londoners all around them died of the horrible disease. I do wonder how he could have tolerated the carts full of dead bodies travelling through the streets as he drank his draughts of healthful herbs and marvel that he can sleep of nights with the lives of tens of thousands on his conscience. Let this be a record of this gross misdeed, though it be too horrible to relate during my lifetime. I should surely lose my life for this indiscretion if it be revealed.' "*

"Oh no," Sarah breathed, sinking down onto the chair next to me. "Oh no . . ."

There were no words for the next few minutes. What we had just read stood in such stark contrast to our own idyllic life together that we felt horribly guilty about those lives lost, so needlessly. *Tens of thousands.* But then, according to human nature, in the next moment we felt only gratitude that *we were alive.* We needed to make the most of each moment. I sensed—no, I *knew*—that Sarah shared my thoughts.

It was a moment of closeness . . . fostered by a horrible, deadly, dark secret.

"Alex, I want to *live.* With you. If anything ever . . ."

"Sarah. We'll be all right. Everything's going to be all right."

We held each other until we felt better . . . both of us. Then Sarah slid a chair in front of the door, though it was double locked, and we sank into oblivion in each other's arms.

The power of marriage is seriously underestimated.

Two hours later, I woke abruptly from the sleep of the

dead and realised I still needed to take my contact lenses out—at least for a couple of hours. As I rose from the bed, gently removing Sarah's arm draped over my chest and placing it by her side, something across the Green caught my eye. Was I seeing things? I blinked and looked once more at the upstairs windows of Rauner Library. There it was again! A flash of light had shone ever so briefly; no question, someone was in there with a torch.

Rauner had been dark when we returned to our room. Had we led whoever *else* was searching for the Pepys documents there? But how had *they* got past the sophisticated security system? I wondered exactly who was in there and what they were doing . . . and was glad Sarah had brought the butter churn contents with her.

I checked to be sure that the papers, now stowed in protective envelopes, were still safely taped to the bottom of the large bureau. They were . . . for the time being. So worried was I that after removing the lenses I put on my glasses, got out the documents, and transcribed them. I stowed the transcriptions in the back pocket of a pair of jeans, slid off my glasses, and climbed back into bed as the first hint of pink appeared in the east.

Even if we had led someone else to Rauner, there was nothing left for them to find. A smile spread slowly across my face; I let my eyes close.

Nothing left to find, I thought drowsily . . . unless they found *us*.

My eyes snapped open.

CHAPTER 15

God knows what will be the end of it!

Such mad doings there are every day among them!

And from all together, God knows my heart, I expect nothing but ruin can follow unless things are better ordered in a little time.

SAMUEL PEPYS

When I awoke, Sarah was looking down at me with such excruciating tenderness that I wouldn't have moved anything but my eyelids for the world . . . only I couldn't resist lifting a hand to touch a lock of her silky dark hair, hanging tantalisingly close.

"Your bruises, Alex—I'm sorry. It's nearly eleven . . . we've slept for seven hours."

Little did she know I'd spent much of it fearing a rattle at the doorknob.

I had no interest in the bruises, and I sat up immediately. That is, I tried to sit up but quickly sank down again.

"I thought so," Sarah said. "I've ordered room service. We'll take it one moment at a time. Everything's going to be all right."

The next thing I knew she was moving to answer the door. When I next dared to open my eyes, a trolley had appeared in the middle of our room. Sarah was standing at it, gathering goodies for us on a plate. I thought I smelled . . . did I smell . . . ?

"Sarah, darling, if you're some sort of angelic apparition I don't think I can bear it."

"I'm no apparition. And the Breakfast King *will* have his breakfast." She came towards me smiling, bearing a plate of my favourite breakfast foods, the most prized of the day. We all have our little foibles; on holiday, one of mine is breakfast. Better yet, because Sarah knew me so very well, she'd ordered the unlikely combination of French Toast (a taste acquired from Dartmouth dining hall days) and scrambled eggs.

Were all husbands treated like this? Had I married a goddess of pleasure?

She sat on the edge of the bed, inches from me, aromas wafting temptingly from the plate she carried. She all but waved it beneath my nose.

"Eat well, my love. We have a big day ahead of us."

Had I realised just *how* big, I'd have stayed in bed.

Like a fool I not only ate but rose, showered, and prepared to meet the day. "We should see Mattie first," I said, transferring the transcriptions from the jeans to the back pocket of the trousers I wore.

"Absolutely. She should know everything first."

I told Sarah about the transcription as we set off for the hospital; she nodded her approval.

Ten minutes later, having stopped to pick up a bouquet

of flowers, we were at Mattie's bedside. She had that same disconcerting look—delicate yet powerful—that I remembered from dating her, even with the bandages encircling her head. Moose had met his match. He sat at her side, holding her hand.

"Alex!" she exclaimed as we entered the room. "What happened to you?"

I smiled. "You shall soon know all. I'm delighted to see *you* feeling better." And I was.

"How are you today?" Sarah asked.

"Okay," she replied a bit warily, looking a bit like a pirate in her bandages. I couldn't help but recall one night when she'd . . . but no. The past was firmly in the past. In fact, sometimes it was better to pretend the past had never been.

But how did one stop memories?

"So tell me. What's the good news?" Mattie sounded as perky—no, aggressive—as ever. How could someone so small carry such weight?

"I'm glad you're feeling stronger, Matt." Inwardly, I cringed at the use of the intimate nickname before my wife—force of habit only—but Sarah showed no reaction. But then, Sarah was exceptional. "Because some of this might come as something of a shock to you. Are you sure you're up to . . . ?"

She and Moose beamed at me, holding hands. "For heaven's sake, Alex," Mattie scolded, rolling her eyes for our benefit.

I got the message. So much for gentleness. If she wanted it that way . . .

"Okay." I cleared my throat, all business. "Sarah and I broke into Rauner last night. We were able to obtain what

I have come to call The Butter Churn Papers from the Frost Farm Bequest. In them we found the most remarkable diary entries of Samuel Pepys, torn from his diary and obviously carried to the States by the emigrating relatives of his servants."

This was densely packed information, but neither of them needed babying. Both Moose and Mattie were staring at me. Before she could say anything I carried on. "By far the most valuable item, you'll be glad to know, is the one you hid behind the Treasure Room mantel."

As I watched Mattie, I longed to compare notes with Sarah. It seemed to me there was a touch of greed—something unbecoming—as Mattie waited for me to go on. But then her entire career might hinge on this . . . That was it. *Ambition.* It was naked ambition I saw in her eyes. To her credit, she remained silent.

"It wasn't written by Pepys, Mattie."

Perhaps it was cruel. But I needed to know how much she already knew. The answer was very clear: she knew nothing.

She was devastated. Before she could unravel too far I continued.

"It's *better* than Pepys."

My ex-girlfriend stopped on her slide into a very deep funk and tilted her bruised face at me.

I smiled at her. "My friend, you have secured your future. What you've found is a letter from King James II to Samuel Pepys, thanking the latter for personal tutoring in Shelton's Tachygraphy. This letter is worth far more than something from Pepys ever could be. Here—I transcribed it for you." I handed her a hastily scrawled page of Hanover Inn stationery.

Mattie snatched the sheet, scanning it avariciously. She knew very well what this meant. She knew it meant more than the book value of such an item; it meant her career. Then she got hold of herself. Being Mattie, she feigned an attack of *mal de tête*; I suspected she was eager to speak privately with Moose. Good manners dictated that Sarah and I leave immediately.

As we stood at the door, I delivered the coup de grâce. Quietly, I said, "Moose, it's a shame Mattie's not feeling well. There's a lot more to tell."

He gave me a look of longing, of commiseration.

Poor Mattie. She sat up a bit, passed a hand over her forehead, and said softly, "No, don't go. I'm all right, really."

"Another time," I said, and ushered Sarah out of the room.

Outside the hospital building, Sarah asked, "What do you think that was all about? She almost acted as though we're on different sides of this, instead of helping her out. I thought she was going to jump out of the bed and beg you to tell her more."

I grinned at her. "I know. I have very little patience with her brand of manipulation. Thank God you're not like that," I said fervently.

"I'm glad you're still happy with your choice," she replied with surprising gravity. "It's an odd feeling to be with you and Mattie. You're obviously still close."

I gave her a peck on the cheek and said, "Rest assured, you have nothing to worry about."

All the same, I hoped her mind hadn't leapt to Pepys's extramarital dalliances.

She snuggled close as we walked, attaching herself affectionately to my upper arm. Normally I loved this; today it set off a fireworks display of pain.

"I'm so sorry," she said sincerely, pausing to deliver a kiss to my cheek. "My wounded hero. What's next?"

I sighed. "I'm thinking another visit to The Pet is in order. Not to torture you, because I can tell you don't like him. Just because—well, I feel we should."

"You're going to tell him what you found?"

"Of course!" I gazed at her in astonishment. "Surely you don't think I would keep something of this magnitude from my Pepys mentor, of all people!"

She shrugged. "I just didn't know how many people you wanted to tell, and how much you trusted him."

With that notice of the degree of antipathy she felt towards Pettifer, we went straight to the car. Before we'd left Hanover I entered his phone number on my mobile. It wouldn't do to show up unannounced.

"Hello?" a gruff voice answered. I didn't know who it was, but it wasn't The Pet.

"Hello, this is Alex Plumtree ringing for Pettifer." No response. "Is he in, please?"

"You were his student, right? Just here the other day?"

"That's right." Could this be his son? "Are you Lane?"

"Yeah. And my father's been missing since last night. I'm getting worried about him. He takes medication now, you know. He *can't* miss it."

"Do you mind if my wife and I come over to talk? Maybe we could help."

"Please. I'll be here."

"We're on our way."

Lane, his father's only child, had "gone the long way round," as his father had put it many years ago. He'd passed through a difficult patch and Pettifer had decided strong medicine was in order, particularly as the boy showed no interest in going to college. Lane had been shipped off to New Zealand to work on a horse ranch just after Sarah and I had graduated. These many years later he was still enamoured of farm life and put his skills to use at the College's equestrian facility. I was curious to see what sort of man Mattie had found so attractive.

When Lane came to the front door of the farmhouse, he looked like an exact replica of his father—leggy, tanned and strong—with a thirty-year advantage. He proved to be as hospitable as his father, and likeable in a strong, silent sort of way.

"Please," he said, urging us in. "Sit down. Coffee?"

When we were all seated in the comfortable room, coffee in hand, he began. "This is really unlike Dad," he said, sitting forward in his father's rocker. "Not only is there the matter of the medication, but we have a sort of routine. Once he and I patched up our differences, we've talked first thing every morning for years." He shook his head. "I don't like it."

An idea was developing in the dark recesses of my mind, and I didn't like *it*, either. Sarah gave me a significant look, as if she might have had the same suspicion.

"I don't know if this means anything, but your father spoke at our class dinner last night," I told Lane. "He was substituting for someone."

"He didn't mention it to me." Lane frowned. "But why is that important? Did he seem all right?"

"He was spectacular, as usual. He dressed as Shakespeare and hit all the high spots . . . or should I saw low spots?"

Lane smiled.

"But there was something odd about the conclusion of his speech," Sarah interposed. "Actually, now that I think of it, I'm not even sure he intended it as the conclusion. He suddenly just *disappeared* into the darkness. We kept applauding, but he never returned. We all decided it had been your father's idea of a dramatic ending."

I picked up the story. "After dinner I walked round to the front of the tent, where the platform was, and had a look. Even accounting for drama, I thought it was odd that your father didn't return to acknowledge his applause. But there was nothing out of place; no hint of why he might have disappeared."

"Maybe I'd better see if his car is abandoned somewhere—I'll check the boathouse and that side of the campus."

I knew I'd still left out part of the story. "I wish I didn't have to tell you this, Lane, but last night a friend and I were in the old boathouse. We were attacked by some very unpleasant people—they'd have killed us if our friends hadn't come down the path."

Lane shook his head. "You know we had some trouble in Hanover just last year. I thought all that was over."

"A whole cluster of nasty incidents this weekend

seems to have something to do with a recent find at Rauner Library. It's to do with Pepys, your father's speciality."

"Bunch of nutcases. Never could understand the Pepys thing." He stood impatiently. I could imagine that the crusty cowboy would have little use for anyone who lived for lace collars and entered the king's "closet" with the monarch. "I'm going to see if I can find him. Call me later."

We were climbing into the car as he sped off in a dark green pickup truck.

"How could I not have realised?" I asked.

"How *could* we have realised?" Sarah said soothingly. "You have to admit, Pettifer is a dramatic person. His exit seemed perfectly in character—a nice touch."

We stopped back at the Inn to reconnoitre; we'd decided that in view of events we'd have to extend our stay. God willing, this would all be sorted soon and we could get back to our honeymoon on the *Carpe Diem.*

"Mr and Mrs Plumtree?" The desk clerk looked almost frantic to catch us as we passed the front desk. "The President of the College has been trying to reach you. If you'll give me a ring when you reach your room, I'll connect you."

Sarah and I exchanged a look. "All right," I said. "Thanks."

"There were several other messages for you as well," he added, and handed them to Sarah. We smiled our thanks and went towards the staircase.

"Alex, take the lift just this once. It won't be the end of your good habits. Look how you're walking!"

I went obstinately to the fire door leading to the stairs. Sarah sighed and followed.

"Damn," she muttered, shuffling through the messages. "They've found me."

"Who?"

"Work."

I stopped cold on the staircase and turned to face her. "You can't be serious. Sarah, darling, I thought that just for this week—"

"If you think I told them where we were going, you're badly mistaken. My parents must have finally given in. Maybe it's something important." I could hear her slipping into work mode. The problem was, in Sarah's work, *everything* was important. If they were calling her it could be anything from a government falling to an economy collapsing. My wife seemed to get only the juiciest of crises.

While I rang down to the front desk, Sarah pulled out her mobile and started punching at the keypad. "Yes, Mr Plumtree. Hold on, will you?"

In mere moments, the College president, James Bright, was on the line. He was a pleasant, jovial ex-history professor who had immediately captured the hearts of students and alums alike. I was pleased and honoured to speak to him personally.

"Alex? This is Jim. Sorry to bother you. How are you enjoying your reunions?"

What could I say? That murderers seemed to lurk behind every college building and bookcase? That I had nearly been killed twice in one evening, and my friend the night before? "Very much indeed, sir. The more so because it's my honeymoon."

"*Really!* I'd say you were quite noble to return for reunions under the circumstances. Oh, and congratulations on joining the Friends of the Library board."

"Delighted to help in any way I can."

"Glad to hear it! Because I have an important favour to ask of you."

"Yes?" I queried, though privately I thought I'd nearly reached my capacity for performing favours of any sort, for everyone but Sarah.

"We have a most unusual visitor here this weekend, a fellow countryman of yours . . ."

My mind flew to the "countryman" who'd intended to throw me and Moose into the Connecticut River.

". . . with a most fascinating ancestry. You know that it was the second Earl of Dartmouth who made it possible for the College to be founded in 1769. Well, this is a man who has come into ownership of Earl Dartmouth's papers. He's interested in making a significant donation of books and papers to the college. I won't mince words, Alex: we need to pull out the stops to make him feel that we value him here. It would be a shame for those papers to go anywhere but Dartmouth, and he's actually hinted that if he's not very pleased with everything, he'll donate them somewhere else instead.

"I had dinner with him last night, and Dean has spent the morning with him. This afternoon he's requested a drive to Mount Washington. It takes some time to get there, as you know, and I thought you'd be just the man to spend it talking to him about book-related issues—especially in view of your role at Rauner. Oh, and did I mention he's an oarsman? I hope you'll help us out, Alex—please?"

"Er, would you mind if I conferred with my wife for a moment?"

"No, no. Of course not. I'll hang on."

I put down the phone and went to Sarah, who was hunched over her own phone and making notes in some personal shorthand of her own. Interesting, I hadn't seen it before. She looked up, then told the person on the other end to hold on. "Alex?"

"I'm needed to help secure a library donation this afternoon of some papers of the Earl of Dartmouth's," I said softly. "*The* Earl of Dartmouth, as in 1769. The potential donor wants to go on an outing to Mount Washington. . . . I'd like to help, but not if it'll ruin our plans."

"Alex, I'm so sorry. This little problem is going to take me all afternoon to iron out. You'll be glad to know, however, that I'm refusing to go to London immediately; if they want my help, they can have it long distance."

"Good girl. But you'll have dinner, etcetera with me, won't you?"

"Especially the etcetera. Guaranteed." She threw me a kiss and went back to her conversation.

"President Bright? Yes, sorry, *Jim*. It will be an honour to help."

"Wonderful! I'll have a driver pick you up at the Inn in, say, ten minutes?"

I laughed. Nothing like being railroaded. But somehow with him it was hard to mind. "Yes, fine."

As I gave Sarah a hug, tied on my running shoes and went down to wait on one of the Inn's porch rockers, I wondered if I would ever have ordinary days like other people. Days when there was nothing to do. Days when no one went missing, days when my life wasn't threatened. Honeymoons without international crises or College pleas for assistance.

No, I decided, with cheerful resignation. Probably not.

I plucked a copy of the Sunday *New York Times* off of the seat of an inviting rocker, but shopped short at the sight of the two thirty-six point headlines. This being America, the New York Yankees shared the spotlight with the headline that shook me to the core: "*Britain Rocked by Riots, Terrorism in Wake of Struggle for Crown.*"

The disturbing article went on to say that the Queen appeared not to be recovering well from her accident. Religious groups were protesting the possibility of Prince Charles ascending the throne in increasing numbers. Still others were running about with placards bearing the face of Prince William. Unknown parties were continuing to cause fires to break out through the City, despite a close watch by police and paramilitary forces.

To make matters worse, Prince Charles had evidently visited a holistic health centre in Kent and, in an effort to lend credence to their work, commented that he himself takes a certain herb reputed to stave off memory loss. A pensioner had hurried to his local surgeon to get some of the herb the next day, and was told he couldn't get it on the National Health Service. The anti-Royalists were having a field day with the story, playing up the fact that royals have access to medicines that their subjects don't.

We were reliving the plague herb story in our time.

But that wasn't all. A box on one side described a "mystery man" who was seen near the Queen's horse shortly before her accident. Police were searching for him.

I was certain that I knew now what Sarah's phone call had been about, and why Ian or her parents had seen fit to interrupt us. Despite the disastrous news from home, I felt a touch of pride that my wife had been called in to save the day.

A Dartmouth-green van bearing the college crest pulled into the Inn's porte cochere, and I stood to perform my own humble service.

CHAPTER 16

Pretty odd company . . .

But when others discover your fear, and that discontent produces fear, they will be discontented too, and impose on you.

And now this do make all people conclude there is something extraordinary in it, but nobody knows what.

SAMUEL PEPYS

The owner of the Earl of Dartmouth's papers, one Vivian Porter, proved to be a delightful gent of perhaps sixty-five. He reminded me a bit of Ian. Although everyone in Britain knew the Porter name, I was surprised that I'd never met or heard of Vivian, especially considering that he was a collector of such important papers. Still an active oarsman, he was keen of mind and strong of body. From the moment I joined the jolly College van, which also contained a driver, a youngish man, and a frosty Patricia Bailey, I knew that the afternoon would be far from a chore . . . no matter how much grovelling and cossetting Vivian would extract from us for his precious papers.

"Good heavens, Plumtree, this *is* a pleasure! Knew your father well. I daresay he'd be very pleased to see how you're carrying on. Oh, this is my man Jonathan.

Jonathan, Alex Plumtree." The young man nodded at me from the back of the van. "And you know Patricia." Patricia widened her eyes at me; she hadn't forgiven me for the late-night call to arms at Rauner. "Now tell me what you know about this quite remarkable peak we're about to visit. Been up it, have you?"

This set the pace for a dizzying whirlwind of conversation that flitted from subject to subject and nation to nation almost faster than the mind could follow. I bided my time in discussing Porter's intriguing donation; it wouldn't do to rush it. Besides, we had so much in common it was almost absurd . . . or else he was skilled enough socially to make it appear so.

It took over two hours to reach the base of the mountain. When we arrived, I was fascinated to see the distant and formal service Jonathan provided, from opening the car door to offering a windcheater to his employer. Having grown up entirely without servants myself, it always intrigued me to see the invisible lines that defined such a relationship.

"I've never been up the cog railway before," I offered, as Patricia purchased tickets for all of us. "This will be a treat."

"Ah, let me guess. You normally *run* up the mountain, I suppose." Vivian laughed, but he was spot on. We used to run down, too.

I smiled. "I'll bet you'd give me a run for my money, Vivian."

"Indeed I would, my boy. Jonathan, too. Did you know he won a triathlon in England this spring? I know the Americans do that sort of thing all the time, but I find it quite remarkable."

"Impressive," I said, viewing Jonathan through new eyes. "How did you come to do the triathlon?" I asked him.

He shrugged. I had the impression he didn't really know how to smile. "Let's say I enjoy extreme exercise."

We said no more about it then; we all got aboard a car of the train and settled in for the ride. Vivian arranged it so that I sat next to him. To my surprise, he chose the moment that the noisy car began to rattle along its metal path to get down to business. "Now Plumtree. I'm exceedingly glad to have the chance to talk to you today. You see, very few people are acquainted with the sort of historical papers I'm talking about giving to the College. They're priceless, actually, in that they contain a record of the entire process of the second Earl of Dartmouth coming round to give money for a College that would teach the Indians—I mean Native Americans—about Christianity. In your opinion, is Rauner adequate to house such papers?"

"Certainly, sir. Surely you've seen the library for yourself?"

"Patricia is giving me the grand tour tomorrow; evidently the head man's away. I'd like *your* opinion."

"Dartmouth College has taken every possible care to make Rauner the finest special collections library, from security to lighting and humidity. . . . I assure you, you wouldn't regret housing your gift there. And you can imagine the great value the Dartmouth papers—I've heard just a bit about them—would have to the College. It's not every day that something with such specific value to a particular institution comes along. As a Dartmouth alumnus, I personally hope you will make them available to the College. As a group we're very fond of tales pertaining to the College's earliest days. No doubt you've heard—we're quite a loyal bunch."

Even as I made my soft and sincere sales pitch, I had a feeling that something was amiss. How could this man have flown all the way here, and done no research on Rauner? Surely Phil Cronenwett would have sent him materials reassuring him as to the quality of the facility, and the treatment of the gift. Something didn't ring true.

Naturally I couldn't tell Porter that, nor could I discuss it with Patricia—so I simmered with disquiet all the way up the mountain. Eventually, after more chatter (during which he spoke knowledgeably about the Plumtree Collection) we arrived at the end of the cog railway, the summit of Mount Washington. At least, I thought with tongue in cheek, the subject of Pepys hadn't come up.

"Good heavens, what an exceedingly desolate place!" Vivian exclaimed.

I knew what he meant. Desolate, majestic, and incredibly beautiful at the same time. We stood at the top of the world—but how odd it was to stand here without being utterly exhausted from the long run up. Mount Washington was very old, and therefore well-scrubbed looking. It was cleansing to the soul, too, somehow—the highest, wildest, coldest, most unpredictable peak in the Presidential Range. The weather observatory station up here added a certain prestige, making the mountain the oracle of peaks, the one worthy of special study. A modern, attractive building near the summit housed not only the observatory but a museum and was manned year-round. Antennas for radio station WMTW also bristled from the mountaintop.

"What's that over there?" Jonathan asked, moving quietly next to me. We stood on a safe plateau, near the mountain's highest point but not precipitously so, a spot intended for the general public.

I followed his eyes past the building and antennas to a bright yellow sign some distance away. I smiled with fondness. "Ah. That's to warn people away from a rather drastic dropoff. It falls off for about forty feet just there to a place called Dead Man's Ledge—now there's a nasty, unforgiving bit of rock. I went down there on a dare once. Lucky to have survived, I think."

Jonathan was shaking his head, ever the serious athlete. I could tell he was intrigued by the challenge of descending a sheer wall of granite. A moment went by. We watched Vivian tell Patricia a story about his mountaineering exploits in Nepal in the fifties, oblivious to the scenery. Jonathan's attention returned to the ledge, far across the summit area. I saw him squint at the neon sign. "Would you . . . ? No. Sorry."

"What?"

He seemed fascinated by Dead Man's Ledge. "I was just wondering . . . since they're busy just now, d'you think you could show me how you got down there?"

"Sure." I'd got my word in with Vivian, after all. Why not enjoy a trip down memory lane? The old body might be a bit creaky after my recent exploits, but it wasn't out of commission yet. I doubted the others would even notice we were gone.

We began the hike over to the ledge when to my utter disbelief I saw one of our heavyweight eight just ahead on the path. "OSO!" I bellowed. It was almost comical, the startled look Jonathan gave me—as if I'd lost all my marbles in the space of a moment.

"BUDDY!" Oso, "the bear," came running and gave me a characteristic bear hug. "What're you doing up here?" He eyed Jonathan. I could read the question in his eyes: *Are you crazy? Where's your lovely bride?*

I know, my eyes told him back. *Business trip.*

I said, "Oso—I mean, Dave—this is Jonathan, visiting from England."

"*Great* to meet you!" Oso said with his inimitable enthusiasm. He had started a mail-order computer company that now had one of its machines in virtually every home in America. Sometimes it seemed to me he'd done it on enthusiasm alone.

"And you," Jonathan said quietly, with characteristic English reserve. He kept his hands locked firmly behind him. I could almost hear him thinking, *Just don't hug me.*

"Buddy, a few of us are extending the reunion tonight, back at the Inn. Want to join us? Or do you have . . . *other* plans?" He raised his eyebrows. Clearly, he was thinking of Sarah.

"I'd love to, Oso, but . . . well, I'll have to wait and see."

Oso, the highly trained salesman, took it all in with perfect understanding. "Fine. If you decide to join us, you can always ride back with us. Plenty of room . . . we could go straight to my place and start the party."

"Thanks, Oso." We shook hands, grinning like a couple of idiots. We had an absurdly rich treasure store of memories. "Hope to see you later."

I noticed Jonathan taking all of this in with rapt attention. *Talk about a foreign culture . . .* Even as Oso ran to join his latest in a string of long-term, live-in girlfriends the Briton watched in disbelief.

Jonathan quickly got hold of himself and started asking more questions about Dead Man's Ledge. "How did it get its name?"

The transition was so abrupt that it took me a couple of paces to adjust. How could two English-speaking cultures be so very different? "Er—someone did actually die out there, as you might guess. It's also quite atmospheric, desolate, in a way. I suppose people name these things to remind others of how dangerous this mountain really is."

At that, I saw him glance around in an attitude of what might have been apprehension. I'd had the same feeling when I was twelve, when my grandfather—my mother's father—had first brought me up here on a hike during one of my Boston summers. Although the mountain didn't *look* particularly threatening, the number of people who died up here every year after embarking on simple day hikes was sobering. Experienced hikers understood and feared Mount Washington. There was no use explaining all this to Jonathan; he'd only think I was exaggerating. And God willing, as we were going back down on the cog railway, he'd never have to find out for himself.

In seven minutes, we reached the dropoff to the ledge. As we stood several feet from the edge I said, "I hope the others won't worry about us." I glanced back at Patricia and Vivian, now a considerable distance away.

"I shouldn't think so," Jonathan said. "Vivian will be regaling Patricia with tales of his exploits in the Himalayas. And they're perfectly safe there."

Reassured by this, I crouched with him at the head of the ledge. Here, we were far beyond the path taken by casual cog-rail passengers and off in a world of our own. The majesty of the peaks we overlooked, dark rock with patches of white summer, never failed to fill me with awe.

From this view, the rock ceased to be smooth and ancient and took on a sharp, craggy look. It was much more hostile, somehow—and why then more beautiful?—for its violence. It almost seemed that by merely looking we might fall away to eternity, all the while amazed by the infinite beauty of the harsh, rocky space.

We stared for a moment in mutual wonder, which was why it surprised me all the more when he said quite suddenly, "Get down on the ledge. *Now*." The small, dark nose of a gun with its sinister eye pointed at me from his jacket pocket.

Another evil Englishman? If this kept on, I'd start to believe Hollywood about some native lack of goodness in my fellow Britons.

"Jonathan, what do you—"

"You heard me. Do it now or I'll shoot." He looked over the sheer dropoff. "I could kill you now, or I could make it look like you accidentally did yourself in. If I were you, I'd take the last chance you'll ever get."

I gaped at him. "What . . . ?" I had in no way associated him with the Pepys affair, and so was all the more stunned. Was Jonathan acting on his own, or was he carrying out Vivian Porter's wishes?

Yes, I could see it now. Vivian's unlikely ignorance of Rauner. How brilliantly—creatively—they'd pulled this off, eliminating one of their main obstacles to keeping the papers secret forever. And there would be no trace of the crime.

I sighed. "I don't suppose there's any point in . . . no." I raised both of my hands, palms towards him, in a gesture of understanding and wary cooperation.

As I turned to start the descent, I thought of how I

might have avoided coming to this point. I might have started by not being so helpful to the College. It was trying so hard to do the right thing that seemed to cause all the trouble.

I remembered with surprising accuracy what it had taken to get onto the ledge as an undergraduate. First of all, a sense of immortality and superhuman strength (forgive me, I was nineteen). Second, luck. Avoiding a slip on the minuscule hand- and footholds was a near-miracle. As I chose each vitally important handhold and toehold, I played for time and thought about strategy. As Pepys might have said, Lord! but I was glad for all those chess games with my father and grandfather.

Pepys. I never wanted anything to do with the old windbag again.

But strategy . . . that was the—

In one heart-stopping moment, my hand slipped and I hung with my feet twelve feet above the ledge. If I fell now, I'd bounce off the ledge and fall to my doom. Every movement had to be calculated for a slow, careful landing on the twelve-by-forty-eight-inch-ledge.

There's another lesson here, Alex, I told myself. *Why were you bragging about your exploits? He'd never have known* . . . But then I wondered how he could possibly have spotted Dead Man's Ledge on his very first visit to Mount Washington. Impossible. He'd watched for opportunities and engaged my pride.

It was amazing how fast these thoughts occurred and receded—hundreds of them per minute. Is this what people meant by having their life flash before them?

I was perhaps one third of the way down, and all too aware that getting back up, should I be lucky enough to have the chance, would be infinitely harder. "What will you tell them?" I asked, willing a quarter-inch outcropping of granite to become a fingerhold. "Won't they ask where I've gone?"

"Won't you die anyway?" he asked casually. "Actually, you've made this very easy. You ran into a friend—none of us could avoid seeing the two of you carry on. You decided to go back with him. Now get on with it."

I longed for a replay of the night before, when The Boys had come trotting down the boathouse path to my rescue.

"Aaaggh!" I cried out as a rock flew hard into the knuckles of my right hand, which was tenaciously gripping a tiny bit of something by the fingertips. Jonathan was accelerating my demise.

I closed my eyes and held on out of sheer terror. I'd felt enough pain in my life to learn that the will was stronger than sensation. I could feel my hands slipping—they weren't used to clinging to microscopic bulges of rock. So I kept moving, which had no doubt been his idea.

"Just coming!" I heard him call, all calm competence, and said a fervent prayer that his malice would be uncovered. How many mountain accidents, I wondered, happened like this instead of a sudden surprise of cold and wet, with no time to get down? Come to think of it, it was the perfect place if you had to get rid of someone. . . .

My running shoes—hell, might as well revert—*trainers* were three feet from the ledge when I decided to drop down. It was a risk, but who knew what my tormentor would do to finish me off from above if I didn't huddle against the ledge and become invisible to him?

In the next moment, I found out just how sound my

strategy had been. Because a millisecond after my feet had hit the narrow rescue of the ledge, I glimpsed a large object hurtling towards me at rocket speed. I hugged the mountain, willing it to miss, but it was so close . . .

Bang! It glanced off my temple and knocked me sideways. Teetering on the edge of eternity, I began to fall backwards ever so slowly and struggled to compensate. I regained my balance, and then . . . no . . . falling again. Something was in my eyes, clouding my vision . . . but I did, just, get onto my hands and knees. Dizzy, I knew I'd been knocked on the head and couldn't expect to hold the position for long.

I heard footsteps recede from the top of the ledge. Jonathan was gone.

CHAPTER 17

Wakened about two o'clock this morning with a noise of thunder, which lasted for an hour, with such continued lightings, not flashes, but flames, that all the sky and ayre was light; and that for a great while, not a minute's space between new flames all the time: such a thing as I never did see, nor could have believed had even been in nature. And being put into a great sweat with it, could not sleep . . . and that accompanied with such a storm of rain as I never heard in my life.

But Lord! To see how unlucky a man may be by chance!

SAMUEL PEPYS

With grim irony I ran through all the things I'd told Vivian and Jonathan about Mount Washington's unpredictability. It was absolutely true that without a coat, without shelter, it was quite possible that I wouldn't survive the night. Yes, it was June—but in the mountains June was as unpredictable as March. It was early. Early enough for plenty of rain, wind, even snow. . . .

The sun was still shining. At half-past four by my watch, I counted it as one of two conditions to my advantage. The other was that Sarah would know something had happened as soon as I didn't return in time for our dinner date.

Or would she? She might be busy defending the free world. Or Jonathan might tell her I'd gone with Oso. . . .

And then I recalled our debate about getting a search party out for Mattie, and how futile it had been. Why? No one knew for certain she'd been on the mountain. The way Jonathan would tell it, no one knew for certain *I* was on the mountain, either.

Definitely leaning towards the hopeless side of the scale, but not yet decisively tipping the balance. Even as I perceived the darkness of the situation, I knew it was loss of hope that would kill me . . . if I let it.

My sole option was apparent: sit and wait. If it weren't for the head injury, which had now caused blood to flow in ominous quantities onto Dead Man's Ledge, I would try to climb back up the rock face. By now, Jonathan would be on his way to Hanover, telling them that I was coming back with Oso.

In the way that one catastrophic event often follows another, I felt a puff of wind. A glance skyward told me that I was not going to be fortunate with the weather. An enormous thunderhead was shooting plumes of cloud upward by the second. The lead-grey bottom of the cloud roiled and seethed like a brew in some evil cauldron. A thunderstorm . . . lightning.

I had to act quickly. I got up off my hands and knees, thinking that it might be better to try to climb the rock face and get to the weather observatory before the storm started. But I'd no sooner stood up straight than light-headedness overtook me. I had to sit down fast. Even this was a challenge on the narrow outcropping.

I fought wooziness with all my might. Rotten luck that

I hadn't had anything to eat since our late breakfast that morning. Even some water would . . .

I came round as rain lashed my face and thunder boomed. With deafening volume, the crash echoed threateningly between the rock faces of the mountains. It was much colder now, and darker. Nearly six o'clock, my watch said; far from dark . . . so this was storm light. The lightning looked like constant flame more than flashes. With shock I thought of the narrowness of the ledge and marvelled that I hadn't rolled off. But I of all people knew about the powerful instinct for self-preservation.

The rain bucketed down in sheet-like waves. It was stunningly cold. I huddled closer against the rock—though everything seemed equally cold and wet now. From my excellent vantage point, I saw with profound dismay that the storm cloud was roughly the size of China. It spread, decorated with the flame-lightning in a constant and impressive display of power, literally as far as my eye could see. I knew all too well what this meant. The torrent wouldn't stop for hours.

And then . . . even as I noticed how large the storm was, the wind seemed to abate. This storm was going nowhere: it would park over Mount Washington and pummel it.

I again considered risking the climb up the face, but now had two strikes against me. First, after the knock on the head I wasn't up to pulling myself up. It would take all I had on the best of days.

Second, the rock was now slippery with rain—awash with it. Those pencil-thin fingerholds would offer no purchase. My best—no, my *only* chance was to hunker down and weather the storm.

I must have drifted in and out of consciousness. Suddenly, by my watch, three and a half hours had passed. Half-nine and the storm raged on, though the lightning seemed to have diminished.

By now Sarah would certainly be wondering where I was. But she knew me better than anyone else. She knew I'd have called if there was a change of plans. Moreover, she knew I *never* would have cancelled dinner with her, honeymoon or no honeymoon.

This thought was the greatest comfort I had.

I closed my eyes and remembered the time I'd earned my first *real* dinner out alone with Sarah. To avoid her lecherous boss—in a job that I now knew had been a cover for her real work—Sarah had told him she had a date for the evening at a particular restaurant. She'd recruited me, the safe friend, to take her in case he came to check up on his employee. He had, and I'd saved the day—or so she said. That was the first time she'd seen me in shining armour.

Perhaps it was the thought of that happy night when our courtship began . . . but I felt almost warm. Perhaps the temperature had risen, despite the rain. I felt *good*—in a drowsy sort of way.

I'd gone just far enough down the path that I didn't even recognise the familiar harbingers of hypothermia. But an eerie thing happened; Sarah's calm but clear, insistent voice said from somewhere close by: "Alex! You mustn't go to sleep! Come on—*wake up*!"

My mind was in such a fog that I actually peered around, as if she might have somehow joined me on the ledge. She wasn't there, of course . . . but there was no doubt she'd spoken to me. It was like a slap on the face—a life-saving one. I saw my situation with frightening clarity.

Of course! I was sinking into the hiker's classic trap. My body was shuddering in an involuntary attempt to keep itself warm. I was *cold*, not warm.

Get moving, Alex. I embarked upon a routine of pumping my arms, stamping my feet, and every now and then even a half sit-up. Had anyone been watching, they'd have had a hilarious time—I'm sure I looked like an overturned beetle, struggling to right himself.

As I exercised my body, my head began to ache, but my mind started working. It went immediately to the reason for my exile on the ledge.

The result was several disturbing insights into why certain people might have been motivated to kill for the Pepys papers.

Think, Alex, think. Who wanted those Pepys papers to remain hidden more than anyone else? *Think.* What was in them?

What was in them, what was in them . . .

I focussed my mind with an effort. In Mattie's find, King James II thanked Pepys for teaching him shorthand. In the Butter Churn find, Pepys condemned Lord Dartmouth for his ill treatment of the natives in Tangier, and told the secret of the plague herb . . .

Mmm. As I wound up my arms for another invigorating go round, I found myself getting somewhere. I was not only feeling more like myself, but I at last saw a credible reason for not only paper-poaching but actual violence.

Still on my back, I pretended I was bicycling up a very long hill; it worked quite well. How could I not have seen this before? Beloved Dartmouth College. If Lord Dartmouth's ill-gotten gains in the seventeenth century, which translated into the College's ill-gotten beginnings in the eighteenth, were made public the College would face a flap worse than any that had plagued it to date.

Something had been nagging at me since last night— er, early this morning: Dean's presence in Rauner. What in heaven's name was he doing in Rauner Library in the middle of the night? He, unlike anyone else but the President and the Provost represented the College. What if the College simply couldn't bear another round of bad press after the unfortunate affair of the year before, and had decided to avoid any potential damage by preventing publication of the Pepys find?

The press would have a field day.

And of course the College had asked me to come with Vivian Porter and Jonathan, knowing I wouldn't refuse to help. How remarkable that I could see it out here, on a rock ledge hundreds of feet above the nearest level surface, when I couldn't see it some two hundred feet from the College's administrative offices in Parkhurst Hall.

I'd stopped stamping, stopped thinking for precious moments. This time, even more eerily, it was my Bostonian grandfather's voice that came to my ears as clearly as if he were sitting next to me on the precipice. *You must carry on, Alex.* My grandfather, a devoted Dartmouth alumnus, had taught me my most valuable hiking and camping skills; I'd even learned how to bivouac from him. If I had survived all those breathtaking, challenging trips with my grandfather Lodge, I couldn't let a small ledge barely off the public stamping ground of Mount Washington—though forty sheer feet below—finish me off.

The rain had let up now, and the wind was picking up again. Good. The others embroiled in this Pepysian peril—Mattie Harding, Charles Mattingley, and Pettifer Bartlett—each had something at risk. But would they really resort to something so base as violence? Mattie herself had been badly beaten, her home ruined . . .

I felt myself fading away. Renewing my efforts, I reached still further down the path of Pepys association and stepped up the pace of my calisthenics, noting with relief that the rain had almost stopped completely. The wind was blowing constantly, chilling me as it puffed the storm clouds off to some other unlucky peak. To reward my efforts, my brain came up with a nastier thought by far. What a shame that I was such an imaginative sort . . .

Wouldn't it be too horrid if Mattie, or Mattie accompanied by her Uncle Charles, had some private plan for the papers?

Good heavens. What if Charles had hired the British crowbar wielder to attack Mattie, to make it look as though she were innocent? He'd been a little too enthusiastic, unfortunately for her, but he'd certainly come through.

And Pettifer . . . if he hadn't disappeared so worryingly, I'd find a reason to think my old teacher could have a role in all of this. A first whack at the Pepys find, perhaps, to secure his position amongst scholars as the ultimate Pepys authority. I recalled how vigorously he protested the veracity of the find, perhaps too vigorously; how he had lamented the absence of new Pepys material.

The thought of so much duplicity was overwhelming. Not one, not two, but *three* parties might possibly be engaged in trying to keep the papers a secret, and/or murder anyone who had seen them.

One thing I still didn't understand: how did all these people *know* about the papers, and their contents? Mattie had seen the letter written by James II, though she hadn't known what it was. She'd assumed it was the Tangier Diary Extension; she had told her Uncle Charles and me. I had found the Butter Churn Papers days after the attacks on Mattie had begun . . . they *were* the Tangier Diary Extension. I had told only Sarah. Oh, and I'd mentioned them to Moose, but aside from Mattie, no connexion existed between Moose and Pepys's writings.

Good Lord, but it was cold. The wind was going right through—

At that moment, I realised I was sitting on the ledge waiting to die. If I didn't get myself off it, no one was going to come for me . . . Sarah would have no way of knowing where I was.

I had to try to get off the ledge. My watch (God bless Lisette for the gift of the lighted-dial model years ago) said only ten o'clock. Sopping wet, without any kind of extra clothing or shelter, I knew I might reaffirm the ledge's nickname by morning if I didn't get moving.

I stood slowly and leaned against the rock, facing oblivion. So far, so good . . . but I would have to take my time.

I reached up and felt on the rock face for the first fingerhold. The granite was not slippery, though damp; my fingertips found sufficient purchase. The wind had done more than blow the storm away and chill me to the bone; it had made the rock manageable.

With the toe of my trainer, I felt for the first toehold and found it about one foot off the ledge. I stepped up and reached for the next handhold. A feeling of unreality had taken over; I felt as though I were watching my own progress from a distant vantage point. *But I was climbing.*

It unnerved me not to have any visual clues about the wall. As time went on, I found that climbing blind was doable, if damnably difficult. After half a dozen successful upward steps I knew I was roughly one quarter of the way up. The muscles shook in my arms and legs, and an increasing lightheadedness worried me, but I reached for the next handhold. As long as my fingers didn't refuse to grip, as fingers would when they got too cold and weak, and I didn't completely lose consciousness . . . well, I *couldn't.* I *wouldn't* die tonight.

But two more footholds towards safety, I felt the lightheadedness taking over; even felt—from my distant mental vantage point somewhere far above—my hands releasing their grip. The spectator—it was me, but *not* me—shouted a brusque, unsympathetic warning. *"No!"* I heard him shout, and renewed my grip just as I began to feel myself tilting backwards. I clung for a moment, panting from fear as much as exertion, and gathered myself.

"Do it for Sarah," the spectator urged. "You can't fail now, it would take as long to get down as it would to get up. You must keep going . . . come on, now, next toe . . ." The circumstances were bizarre enough that talking to myself seemed quite normal. I wasn't exactly certain who was talking to whom.

But then it happened. My foot slipped off its narrow

perch and the surprise of it, combined with the down-
ward pull, caused me to lose my handholds. I grasped at
every tiny bulge and indentation in the wall, but my upper body drifted farther from the rock with every second.
I felt myself inexorably leaning backwards, out over the
abyss.

The spectator was silent.

CHAPTER 18

*... it is a miracle what way a man could devise to lose
so much in so little time.*

So we are all poor and in pieces, God help us!

SAMUEL PEPYS

This is it ... this is it ... I felt no panic, only sad acceptance.

I slid on and on, my fingertips bloody from clutching
desperately at the rough granite, until I must surely have
been *below* the ledge. Perhaps I'd got higher than I realised ...

But then my feet hit the ledge—hard. I was dangerously off balance. Only the tips of my trainers rested on
the ledge; the rear halves of my size twelves jutted out
over thousands of feet of unbroken desolation.

With an instinctive, tragicomic windmilling of my
arms, I felt myself losing, winning, and tragically losing
again ... this was *really* it. I was falling.

Please, God! I had failed; but in desperation I begged
to be saved. In the instant that I felt myself beyond the
point of no return, I felt life fully. Everything from the
majestic desolation of that place to the way Sarah's skin
felt under my hands, everything from the privilege of in-
habiting a body and being alive in it to the rush of the

wind . . . I saw everything for the astounding wonder that it was.

And then I found that my prayer was being answered—but as usual, not in the way I anticipated. My descent had been slowed through desperate clutching at the rock, sheer friction, and in the last second before I teetered backwards to my demise, I was somehow able to lean forwards. Almost as if the spectator had taken over and was guiding me by remote control, I turned the fall to my advantage and leaned into the rock, catching myself on the ledge with my arms, elbows out. My arms felt as though they might be wrenched out of their sockets, but I found myself clinging to the rock; that was all that mattered.

There was still every possibility that I might yet fall, but I'd been given a second chance. With what seemed my last ounce of strength, I hauled myself up slowly and carefully until I lay on my starting point once again, weak and panting. I was not as cold as I'd been before making the futile climb, but I was shakier.

Some time passed as I recovered from the ordeal. In addition to giving me the fright of my life, it had been exhausting. To my surprise, though, when my breathing returned to normal, I began to fear succumbing to exposure on the ledge more than attempting the climb once more.

And so the spectator watched as I started again, questioning the wisdom of such a manoeuvre with a much-weakened body. Perhaps it was because of the practice, perhaps it was because I was twenty times more careful on the second try. But this time I clawed my way to the top without stumbling. Over the edge, on glorious terra firma, I collapsed in a heap, too spent even to move. The wind was blowing furiously on the bald, unprotected summit; I'd been fortunate that the ledge was somewhat shielded from the wind.

When I could, I stood and made for the weather observatory-cum-museum. I was grateful to know my way around the mountain; all those gruelling runs had paid off in more ways than one. My eyes easily picked out the outline of the weather station and I made a beeline for its light and warmth.

In the way of true mountaineers, the building was not locked. This environment was too extreme to deny refuge to anyone who needed it. I stepped inside with gratitude and closed the door on the chill, singing wind, then felt a rush of overwhelming relief and sagged against the wall. For an instant I wondered if this was all a hallucination, a sort of mirage while I was still out on the ledge slowly losing my mind. But the smell of coffee nearby brought me to my senses. I lost no time in heading towards voices and kitchen sounds at the end of the hall. But before I'd gone more than a few paces, a bearded man of about my own age appeared out of the doorway. He was sipping a hot drink while obviously searching for whoever had just come through the door. He caught sight of me and stopped abruptly; steaming liquid sloshed onto the linoleum floor. Without taking his eyes off me, he thrust the dripping mug away from his body. "Hiker?" he asked, with a nod.

"Sort of." My voice sounded odd, scratchy. "I had— well, a climbing accident." Easier that way, for now. "Dead Man's Ledge," I rasped, by way of explanation.

He nodded and lifted his shoulders as if this was unfortunate, but not to worry. The moustache and the beard parted into a smile. Yet his guarded stance with the mug told me he was more than a little on edge. "You're going to be okay. Come on in." He reached a hand around the back of my arm and ever so gently guided me forward. So solicitous was he that I began to wonder quite seriously how distrubing my appearance was.

"You'll be all right," he reiterated, as I looked at him askance. Then in a more business-like tone, he said, "Ken? Nancy?" We entered what appeared to be a kitchen. I saw the only two people there, a man and a woman, stiffen. Immediately, they put down their drinks, stood, and came towards us. "Hello—and you are . . . ?"

"Alex. Alex Plumtree. And I do know better than to be on Mount Washington like this . . ."

"Please. Why don't you sit down," Nancy said. I appreciated her decisiveness, her earthiness. She sat down next to me. "Mike, get Alex one of the blankets—and some tea. Please. Tea all right for you?" She seemed to study me.

"Wonderful. Thanks. Yes."

"Okay, Alex, what's happened to you?" Ken asked. Immediately I sensed he was the medic among them; something about his calm, his powers of observation. I felt he might start bending limbs and conducting reflex tests if I weren't careful.

It was then, when I knew everything was going to be all right, that I began to fade. I didn't have to struggle any more. But suddenly the image of Sarah, sitting in our honeymoon suite wondering where I was, brought me to myself. "Yes, er, I had a fall—or two—but does anyone have a phone I can use?"

Nancy stood and picked up a handset from the worktop. "Here. While you call, can we start cleaning you up?" With a wry smile she nodded at my head.

"Um—yes, thank you so much," I said. "Very kind."

Mike brought a heavy fleece blanket and put it round my shoulders. I started to punch in Sarah's mobile number, but my fingertips were so raw, and my hands shook so much, that Nancy took the phone. "I'll do that for you," and entered the number as I dictated it.

Sarah didn't answer; I left a message. "Sarah. I've had a spot of bother on Mount Washington." My voice sounded oddly formal, but I carried on. "You could ring me on"—"what's the number here?" I turned to ask Ken.

He told me and I repeated it. "I'll be in touch, darling. Everything's all right."

Mike set down a cup of steaming Darjeeling at my elbow. "Thanks," I said.

He grinned. "You do realize we're going to want to hear the whole story, eventually," he said. Ken had washed his hands and was lifting a large metal box marked "FIRST AID" onto the table next to me as Nancy returned from the sink with a clean, damp towel. I drank the tea greedily as she spoke. "We don't have real medical or lodging facilities up here," she told me. "But we can fix you up a bit and then drive you down to the AMC at Pinkham Notch—they'll put you up for the night."

Pinkham Notch was, I knew, the site of the Appalachian Mountain Club's visitor centre and lodge. Whenever we hiked or ran up the mountain, we signed the registry book there before starting out, then marked ourselves off upon our return. Rangers were on hand at the centre to give advice on weather and trails, and to help in emergencies.

"First we'll see where we are here," Ken said, and delicately began cleaning off my face. I couldn't feel anything at all, and thought it was fortunate that numbness took over at times like these.

"You're pretty scraped up, but from what I can see, the worst of it is a bad gash on your head."

"Mm. A rock fell on me from above."

"Ouch," he said. "Must've been a big one. How do you feel?"

"A bit strange, actually—numb. But not so cold now." The violent shaking had ceded to more gentle tremors.

"Let me get you some more tea," Mike said.

I was downing the second cup when Ken finally got to the gash. He was careful to keep his voice offhand as he said, "From your colouring, and because this was a head wound, I'm pretty sure you've lost a lot of blood. But a bigger problem might be concussion—we aren't going to be able to let you sleep much tonight. There's some swelling around this cut, too. After I patch it up with a butterfly bandage, I'll put some ice on it."

I began to feel very sleepy indeed, and drifted off into a dozy state, though awake. Ken, Nancy and Mike talked amongst themselves and I heard them, but was not part of the conversation. After a bit I was aware of being loaded into the front seat of a truck with Ken, and I heard him say as the truck roared to life, "All right, Alex, we've redialled that number you called earlier and told Sarah you're going to be at Pinkham Notch. She says she's coming to meet you there tonight. But can you tell me who Jonathan is? You've been talking about him. Was Jonathan with you on your climb?"

His voice was so far away. I shook my head, intending to answer, but it was too hard to get the words out. Still, his mention of Jonathan started some sort of process in my addled brain, and the thoughts began to roll. Jonathan . . . now that I knew that he and Porter were somehow involved in the Pepys-related violence of recent days, I could go to the police for help. Once the culprits were exposed and locked up, the problems would surely end—unless there were others involved.

But then a much better alternative presented itself: I could do something to end this mess immediately. If I were to call the press together and reveal the contents of the finds, translating them publicly, there would no longer be any motivation to keep secrets. People might try to prove that the papers were forgeries, or otherwise discredit them. But they would have no reason to destroy those of us who knew of the papers. Enormously relieved by this, I must have drifted off again.

The next thing I knew, Ken and I were being ushered into the Pinkham Notch AMC lodge by a ranger. I heard them talking around me, and to me, but I was so tired . . .

At last, a bed loomed before me and I sank onto it with gratitude. But no sooner had I laid my head on the pillow, it seemed, than the ranger was waking me up again and prodding me to talk. This happened time and again, until I rather rudely begged him to let me sleep.

At that he smiled and said, "Yeah, you'll be all right," and I sank once more into oblivion.

"Alex?" I felt a gentle prod on my arm and struggled to open my eyes. But a symphony of sensation struck and I slammed them shut in agony. A moan escaped my lips before I could stifle it.

"I'm sorry, darling." Her voice was pure compassion. "Your head must feel awful."

I could feel every heartbeat bang in my head; a demon with a sledgehammer was giving his all. My entire body throbbed in empathy. The mere thought of nodding was painful. I managed not to groan again as I whispered, "Yes." I wanted to tell her how grateful I was to see her again, to be alive, but would take that on later.

"Sorry I had to wake you up," she said softly. "Just checking. I know you're exhausted—and no wonder. I want to hear all about what happened later. We've had a doctor look you over. You're pretty badly beaten up, but you're going to be fine."

She sat quietly for a minute. Yet another of Sarah's delightfully endearing qualities was that she didn't talk incessantly. The comfort of having her near was enormous. After a bit she said, "You should have something to drink, Alex. Here."

I prised my eyes open again. Sarah gave me an encouraging smile and held up a plastic container of something orange. Every muscle was sore, even the ones in my fingers. Rock climbing. I took the orange stuff and drank it. I saw that it was daylight; an industrial-looking clock on the wall told me it was half-past twelve. I *had* slept a long time.

"The doctor left these for you; they might help you through the next few hours." She shook two tablets out into her hand and traded me a glass of water for the empty orange drink container.

It all seemed a huge effort. "Good," Sarah said. "Go back to sleep darling. I'll be right here."

———

The next time I achieved consciousness, the curtains in the room were drawn, but a light burned dimly on a table across the room. I wondered what had brought me so wide awake. Soft breathing from a chair at the foot of the bed told me Sarah was there. She looked fragile in sleep, her head tilted slightly back and to the side. Tears came at the realisation of how close I'd come to never seeing her again.

I wanted to get her away from danger . . . who would ever have thought there could be such skullduggery in our peaceful New England college town? But for the sake of Mattie and Pepys's posterity, we would first have to set the record straight.

Wide awake, I went over the rough plan that had come to me in the weather station. Was it Monday night now? By Wednesday morning I'd have Sarah back in Nantucket. And when our honeymoon was over we'd find out just what Pepys meant about a "private library."

We had nearly made it through another bibliodisaster. Sarah shifted in her sleep, her long, graceful neck stretching and turning so her head settled on the other side of the chair back. I felt a profound tenderness and protectiveness towards her.

I continued to watch her sleep as my thoughts drifted from the subtle changes I'd noticed in her over the years—smile lines and happy crinkles around her eyes—to what our children might look like, to what she'd look like in the fullness of maturity.

When my eyes slid closed again, I was smiling.

CHAPTER 19

But it is pretty to see what money will do . . .

*. . . [it] makes me a little proud, but yet not secure but
we may yet meet with a backblow which we see not . . .*

But I must observe the force of money . . .

SAMUEL PEPYS

Sarah and I left the ranger lodge at eight o'clock the
next morning, having said our thanks not only to the noble weather observatory staff by phone, but also to the
rangers. They'd prepared a small ceremony that morning,
complete with coffee and doughnuts, honouring the man
who'd survived a night on Dead Man's Ledge.

"Come work with us *any*time, Plumtree!" one of them
shouted as Sarah drove away.

"In their dreams," she said wryly. "As if you don't encounter *enough* risk in the world of book publishing." She
shot me an assessing look. "You're beginning to seem a lot
more like the Alex Plumtree I know. There was a look in
your eye when I first saw you that terrified me."

"Anyway, that's over, thank God." She shivered in the
sunlight. "Now that we're alone again, Alex, I have something important to tell you. I've a theory about what's
been going on at home."

"In England, you mean?"

She nodded and shifted up. Her long, brown leg extended gracefully towards the gas pedal . . . her *strong*, brown leg . . .

"I think it's very peculiar that the succession crisis has spawned a *religious* crisis. How often, in the recent history of England, have the two had anything to do with each other?"

For the first time in our marriage, I felt a cultural gap looming. *Don't panic, Alex, this is normal in intercultural marriages.* "Darling, it's not your fault, but you've just committed a rather typical American gaffe. The two issues have had a great deal to do with each other in recent history—in Pepys's era, for instance."

She looked at me askance and actually laughed. "Alex! I'm not speaking in an academic sense, here. The seventeenth century is not exactly *recent* history."

"From whose perspective?" I asked, keeping my tone carefully neutral.

"All right, I take your point." I could tell by the sound of her voice that she was smiling. She wasn't sorry to be having this discussion; didn't mind being reminded that there were other ways to look at things.

"I'm only saying that it's peculiar, Alex. It's as if the one cause might be *using* the other to get its way. Those violently opposed to the Prince of Wales taking the throne may well have persuaded the more conservative religious faithful to take a stand. If you know what I mean."

"Mmm. I know *exactly* what you mean. In fact, the very same thing happened in Pepys's day. The fire was part of it then, too."

"*What?*" Sarah looked as though I'd just told her the world was flat, after all.

"Of course. There's a reason the British keep repeating that phrase, '*Plus ça change, plus c'est la meme chose.*' Pepys called one faction 'fanatiques.' The 'fanatiques' thought the world was going to come to an end at any moment. They were non-conformists with the Church of England. But there was also suspicion of a 'popish' plot, a bad word in England during those times. Remember, people were incessantly worried that the French and others allied with the Pope were going to try to claim England politically. The whole episode is particularly diverting when you think that many of the royals *were* Catholic, and only concealed their affiliation for political reasons . . .

"But sorry. I'm getting carried away again. Back to the present. The point is, in the 1660s King Charles II had it coming at him from both sides, and so does our modern-day, temporary 'King Charles.' Only now it's in terms of conservative—well, at least '*keep the C of E tradition*'—vs pan-theist."

It was a sign of how far I'd travelled down the path towards acceptance: I no longer found these wild coincidences between history and the present bizarre . . . though I certainly perceived them with a sense of awe. And if I were wise, I thought, I'd use them to help me work out what exactly was going on with the Pepys papers.

During the rest of the drive, I discussed my plans for an announcement to the press with Sarah. She got on her mobile and rang an old school friend who was now the proud proprietor of one of Boston's busiest public relations firms, who agreed to arrange it for three o'clock that afternoon. If all went well, we'd have America's best-known bibliojournalist meet us in front of Rauner.

Then it was back to Nantucket . . . and back to what a honeymoon was supposed to be all about.

When Sarah parked the car in a coveted space opposite the Inn, it was already eleven o'clock. I levered myself stiffly out of the car, dreading the warning call I felt I should make to Dean before the press conference. I dreaded it not only because I now suspected that he'd taken a rather active role in trying to get rid of me, but I thought he might go berserk at the prospect of more adverse publicity for the College—especially anything smacking of dirty money.

I told myself that at least Dean-Dean was unlikely to come after me at the Inn in broad daylight.

Back in our room, I installed myself on the bed for the difficult phone call. One of the joys of Dartmouth College was that it was still possible to call a central number, and be put through to virtually any college employee by an operator. "Dean Small, please," I said, watching my wife toss her handbag on the bed and run her hands through her hair.

With anticipation I saw that she was coming to sit next to me—but before she got to the bed she stopped short and bent over the bureau in an attitude of alarm. Swiftly, she patted the bottom of the bureau, then bent to inspect it more closely.

Hurrying to me, she leaned close. "The papers are

here," she whispered, her lips brushing my ear, "but someone's been in the room—the drawers have been opened. It might have been a professional job. Be careful what you say—listening devices."

I felt a sinking feeling at the very thought of anyone taking the priceless papers.

And *listening devices*? Was it the British pair who'd tried to make us disappear at the boathouse? Or my friend Jonathan, hoping to learn the whereabouts of the papers from Sarah? Mattie and Moose?

The problem with these intrigues was that I began to distrust *everyone*. Of course the College still had to be at the root of it . . . and I couldn't escape the fact that the College owned the Inn. In an official crisis ye olde alma mater might be able to gain access to a room key . . .

"Who do you think?" I mouthed to my wife.

"We'll find out after three, maybe." She didn't seem terrifically worried as she gave me a casual kiss—after all, thieves and intruders were nothing unusual for her (or me, for that matter).

Dean's smooth voice came down the line. "Alex! Are you still in Hanover?"

"Yes." Only just barely, and by the grace of God, I thought.

"Good. I was afraid you'd resumed your honeymoon and left me knee deep in—um, *this*—alone. Patricia was more than a little perturbed at the way you deserted her with Vivian Porter—to go off to some party, she said. And then Porter disappeared, once they got back to town, without saying boo. Extraordinary." He lowered his voice. "Any news?"

"Er . . ." I couldn't tell him over the phone if it was bugged; I'd have to meet with him in person.

I had an urge to laugh at Dean-Dean's outrageous accusation that I'd abrogated my responsibilities with Vivian Porter, when he'd nearly had me killed—all for the College's sake.

"We need to talk, Dean. There have been some developments I'd like to discuss with you . . . do you have a few minutes? I could pop over to your office."

"Of course I'd be delighted—but I have a better idea. Have you seen the new exhibit at the Hood yet? Pepys's diary is part of the display."

"Really?! No, I haven't seen it." I'd heard about the Plagues and Famines exhibit at the College's art museum and despite its cheerless title had certainly intended to see it over the weekend—until events careered so wildly out of control.

"I'll meet you in front of the Inn; we can talk as we walk through the exhibit. I must say, I'm eager to hear what's developed."

And so I changed clothes as quickly as I could, claiming a kiss and hug from Sarah.

"Want me to talk to Mattie and Moose?" she whispered in my ear. I nodded, shuddering with delight at the closeness of her. Wanting desperately to linger, I got myself firmly in check and proceeded with assorted creaks towards the lift.

Dean came striding across the road as I stepped out onto the porch. He was the very picture of a preppie academic administrator, his khakis deliberately several inches too short and his horn-rims standing out starkly against his freckled skin. His look of pleasant greeting changed instantly to concern as I stepped out to meet him.

"Alex! What *happened* to you?!" He seemed genuinely taken aback; I was struck with a wave of shame for suspecting him of involvement in my ordeal. Still, it was the College that had arranged for me to accompany Vivian Porter up the mountain, and they did have the best motive. . . .

"I'd like to talk to you about that," I answered evasively. Few people were out on the paved walk with us; a lone student on a motorised scooter glided past, his discman blaring tinnily. Just to be safe, I glanced around but saw no familiar faces—friendly or otherwise. "Vivian Porter's companion arranged a little rock climbing 'accident' Sunday. I had lots of time to think it through in the great outdoors: the papers we've found are rather damning to the College. I'm afraid that led me to an unpleasant conclusion: perhaps someone thinks that if they get rid of me, they'll get rid of the problem."

Only then did the disturbing thought occur that Jonathan hadn't been at all concerned with learning the whereabouts of the compromising papers. In fact he hadn't even mentioned them. Why hadn't he tried to find out where they were, in order to destroy them? The College couldn't have known where the papers were at that point. This was sinister indeed; it meant they were confident of controlling the papers. Someone at Rauner? Dean?

And then a *worse* thought dawned: what if the papers were no longer safe with Sarah at the Inn? No, I told myself; Sarah was easily equal to any situation that might arise.

Dean stopped in front of the Hopkins Center—the arts building—and faced me. First he was stunned, then indignant. "What do mean he arranged an accident? Are you saying he *attacked you?* Did—did you call the police? Is he in custody?"

The huge letters across the top of the Hopkins arts center announcing that night's Film Society offering screamed "PAPER CHASE—8 & 10" immediately over Dean's head. If I weren't a bit fed up with the situation, I'd have thought it funny.

When I didn't respond immediately, he became angry. It was as if a cloud passed in front of his face. "Wait just a minute! Do I understand that you think *Dartmouth College* arranged to have you attacked?"

I held up a hand. "Dean, I don't know what to think. *Someone* tried to have me killed, and the College has a better reason than anyone. I can assure you, I don't like saying it any more than you like hearing it." I sighed. "Yes, Sarah did call the police, but as you told me over the phone, both Vivian Porter and Jonathan seem to have disappeared." We turned down the pathway towards the museum.

"This is shocking . . . all this violence . . . over what might have been such a boost for the College. If only this blackmail threat—and everything—hadn't ruined it all." He shook his head and put out his hand to push open the door.

"Dean."

Hearing something in my voice, he hesitated with his hand on the brass plate.

"I'm putting a stop to it. Once the papers and their contents become public knowledge, *no* one will have reason to continue this. No more intrusions to Rauner, no more attacks—and the College will still have its public relations coup. Naturally I wouldn't say anything negative about Dartmouth. I've arranged a meeting with a Boston journalist to make it all public."

Under different circumstances, the look of horror on his face would have been comical. His mouth hung open; his eyes widened to dinner-plate proportions. "Oh no! Alex, you mustn't. Don't you realise what you'd be doing?"

"Yes, I see exactly what I'd be doing. Look, I know you've faced your share of crises too, Dean. The only way is to get everything out in the open. And you needn't worry; we've chosen the perfect journalist for the job. She's the one who covered the Shakespeare hoax last year at Yale."

He shook his head vehemently. "No, no, *no*—you don't understand. One more bad blow to the College, and . . ." The thought was so horrible to him that he couldn't carry on.

Then I saw what I hadn't before: Dean's job was on the line. He personally would suffer if the College were cast in an unattractive light just now.

"Dean, I'm sorry if it makes things difficult for you . . ."

The horrified look was now overlaid with exasperation. "It's not *me*, Alex, it's—oh, *damn!* I shouldn't be telling you." He glanced around as if someone might be eavesdropping, but at noon on a summer weekday visitors weren't flooding into the museum. We stood outside the door, speaking in intense whispers. "It has everything to do with the donation, don't you see? You know about Porter's offer. What he pledged to give put us in a unique position among colleges of our size. If this unpleasantness is revealed about the College in these papers, he'll withdraw his donation."

I was incredulous. "Look, Dean, you must realise that I've worked it out. I *know*." And I did, although it had only come clear as I said the words. *The College planned to trade the Pepys Tangier Diary Extension for the Earl of Dartmouth's papers.* It had to be; it made sense. Why else would Porter have appeared with his donation just now? And how else could the College decently get rid of the nasty secrets about its past in the Tangier diary extension excerpts? But they must be going wild trying to find the blasted things. "I know about the—er—exchange."

The look on his face was priceless. I was either exactly right, or he thought I was a raving lunatic. "You *know*? But . . ."

"You'd be making an enormous mistake! Don't you find anything odd about the offer to trade the Earl's papers for Pepys's dirty secrets, and the blackmail attempt? Not to mention sundry attempts to kill me, Mattie, and evidently Pettifer—the only people who really know about the Pepys finds. Dean, I strongly suspect Porter is a fraud. When I met him, I was surprised I'd not heard of him, given his collection. And look—do respectable donors suddenly *disappear* as he has?"

"Alex, I'm sorry you've had to go through so much. Forgive me for saying it, but it was extremely arrogant of you to barge into the College's business like this—while Phil is away on vacation, too. Don't you think he deserves to be in on this?"

I understood his need to recover, even admired his tactics in trying to delay the announcement. But I was as determined as he was. Not only my life, and that of my wife, were at risk . . . the remainder of my honeymoon hung in the balance. No man would give that up without a fight. I decided to play for time.

"How about that tour of the exhibit you promised me? We can discuss this Pepys mess later." Maybe I could calm him down, talk some sense into him. It was clear that he had no desire to prolong our encounter, but ever the diplomat, Dean did his best to stifle his irritation.

He led me down the plushly carpeted hallway into the depths of the museum. The air smelled delightfully of rare, exotic scents; perhaps it was the oils of the paintings themselves that gave off that distinctive museum aroma.

A solid-looking matron with a carefully coiffed page-boy was coming out of a room labelled "THE ART OF PLAGUE AND FAMINE" as we approached the doorway. "Dean *Dean!* You're back." She beamed at him. Her nametag announced that she was a docent with the distinguished moniker of ROBERTA.

"Um, yes." Distracted as he was by our discussion outside, he remembered his manners. "Roberta, this is Alex Plumtree, newly appointed to the Friends of the Library board. Alex, Roberta is our expert on the exhibit; she did graduate work on plagues in literature. In fact, Roberta, since you're here today . . ."

"I'd be delighted." She beamed and ushered us in, beginning with the Middle Ages and some truly nightmarish paintings dealing with unpleasantries I'd rather not mention. We moved on to the time of Milton and *Paradise Lost*, and I was interested to see a reproduction of a page of the original manuscript. "While *Paradise Lost* does not specifically address the plague that struck London at the time of its writing, it is believed that Milton's relation of the struggle between Satan's fallen angels and the hosts of heaven may have arisen from the author's own battle for survival." As she ushered us from one tastefully arranged display to the next, I was impressed by the depth of Roberta's knowledge.

"And here," she announced, looking very much like the cat who'd swallowed the canary, "is perhaps our rarest item." As I gazed at the black and white engraving, I saw that it was surrounded by familiar quotes from Pepys's diary detailing the dastardly effects of the plague on Londoners. I noticed too, that while the Dean had moved at a measured pace through the exhibit until now, at this point he'd stopped dead.

Roberta continued, "The story behind this anonymous engraving—no one knows if the story's true, of course— is that an herb was found in Tangier that was known to cure the plague. In fact, Lord Dartmouth—a number of generations before the Dartmouth for whom the College was named, of course—was sent to Tangier with Samuel Pepys to report on England's establishment there. Over here at the left," she raised a manicured nail to the glass, "you can see the natives harvesting the leaves of a tree."

"Roberta, you must tell Alex what you found in your research."

The docent tried to hide her pride, but was betrayed by blotches of colour that suddenly dappled her neck. "I travelled to France to read a great many materials that had recently been unearthed from a French monastery. It is possible that no one had read the particular account of events in the 1660s that I found in my studies. I chose it because it dealt specifically with the plague in England,

and contained the first-hand reports of those who passed through the area near Calais on their way to England. We must remember, of course, that the French and the English were not especially fond of each other at the time. For the French, Anglophobia was next to godliness."

I smiled. The study of history always revealed the same truth: times haven't changed much over the centuries. Roberta caught my smile and reflected it.

"According to the scribe's account, although to my knowledge this is not documented anywhere else, King Charles kept the precious herb solely for the use of his family and loved ones, and several friends at court. It is thought that Pepys himself may well have received some of this herb, as he was well thought of at court and saw the King and the Duke of York nearly every day. It *has* always been noted that Pepys was extremely lucky to survive the plague, living in the heart of the infected area as he did."

Poker-faced but bright-eyed, she examined me for a reaction and got one. I was intrigued by this story—it had the ring of truth to it. The purpose of England's establishment in Tangier in the seventeenth century had always been something of a mystery. Pepys himself had lamented the waste of money and effort. It had been hugely expensive, difficult to manage, and seemed to offer no benefits. This seemed to be the answer at last.

"Fascinating!" I said. "But this wonderful story isn't told in the exhibit anywhere. Why don't you have it next to Pepys's quotes here on the wall?"

The blotches returned. "Oh, remember—I have no real proof. After all, it's not in Pepys's diary anywhere, and he certainly told *all*! He wouldn't have kept something like *that* back."

Bang! It hit me. Pepys *hadn't* kept it back . . . Those references in the Butter Churn Papers to the plague herb—and his mention of the king keeping it for himself.

Roberta was saying, ". . . but it does make a good story. It doesn't deserve to be a permanent part of the exhibit . . . but whenever I take groups through, I tell my little tale." Giving me a questioning look, she exclaimed, "I must say, no one has been quite as interested as you two! Gratifying to have you take an interest in my obscure little world."

She took us on through the rest of the exhibit, which ended with some truly horrifying works of art based on the spread of AIDS. Through earphones, it was possible to hear a symphony composed on what it felt like to live with the disease. This part of the exhibit was extremely disturbing, and a feeling of despair and doom was still hanging over us as we stepped out of the room and said our thanks to Roberta.

"You're magnificent," Dean gushed, putting a hand on her shoulder attentively. "Do you have everything you need here? Everything all right?"

"Oh, yes. The new director is absolutely inspired. All the docents love him. The Hood's never been in better shape."

Lucky for the Hood that my English boathouse friends and Vivian Porter (not to mention Jonathan) didn't know about that engraving, or it wouldn't be in such fine shape, I thought as I followed Dean out of the back door into the warm June sun. Now I knew exactly what Vivian Porter had been so eager to cover up. Porter was the royal family's henchman. It was also a considerable relief that the College hadn't been at fault after all.

But now I had a real dilemma. Sarah and I held the cards—or rather the diary pages. Did we help smooth over the difficulties at home, in England, by somehow keeping them secret . . . or reveal the truth for posterity?

If I'd been thinking clearly, I'd have known that even this conundrum was too simple: it couldn't all be so easily wrapped up. By now you'd think I would know to look at the character into whose shoes I'd been thrust. If I'd considered old Samuel more carefully I'd have seen another contradiction in him: Pepys was a simple man in his instincts and tastes, but he'd had to be extraordinarily calculating to stay alive in his world of justice-by-guillotine. A powerful new villain was always coming out of the woodwork to undo Pepys, and time and again he'd had to recruit his friends, intelligence, and good reputation to slither out of his many political difficulties as head of the Navy.

Sadly, I am not now, nor will I ever be, as calculating as Samuel Pepys—but like the diarist, I was fortunate enough to have a particularly powerful friend come to my aid.

CHAPTER 20

In the afternoon my heart was quite pulled down . . .

God keep us, for things look mighty ill!

This did unsettle my mind a great while . . .

SAMUEL PEPYS

Back in the honeymoon suite at the Inn, I patted the underside of the bureau and felt a rush of horror. The papers were gone! In disbelief I got down on my hands and knees and peered, panicstricken, at the smooth underside of the furniture. But in the next moment it occurred to me that Sarah might have taken them in preparation for the meeting. Yes, almost certainly that was the explanation—after all, the room hadn't been ransacked.

Comforted by this thought, I sank gratefully onto the king-sized bed. Two hours remained before the meeting with the journalist. All I wanted was to—

A businesslike knock sounded at the door. What *now*? Too many possibilities came to mind, from Mattie not approving of a meeting with the bibliojournalist (how *was* Sarah getting on with her?), to a return of the bizarrely aristocratic boathouse attackers. As I scraped myself off the bed to go to the door, I prepared myself for anyone.

Anyone but who it actually was. I swung the door open into the kindly but serious face of a man in uniform. HANOVER POLICE was emblazoned on his shirt in golden yellow thread. "Alex Plumtree?"

"Yes?" Perhaps they had apprehended Jonathan and he'd come to tell me.

"I'm afraid I'll have to ask you to come with me, Mr. Plumtree. You're under arrest for theft."

He took out a small printed card and began to read me my rights; evidently he hadn't made enough arrests in the peaceful hamlet of Hanover to have memorised the litany. "You have the right to remain silent. You have the . . ."

His voice faded as my mind raced down a long, dark corridor of doubt. The most obvious conclusion was that Dean had decided to get me out of the way before Sarah and I could meet with the press.

The policeman with the kind eyes stopped his litany and tucked away the Miranda card.

"May I ask who's bringing the charges?"

"Dartmouth College."

"I see. May I just write a quick note to my wife, in case I can't reach her by phone?"

"Sure."

Under his watchful eye I picked up the pad of paper on the bedside table and scrawled the words, *Sarah—Your groom is in the slammer for theft courtesy Dart Coll. Come when you can—but carry on with plans for 3. Yours, A.*

I left my note inside the door and went along with my captor peacefully. The thought of being jailed in idyllic, peaceful Hanover was almost comical; it was hardly likely to be a harrowing experience. As we rode down in the lift, the poor policeman averting his gaze almost shame-facedly, I remembered that Pepys himself had been im-prisoned . . . if I remembered correctly, he'd just fallen out with the wrong man. As had I.

Think, Alex. What *purpose* had it served for Pepys to be put in gaol? If I could work it out, perhaps I would know why I must endure the same fate. But on the short ride to the police station, I came no closer to seeing a useful pur-pose for it all. In fact, I thought idly, the only purpose it had served was to keep the man out of danger during a very dangerous time.

At the gaol, the officer took my wallet but fortunately didn't search through my pockets; I didn't want to let the transcription of the Tangier excerpts out of my sight. I was allowed to make my phone call, but Sarah's mobile was busy. The officer generously allowed me to try every twenty minutes or so, but after half-past two I began to wonder. *What was Sarah doing on the phone all this time?* It was most unlike her to have the blasted instrument at-tached to her ear. She was supposed to be establishing a united front with Mattie and then Pettifer, if he had sur-faced yet, before the announcement . . . and how could she do that while she was on the phone?

At a few minutes past three I leaned back and turned on the TV in my rather comfortable cell. There was a time when I would have been pacing the confines of the room, boiling with rage and resentment at having been removed from the heat of battle. But there was a new part of me, and she had changed everything. For one thing, she would handle the meeting with the bibliojournalist at least as well as I could. For another, I found that I rather liked sharing the load.

This being Hanover, I hoped for more than basic cable—even in the local clink—and got it. The BBC channel flared to life on the little box. An announcer was standing, looking agitated, on a City street near the Stock Exchange, with sirens, fire trucks, and flames providing audio and visual background. I sat up quickly on the bed.

"... the new fire has broken out near the Stock Exchange. The building has been evacuated, and disaster recovery personnel are on hand to restore operation as soon as firefighters say it's safe to enter the building. No one has been injured so far in what is assumed to be another outbreak of protest to the Prince of Wales's temporary assumption of the role of monarch, nor were any perpetrators found at the scene. Investigators say they will comb the fire scene for evidence, though there are as yet no suspects in the other recent incidents of arson in the City. Yesterday's fire in Threadneedle Street has now been brought under control, but the effort to control the blaze was made doubly difficult by the timed detonation of incendiary devices. Experts say the devices were designed to keep the fire burning over a large area. Back to you, Bernard."

"Thanks for that report. Now let's go to the head of the Stock Exchange for his evaluation of how this fire will affect Britain's financial sector ..."

Fires had carried on as much as a year after the Great Fire in Pepys's time. Political and religious plotters were suspected, just as they were today.

No wonder Sarah was on the phone. I began to wonder if she had even thought of the meeting about the Pepys papers. The journalist might still be standing in front of Rauner, or worse yet, cursing the people who'd asked her to come all the way up to ...

But no. Sarah would not have forgotten.

My ears perked up again as the head of the Stock Exchange faded away from the screen and Windsor Castle appeared in the background, overlaid with a photo of Jonathan. I gaped at the man who'd forced me onto Dead Man's Ledge as the silken BBC voice continued.

"In a development that must greatly displease the royal family this evening, Scotland Yard has found a link between the 'mystery man' seen near the Queen as she was riding on the day of her accident and the Queen's own office. The Queen's staff say that the unknown man—who appeared to be a casual hiker—came quickly into range of the monarch and suddenly flapped his jacket, causing her mount to rear. Evidently the man had once worked for Her Majesty, but now has ties to the Duke of York's staff. Authorities are still attempting to find the suspect, who is thought to be out of the country. And in other news . . ."

Unbelievably, Sarah suddenly stood in front of my cell door. "Alex," she said decisively, as if trying to wake me up. "Alex. This is Elizabeth Mullion. She wants to talk to you."

It flashed through my mind immediately how odd it was that Sarah made no spontaneous explanation why she hadn't come sooner. No apologies, no expressions of sympathy. In an instant, I knew that something was up: she had either arranged for my incarceration, or gone along with it. The journalist didn't look particularly surprised, either. Why?

After a millisecond of doubt, I told myself not to be silly. *Alex, you can trust your wife.* I saw that she was carrying her leather tote bag, and felt certain that the papers were safely stowed inside.

Just as suddenly, at the same instant I knew that my previous flash of insight had been accurate: as Pepys's stay in gaol had ultimately been to his benefit, so my beloved wife had had me confined for my own protection.

It made me smile. Sarah caught the sudden change in my countenance and began to smile herself. Then she started to laugh, and excusing herself with a wave of the hand, turned me over to Elizabeth.

I reentered the fray. "Elizabeth, I'm delighted to meet you. We're so glad you could come to Hanover. I assume you've got most of the story, but what else do you need to know?"

Footsteps sounded on the tiled floor. It was the kind policeman, approaching my cell. "Mr Plumtree? I can let you go now. The College has decided not to press charges." His key clanged in the lock as he released me. He seemed to only just manage not to apologise for locking me up in the first place.

Sarah, having recovered, appeared behind Elizabeth and said, "All right—let's get out of here. Tea at the Inn." As I was released, she turned to Elizabeth and spoke into her ear. "Sorry, Elizabeth. Final destination for today. I promise."

Elizabeth merely smiled and looked from Sarah to me and back again, seeming to enjoy the whole experience. My belongings were returned to me at the front desk—I experienced a fleeting moment of humiliation—and we strode out of captivity into the bright summer day.

Sarah said to us both, as if commenting on the weather, "I think we should wait to discuss this until we have some privacy. We'll take a function room when we get to the Inn. Elizabeth, where did you say *you'd* been on your honeymoon last year?"

I liked Elizabeth. Without a moment's delay she said, "Caneel Bay. The Virgin Islands. Good sailing ... far enough away, and hard enough to get there, that you don't even think of the real world."

I decided to be forthright. Why on earth not?

"Did you know that Sarah and I are on our honeymoon?"

"Not *really*," she said, smiling nervously. "You're not serious. Are you?" Evidently she had noticed that we were having less than the idyllic experience. I saw her glance surreptitiously at the ring fingers of our left hands.

Sarah answered her with a brisk nod.

I said, "Oh yes. But you'll understand, since you're so familiar with the world of books. It's not every day that we get to write our own chapters, is it? By the way, I thoroughly enjoyed that piece you wrote on the Shakespeare hoax last year. You're obviously extremely knowledgeable. Good thing you're on the beat."

"Thank you . . ."

"How did you meet the owner of the forgery?" Happily, she embarked upon the quirky story of deceit in the scholarly bibliophile world and entertained us on the way to the Inn.

When we were comfortably seated round a burnished oval table in a small private room, with tea on the way, Sarah took charge. "All right. Alex, Mattie joined us and told Elizabeth all about her find. Although we couldn't present the actual document—I'll explain in a moment—Mattie described it in detail and showed her a copy of the transcription. But we haven't begun on the *other* find yet. In fact, I have some bad news." She turned to Elizabeth as if to say, *your turn.* The bibliojournalist took a deep breath and began. "I've been investigating the anonymous claim of a Pepys find—the one posted on Pepysiana—for some time. Oddly enough, the one that I assume the posting was about—the letter from King James to Pepys—does appear to be genuine. But the papers you've found in the butter churn—ironically, the supposed Tangier diary extension everyone's been half-expecting to see turn up some day—well, I believe they're a hoax."

I was incredulous. This didn't make any sense. "But how can you think they're a hoax? No one even *knew* about them until I found them." I felt my face flush with anger. "Besides, I've *used* his original diary; held it in my hands. Those papers really do appear to be authentic, right down to the paper itself and Pepys's own hand. What leads you to suspect otherwise?"

Elizabeth looked almost apologetic as she said, "That Pepysiana notice follows the pattern of the Shakespeare hoax precisely. In that case, the posting also came first, and the mention of Yale. Then came the chance discovery of what appeared to be a new Shakespeare play in a box of papers from an alum's estate. So now that you've discovered this find in the Frost Farm butter churn, you can see how I might begin to discern a pattern and become suspicious."

I was stunned into silence.

I felt very much at sea; the papers had certainly looked real to me, but I had to admit that she had a case for a hoax. Why did I feel such an urge to defend them as real? Because I'd found them? *Alex, put your vanity aside . . . just discuss the papers with her from her point of view.* "Well. Why don't we go ahead and have a look at them? You have them, don't you, darling?"

"Um, no," Sarah said, looking down at the table, then brushing a bit of lint off her shirt. "Bad news there, I'm afraid: the papers weren't where we left them."

I boggled. *Sarah, sweetheart! You were the only one who knew where they were!* Whoever had been snooping in our room during our Mt Washington escapade hadn't stolen them . . . but it was true that the papers *had* been gone when I returned from my meeting with Dean. I didn't think much of it; it had seemed reasonable at the time that Sarah would have taken them with her. I wanted to scream. There was something decidedly odd here, but I couldn't seem to piece it together. Sarah would *never* . . .

Sarah went right on. "But that doesn't mean they don't exist, as I told Elizabeth. I saw them, you saw them, and there's been enough skullduggery to make anything possible around here. And we do have the transcription . . ." She nodded at me; I pulled the crumpled, barely legible thing out of my pocket and passed it to Elizabeth. Sarah said to me, "Why don't you do the honours?"

I went over the contents of the Tangier diary extension. I told Elizabeth which words he'd used as code beyond the shorthand, and she nodded as she scribbled in her notebook. She obviously knew a bit about Pepys, too.

Finally she sighed, looking up from her notebook with large brown eyes and a sad smile. "If it's true, this is a sensational story—as you know. But can you give me any *proof* that it's genuine? I'll have to defend it to my editors."

Sarah answered firmly, "No, we can't. And I do apologise. But I hope that in time we'll be able to show you the papers themselves."

What on earth did she know that I didn't? Just exactly what had happened while I was in the Hanover gaol?

Sarah and I walked Elizabeth to a taxi at the front of the Inn. When she was safely away, I turned to face my wife. "My dear, if I didn't know better, I'd think you were holding out on me. Did you have any trouble at Rauner?"

Sarah answered matter-of-factly, gazing out over the Green, "You mean masked Englishmen attacking us as we stood defenceless on the steps? No. Everything seems to have returned to normal, aside from the absence of the papers—or perhaps *because* of their absence."

"You don't seem particularly disturbed about their disappearance, I must say." But if she wasn't going to tell me, she wasn't. I wouldn't beg. We turned to go back up to the room, and still I waited for her to say something.

When the door of the room had closed, she took my head in her hands, a palm on each cheek, and peppered my face with kisses.

"I'm more than a little relieved at all this," I managed. "I was beginning to think I'd married someone with a split personality."

This seemed to entertain her.

"Are you ready to give me some answers?"

"Mmm . . . as long as they don't touch on my work."

"I know, I know: you could tell me, but then you'd have to kill me. Well, answer me this: did you remove the papers yourself?"

She smiled. "You really are too clever for your own good."

"And you and Dean-Dean had me put in gaol?"

"Not angry, are you?"

"Angry? Good heavens, no. You seem to have solved rather a lot of problems all at once. In fact, now that it's been dismissed as a hoax, everyone seems to be off our backs."

"Well, not everyone," Sarah admitted hesitantly. "I'm afraid things are really hotting up on your home front. In fact . . ."

My mobile rang on the desktop, interrupting her. Before answering it I said, "Speaking of the home front, you're not going to believe this. I saw the BBC news in my gaol cell, and the man who spooked the queen's horse was *Jonathan!* Of Mount Washington fame . . . Hello?"

"Alex! Lisette. I am so sorry to disturb you on your 'oneymoon."

I smiled at the sound of her voice. "You're just calling because you want lurid details . . . I know you."

She giggled, then got down to business. "If only. No, my friend, we 'ave a problem."

"Let me have it."

"The Duke of York rang 'imself, all in a tizzy. 'E says with the Prince of Wales's public relations fiasco, 'e needs to get 'is book out *immediately*. Right away. Rush-rush . . . 'E wants to announce the book before it is published to deflect attention from his brother. The Duke was quite funny about it when 'e rang; 'e said the book will make everyone glad *'e* is not the one next in line for the throne! Lovely sense of 'umour, but 'e is not taking no for an answer when it comes to meeting with you—*in person.* 'E seriously wants you to manage it all yourself. I didn't feel I should make the decision for you, so I am afraid I gave 'im your mobile number." There was a pause; I could almost see her wince. " 'E will be ringing you at any moment."

"Thanks, Lisette. I understand."

And it peeved me no end . . . because I hated to throw away such a magnificent opportunity. It was a shame that this personal emergency of his—well, *national* emergency—had had to come up this of all weeks. Well, even though some part of me longed to please the Duke in his time of need, I wouldn't do it to Sarah. She'd suffered enough because of the Pepys mess I'd got us into. I wasn't about to make her unhappy by flying back home from this particular holiday at his summons.

"All right. Enough of that." Lisette shifted gears. " 'Ow are you two getting along over there? Fighting like a married couple yet?"

"Not exactly. I'm happy to say that all is well." I looked over at Sarah, stretched out on top of the bedspread, and thought, *very well indeed*. "Thanks for the call, Lisette—I'll be prepared for the blast."

She signed off with one of her suggestive comments—her speciality. Still smiling, I tossed the phone onto the bedside table and leaned back on the bed next to Sarah.

"Trouble?"

I shook my head. "Not really . . . the Duke of York is rattling my cage. I mean, I've been extremely honoured that he approached Plumtree Press with his book—it's really well done, from what I've seen of it. But he wants me involved personally in rushing this book of his to press, which simply isn't going to happen this week. He can jolly well talk to me over the phone."

"I suppose he's worried about other people not respecting his privacy, or not being equal to the job. He seems to trust you." She fell silent for a moment. "I haven't told you, but they want *me* back in London urgently, too. I told them to forget it." Was there something wistful in her voice? Was this an important opportunity for her, too, that she was missing because of me?

It would be too ridiculous if we were both secretly

wishing we could nip back to resolve these vital issues, but were too concerned about our partner's feelings to say it.

I braced myself, then dived in. "Darling, if you need to go back, we could both go—and then come back for a sail on the *Carpe Diem*."

She looked up at me, startled, her face a disconcerting blank. "Are you serious?"

Uh-oh, I thought. Maybe Lisette was spot on, and we were about to start fighting like a married couple.

"Oh, Alex!" Sarah enfolded me in her arms as if she hadn't seen me in weeks. Still holding me, she pulled away slightly and looked at me as if for the first time. Her eyes were misty. "I never dreamed it could be like this— you're so *reasonable.* We so often want the same things . . . it's such a relief. I imagined I would always have to struggle against my own wishes to satisfy yours. It hasn't been like that at all."

"It never will be. What kind of marriage would that be? Besides, we're a remarkable match—but the incredible thing is that I actually found you. I'll always be grateful to Dartmouth for that."

She nestled close again and sighed. "I'm sorry I wasted so many years, Alex, when we could have been happily married—I mean after Peter. I don't know why I didn't open my eyes sooner."

"I'm only glad you did, my love. We're together now . . . that's all that matters." I brushed her hair back from her face and kissed her smooth cheek. This total contentment, this deep happiness . . . I'd never felt anything like it before. Neither of us wanted to move, to lose the moment, so we remained absorbed in ourselves. At last, no one was chasing us, trying to frighten us or do away with us . . .

The inevitable happened all too soon; my mobile rang. "It'll be the Duke," I murmured into her ear.

Sarah gave me a squeeze and went to start gathering up her things. "Won't he be pleased!"

"Alex Plumtree," I answered. A flood of frightfully plummy English exploded down the line. "Yes, sir—I mean, *Andrew*. I do understand, and I'm on my way back tonight. Would tomorrow suit you? . . . Good! Say, eleven at your office? Fine . . . Well, you're very kind. I'm delighted that you think so. Right— good-bye."

Sarah watched with interest as she packed her bag. "You're a hero," she said.

"No, you are," I answered. "I'm not quite sure how you did it, but you've cleaned up this mess almost instantly, and everyone seems pleased about it. They need you at the United Nations, I think."

"You're sweet. But I'm afraid they wouldn't approve of my methods." She winked at me.

"*I* approve of your methods . . . some of them very much indeed."

"Oh?" She let the lacy nightgown she was folding slip from her hands as she watched me approach.

My answer was a long, slow kiss, and it ultimately led to a bit of difficulty making the flight out of Boston that evening.

CHAPTER 21

But, good God! what an age is this, and what a world is this! that a man cannot live without playing the knave and dissimulation.

Thence I parted, being doubtful of myself that I have not spoke with the gravity and weight that I ought to do in so great a business.

. . . he says that he hath had all the injury done him that ever man could have by another bosom friend that knows all his secrets . . .

But says he takes it from me, never to trust too much to any man in the world, for you put yourself into his power; and the best seeming friend and real friend as to the present may have or take occasion to fall out with you, and then out comes all.

SAMUEL PEPYS

My, you're both looking . . . er . . . *well!*"

Ian met us at Heathrow, looking uncharacteristically drawn—but the twinkle in his eye shone through. He'd managed to absorb my less than ideal appearance with aplomb.

Sarah gave him a hug, while I acknowledged what he'd

been going through. "I'm glad to see Heathrow's still standing, at any rate."

"For the time being," he replied, gazing vaguely round the terminal as if it might burst into flames at any moment. He sighed. "Things have quieted down nicely ... let's hope it lasts."

"It's *Sarah*," I said. "She miraculously sorted out some rather questionable characters and goings-on we encountered in Hanover."

"Ah! I only got dribs and drabs when we spoke over the phone. What on earth was all that about?"

As Ian drove us to the little flat I kept above the Press (Sarah and I wanted to change clothes and otherwise make ourselves human), we gave him some of the highlights of our time in Hanover. I described Mattie's discovery, then my own. "I really thought I'd found Pepys's Tangier diary extension—"

"*No!*" Ian exclaimed.

"Yes—but my lovely wife, with the help of a journalist, exposed it for a fraud. Could have *sworn* it was authentic. Anyway, the document's in the hands of some unscrupulous thief now ... but I still have my transcription. I'll show it to you at home."

"I can hardly wait."

"There were so many remarkable things about that document—the king's orders regarding Tangier, the behaviour of Lord Dartmouth's men in following those orders ... oh! But I wanted to tell you what I learned about the plague herb theory!" I turned to Sarah. "Darling, I never got a chance to tell you—"

I stopped short. Ian, in the driver's seat, and Sarah,

next to me in the back, had just exchanged an odd look—
ever so quickly.

"What?" I asked them. The secrecy in their look made
me bristle. Was there something I didn't know? What
hadn't she told me, and why? Obviously she'd felt able to
tell Ian. "Come on, out with it. I know when I'm being
kept in the dark."

"What do you mean?" Sarah asked.

I nearly said something about their exchange of significant looks. But just before opening my mouth, I heard
how paranoiac and childish it would sound. I shook my
head as if to say *never mind*. If there were things Sarah
couldn't tell me, I would have to learn to live with it . . .

But then why had she told Ian?

Stop it, Alex. For heaven's sake . . .

Ian jumped in to divert me. "So your friend Mattie's
find was authentic? Tell me exactly what it was that she
found."

I described King James's letter to Pepys, thanking him
for shorthand lessons.

"Extraordinary, all these significant discoveries—or
carefully wrought forgeries—hidden away in a remote
corner of northern New England. I might have missed
something, but what does Robert Frost's butter churn
have to do with Pepys?"

Sarah explained about the family of Pepys's maid,
moving to New Hampshire from England and bringing
the papers with them, while I stewed. She reached over
and took my hand, but there was something between us
that made the act feel false.

At the flat, Sarah was serene about the rift between us,
if she'd even noticed it. As I knotted my tie to meet the

Duke of York, I realised with a touch of bitterness that the honeymoon certainly appeared to be over. We kissed good-bye as she flew out of the door to her mysterious duties, and I briefly checked in at the Press.

"Well! The bridegroom returns! How was the beach?" Dee, hastily marking her place in her book, beamed at me from behind her desk. I felt so pensive that it was difficult to summon a smile for her, let alone the obligatory chat. I gave out a few nuggets of information as well as a Nantucket souvenir from the bag of treats I'd brought back for the staff. Then, citing the Duke's imminent meeting, I hurried up the staircase, hoping I wouldn't run into anyone else before reaching the sanctuary of Nicola's office. It was the first time I'd ever wished for such a thing.

My world was changing faster than I liked.

Feeling guilty, I stepped into Nicola's office and closed the door.

Her face lit up as she let a sheaf of papers drop to her desk. "Alex! Lisette said you were coming back early." She took a quick inventory of my face and general demeanour and added, "I know you have a meeting with the Duke— you probably want to know where his book stands. We can catch up on everything else later." She moved briskly to a bank of file cabinets against the wall and pulled out a folder, throwing me a smile as she did. "Good news: the dust-jacket artwork came in yesterday."

"Excellent! I hardly dared to hope. How'd you do it?"

"It wasn't me; it was Tina, in production. I only made a suggestion, but she chose the right artist—someone deeply loyal to the royal family, with a sense of history. He couldn't do enough, fast enough." She passed a copy of it over to me.

As usual, Nicola and her crew had hit the nail on the head: it was a pastiche of photographs of the Dukes of York all the way back to Pepys's time. My stomach lurched at the thought of any possible correlation, however remote, between Pepys and the Duke. But of course there was one; such was the nature of the ongoing title of "Duke of York". The Duke of York in Pepys's time had of course become King James II, the author of Mattie's letter.

Stay calm, Alex. "It's perfect, Nicola. Spot on. I think he'll love it." I looked up from the design. "Thanks for staying on this, Nicola. I think it could be quite important to get the book out quickly."

"Mikka told me they could conceivably have coated jackets in a week. And you know the printers."

I nodded. Our printers in Singapore had often come through for us in our little emergencies; they would put everything else aside for us and run the Duke's book immediately if we asked them.

"Have we finished with the manuscript?" Before we could send it for typesetting, our editors and designers would have to complete their work.

Nicola smiled. "Done today, I'm told. They claim to have enjoyed it immensely."

I breathed a sigh of relief. "Looks all right, then, if we splash out on rush fees and air freight. Nicola, you're amazing. It's as if you knew . . ."

She laughed and inclined her head towards me. "What makes you think I don't?"

Truthfully, at times I did think Nicola had some sort of special insight. Whether it applied only to me I couldn't tell, but her extraordinary perception couldn't be coincidence. I smiled. "You're scaring me. Whatever your gifts, I'm glad you're using them here. Thanks for making this work out, Nikky." Instinct told me to give her a hug, but my overdeveloped sense of propriety reminded me this was no longer acceptable between us—particularly given our close friendship in the past.

With a wave of the cover design, I dashed over to Lisette's office for a " 'Ello, you!" and down the stairs to catch a taxi to the Duke's office.

His private secretary ushered me in, greeting me with unexpected warmth and enthusiasm. If there was one thing I'd noticed in my publishing career, it was that even the high and mighty ooze respect and deference for anyone who might publish their memoirs. It was true that book publishing held power and influence beyond that of most businesses; sometimes that was a good thing. On the other hand, it posed exceedingly dangerous hazards, both mental and physical—at least in my case.

Who knew what the Duke's book would bring? Another flurry of death threats, of running from assassins? Or the laurels of critical and financial success, with the prestige of associating with a royal author?

Most people wished for excitement, intrigue, and unbridled success in their jobs; at this point I longed only for calm predictability.

Waiting for the Duke in a conference room, I thought of all the duties awaiting me. I'd just cut short the one holiday of my entire life when I wouldn't be expected to return phone calls and check e-mails. As a result, I had a frightening lot of work to catch up on, not to mention getting the Pepys Library's money back . . .

But here I was at the Duke's. I tried to put myself in his

shoes. He'd be upset because of his mother's condition, his family's persecution by the public, the terrorism. Like any author, he'd be concerned about Plumtree Press doing the best it could for his book in terms of design and promotion. Happily, I could allay those fears at least.

"Alex!" The Duke bustled into the room and shot me a worried, preoccupied smile. We had nearly the same birth date, but no matter his age, he kept the boyish good looks of his youth, along with a hale-and-hearty, game-for-anything look. "Great to see you again." Sinking into a chair opposite me, he gestured for me to sit. "I must say, it's frightfully noble of you to have come back from your holiday. I am *most* grateful."

"It's a privilege to be able to help—especially under the circumstances. But there's good news all round. This, for starters." I took the dust jacket mock-up out of its envelope and pushed it across the highly polished table towards him.

"I say! *Brilliant*!" He looked at me and gave a little laugh, as if it were almost too good to be true. His eyes returned greedily to the design and stayed there. "You think you can make this happen, then, in short order?"

"Yes, I do—the printers are happy to accommodate us. But you must realise, it'll still be two weeks. That's as fast as any book of quality can be produced."

He nodded. "I understand. God willing, this will all be over by then. We *can* get the publicity going immediately, though, can't we? I've got to get the press off my brother's back—especially with this alternative medicine disaster." The very thought made him run a hand over his eyes.

Privately, I thought I would rather be put on the rack than ever announce another book before its release. I'd tried that unconventional tactic before, and a reviewer had *died* because of it. But could that exact series of events occur again?

I prayed not.

"Yes," I heard myself say. "We can put the word out in advance. We'll use the technique the bookstores use for Harry Potters, the 'order your copy now' tear-off card on a board at the front of the book shops. As far as the press go—"

"We'd prefer to orchestrate that from here, if you don't mind. Things get a bit dodgy for us with the press. We've had to develop our own way of dealing with them."

I could just imagine. At least that was one problem I didn't have . . . the entire world watching me and commenting. The mind boggled.

"You and I have spoken enough about your book that I know you have your own anecdotes, so you're certainly ready for an announcement. We'll draft a press release, and your staff can do what they like to it—if you'd just run it by us after any changes. We'll also provide our list of magazines, newspapers, etcetera—though I'm sure you have your own."

"I appreciate the way you've made this work, Alex. I don't think I've ever had such a positive experience with a businessman before."

"That's kind, Sir. It's my pleasure."

He leaned across the table, grinning at me in a most familiar way, and lowered his voice. "Makes it a sort of family affair for both of us, considering everyone involved, eh?"

I must have looked confused; I had no idea what he meant. *My* family involved?

Once he saw this, he scrambled to explain—or cover up. "It isn't often that everyone in the royal family is caught up in these messes . . . generally the press prefer to take us on one at a time." He flashed his toothy grin and stood; I was dismissed. He reached out a royal hand and shook mine, thanking me again profusely, as we left the room.

As the Duke disappeared, his male secretary stepped forward from his desk to usher me out. He made pleasant chat with me on the way to reception, but in mid-sentence a flying missile careened out of an adjoining passageway. The young man hit the black-and-white-tiled floor hard.

The first thing I noticed after the fact was that the projectile had actually been a rather attractive young woman, who was horrified to see what she'd done.

"I'm *so* sorry!" she exclaimed, stooping to help him up. "I must be careful how I come through there!" As I bent down to lend a hand, I happened to glance through the door she'd barrelled through—straight into the deceitful mug of Vivian Porter.

"Sorry," I said to the fallen secretary, "talk to you later!" Before anyone could stop me, I moved quickly through the door into the room of cubicled offices. Vivian caught sight of me as I approached and—with remarkable fluidity of motion—scooped up his umbrella and fled out the side door. I ran after him and only by the most remarkable good fortune saw his brolly disappear into a taxi gliding away from the kerb.

It was, at least in some way, my lucky day: I caught one just behind him. "I need you to follow that taxi—please!"

My driver, a small, scrappy man with a photo of the

Queen on his dashboard, was happy to oblige. He started the meter and accelerated with abandon through the dignified streets of Belgravia. Vivian led us a merry chase, but my driver was easily the equal of his. We were near the Palace of Westminster when our quarry pulled over and Vivian appeared to give it up. I saw him paying his driver as I took care of mine, and we came face to face on the pavement at last.

He didn't attempt to run; he squinted into my face as if dreading this confrontation. I was aware of my taxi idling at the kerb as if the driver hated to miss the show.

"I'm sorry, Alex," Vivian said earnestly. "I would have preferred to avoid this encounter, for reasons you'll soon understand. But as we're here . . . could I persuade you to join me at my club for a drink?"

He could have knocked me over with his umbrella. I'd hardly expected such civility from a man who *seemed* to have been intimately involved in an attempt to murder me.

"How kind of you." Perhaps I'd learn something at last, I thought.

"Good," he said. "Come on, then." We walked in silence for a few paces. "You needn't be so hesitant about associating with me. I *am* Vivian Porter, by the way—the black sheep of the Porter clan. You might have wondered why you'd never heard of me, but I assure you, my family tries to pretend I don't exist. I want you to know that I had nothing to do with that young man who was hired to accompany me. Dean Small told me about what Jonathan did to you."

"*Dean*? You've been in touch with Dean since disappearing from Hanover?"

He smiled. "We have a great deal to talk about, Alex. I think it's time someone told you . . . though you mustn't let on to your lovely wife."

I searched his face. Considering my wife's occupation, that statement could have more than one meaning. Did he mean that *she* needed to be sheltered from whatever he was about to impart, or that she had been sheltering *me* from some harsh reality?

We were at the door of his club. I was surprised to see that it was one of the most exclusive in London. Perhaps he really *was* Vivian Porter . . . but I would wait until I heard his story to decide.

Sheltered by a massive overhang supported by classical pillars, the uniformed doorman gave Vivian a deep, deferential nod and opened the door for us. We were led past a number of rooms scantily populated with smoking men, many of them alone with their newspapers. At last we arrived in a dark, secluded area where the seating groups were much farther apart. The few other groups in the room seemed to value privacy as much as Vivian and spoke in hushed tones. Their dull drone served as useful background noise—that and considerable snoring.

We settled into deep chairs in the farthest possible corner. Through the window next to us I could see that it had begun to rain. It pattered comfortingly on the aged, handblown panes. He gave a long sigh, meeting my eyes directly. Strange as it may seem, there was something I *liked* about this man—just as I'd liked him in New Hampshire.

"Before I begin, I do need your word—which I understand is estimable—that you will not breathe a hint of this to anyone, Alex. I'm overstepping my bounds by telling you, but it seems unreasonable that you should be the only one not to know . . . especially after what you've been through."

He took a sip of his whopping gin and tonic as I mentally strapped myself in for his tale. "I suppose the first thing I should tell you is that everything—from Mattingley Harding's call to you through Pettifer Bartlett's disappearance—was planned for a very good purpose. Try not to be offended; as you're well aware, our nation is in a bit of a crisis."

I was too shocked to be offended. Reaching for my whisky, I took a reviving sip and riveted my eyes on him.

"I know you're involved with the Duke's entertaining history about the Dukes of York. No doubt you are aware of his effort to illustrate the unsung heroism of these men . . . which casts royalty in a good light. So when a rumour came along that a document suspected of being the Tangier diary extension had been found at your Dartmouth College, it was something of an unpleasant surprise. As a Pepys man yourself, you'll be well aware of the centuries-old rumour that the Tangier extension contains damning information about not only the royal family, but Lord Dartmouth, who was sent to Tangier with Pepys. And if he's tarred, Dartmouth College is tarred with the same brush.

"Mind you, we didn't hear about the rumour through the Internet posting; we heard through Pettifer Bartlett, who'd been asked by Dartmouth College to smoke out just exactly what this discovery was. Years ago the Queen's damage-control staff had consulted with him—no doubt you remember Bartlett's trips to England—about the potential for this plague-herb stuff in the Tangier diary to come out and knock them silly. This was during the Annus Horribilis, when the rumour had come out in a literary magazine yet again. This time, they couldn't stand any more negative publicity."

I stared at him.

"You look upset," he observed with a frown. "Have some of your whisky."

I obeyed.

"Pettifer came up with the brilliant idea of planting a discovery in the Frost Farm bequest. But of course he had to plant something that would throw everyone off the mark . . . and he chose a letter from King James II *to* Pepys."

My mouth hung open; I closed it.

Porter smirked. "Clever, wasn't he? Close enough to the correct item to dispel the myth of the Tangier diary extension, but not too close to raise suspicions. After all, it looked exactly like the page from Pepys's diary, but said nothing at all about Tangier. And then *you* came to Hanover and got your little tour of Rauner, including the Realia Room."

He hefted the gin and tonic and drank deeply, settling his features in an ironic, quizzical gaze as he studied me. "If only Pettifer had known that the story he'd concocted about the Pepys maid's family emigrating to New Hampshire bore the slightest resemblance to truth! The possibility that the actual item existed—let alone that you would find it in such an unlikely place—was so remote as to be nonexistent. Poor unlucky Pettifer. What a shock it was for him!"

I found speech at last. "*That's* why someone set out to kill me? Because I happened to find the *real* diary extension?" I was having trouble reconciling these alternate versions of reality. Only the day before I'd learned that what I thought was the Tangier extension was a forgery . . ."

With apparently sincere regret, he replied, "I still can't imagine anyone unbalanced enough to try to kill you for *any* reason—simply can't fathom it. I really am frightfully sorry. Although I can't tell you who might have done such a thing, I *can* tell you that all of this fear and doubt on the part of the crown and Dartmouth College was set off by a student's prank."

"*What?*"

He nodded. "A student attending the College for what I believe you call 'summer term' is taking Professor Bartlett's seminar on Pepys, and apparently enjoyed a barbecue at his farm immensely. The next day he set about saying thank-you in a most cunning way: he made his professor's dream come true by posting the entry on Pepysiana. It took weeks for Pettifer to work it out. And there, as I believe the Americans say, you have it." He leaned back in his chair and waited for this to register.

These unexpected facts percolated for several moments. "Er—what became of Pettifer Bartlett? Why did he disappear?"

"It reflects well on you that you should ask about your old professor first. He was requested to disappear."

"Requested—by whom?" I asked, bewildered.

"By those concerned for his safety, and with making this discovery of yours go away. By now you'll have worked out that your clever wife orchestrated a way for you to leave gracefully, and get those nasty characters off your back. She produced enough evidence to convince the journalist that the diary extension was a forgery. And since you and your friend Mattie had been very visible witnesses to the skullduggery afoot, sustaining your various injuries at various times, it was decided that Pettifer could disappear believably on a temporary basis—to reappear uninjured later, of course."

"Of course." I felt the first stirring of anger, which had been held at bay by the shock of it all. "And Phil Cronenwett? Was he really on holiday?" If they'd harmed Phil . . .

"By coincidence, he had planned to go away with his family that very week. We simply insisted that he go and not look back . . . for at least *two* weeks." He smiled with infuriating blandness.

"And who, may I ask, was orchestrating Sarah as she put all of this together? Who got her involved?"

He waggled a finger at me. "Certain things are beyond my purview. But she did only come in at the very end. And surely you *know* . . ."

I knew that there had been *someone* . . . but it was not her employer. The Firm, not to mention the International Task Force, wasn't known for taking official interest in Pepys diary discoveries.

One more question. "Vivian, if I may ask, how did you become involved?"

"The sad truth? My own family won't have anything to do with me. But I know useful people in useful places, and I have the right accent. And I desperately need the money." He looked down for a moment. "For once, I was able to do something worthwhile for a cause I care about—"

"Hiding herbs for Her Majesty."

He became distraught; somehow I'd overstepped the bounds. *Good Lord,* I thought. *Now I've done it.*

"I'm—"

He dismissed anything I might say with a tired wave of his hand. "That's just the problem. No ones does understand the loyalty that some of us feel, the need to preserve the royal family and all the good they've done. Why don't you go, Plumtree. Go and leave me alone."

He didn't seem to want to hear anything more from me just then. I went quietly and found my own way out.

Preoccupied, I used my mobile to ring my Pepys Library banker at the temporary office number he'd left me. I'd got through one crisis, and compared to that, finding a quarter of a million pounds seemed little more than a nuisance.

CHAPTER 22

. . . while the business of money hangs in the hedge . . .

The business . . . is hushed up . . .

SAMUEL PEPYS

I've an appointment with Ryan Hinching. My name's Alex Plumtree." Ready for battle, I stood in Reception at the temporary offices of the First City Bank.

"I'll see if he's in, sir. Just a moment, please."

As I waited, I considered the issues I needed to discuss with the banker. While it was true that he deserved great sympathy for his close brush with terrorism, Ryan actually had quite a lot to answer for. First, for not notifying me of the missing funds *immediately,* as treasurer and his liaison to the Pepys Library board. Second, for allowing money to be transferred erroneously, in any amount. I'd discussed the matter with Sarah on the plane back from Boston, and she'd suggested that it wouldn't be difficult for someone to set up an account in my name and transfer the funds into it.

But the real question was how First City Bank could have allowed those funds to be transferred without using the authorisation procedure we'd put in place. For any transaction involving sizeable amounts, all three of us—Urchfont, Mattingley, and I—were supposed to sign our authorisations together, in person. I needed answers.

"You can go up now, Mr Plumtree. Third floor; they'll direct you from there." After the bomb and the fires, the bank had taken space in a huge new building, utterly bereft of personality or design of any kind.

When I finally reached Ryan, I could see that I had underestimated the toll terrorism had taken on his life. He blinked his eyes in a nervous mannerism I didn't recall, and he was far from the self-assured man I'd met last time. The sumptuous office he'd had in the last building had been replaced by a five-foot-square cubicle, and the air was suffused with "new" smell, as Sarah called it: the chemicals of new paint, new carpeting, new furniture, new telephones.

As he ushered me in to his domain he said, "You can see we're in reduced circumstances here . . . but our fail-safe systems did their jobs. It's *nearly* business as usual."

I admired his brave front, and sat in the folding chair in front of his desk.

"No doubt you're wondering how something like your two-hundred-fifty-thousand pound loss could have happened, given the safety procedures you'd put in place. That's certainly the question I'd ask in your position. I'm afraid you're going to be very disappointed in my answer, but I'll give it to you straight: I made a mistake. I caved in to temptation and broke the rules."

When I remained silent, he went on, twisting his designer pen open and closed, open and closed. "I wouldn't blame you for taking action against me, Alex. Even so, I want you to know that I've thought long and hard about it. There's only one thing to be done."

So great was his remorse that I wondered what could be so horrible. I willed myself to be patient.

"Alex, Charles Mattingley came to me and transferred the money. I waived the safety procedures because at first it looked as though Mattingley was putting the money into *your* account . . . to make a purchase of some rare book, I assumed. It seemed logical that you would be the one to make the purchase, as you know the dealers. And as you know, Charles practically *is* the Pepys Library."

It took several heartbeats to absorb this unpleasant fact, which was so far from anything I'd expected to hear. *Charles Mattingley?*

"But . . . have you spoken to Charles about this? He represented it to us as a theft—involving *my* name."

Ryan shook his head miserably. "I haven't told you everything yet . . . he . . ."

"He *what*?" My patience was running out.

"He paid me. He paid me money to do it, more than you'd believe. I manage Charles's personal account; I know him quite well. I *trusted* him. He told me it was nothing more than a sort of harmless prank on you— that everything would be put right in the end. He got me at a good time . . . the children's school fees had got ahead of us, and my wife desperately needs a new car. I took it, Alex. He's been trying to ring me over the last few days, ever since we opened here after the fire. He even came by yesterday, but I had them say I was out. I can't bear to talk to him. I don't know what I'm going to do."

I didn't know what I was going to do, either. Ryan sat on one side of the desk struggling with his knotty problem, I sat on the other side wrestling with mine. Charles Mattingley was the elder statesman of the Pepys Library, in fact of Magdalene College. Who would believe that he'd done such a thing?

Moreover, *why*?

"Did he say anything more about this 'harmless prank'?"

Ryan shook his head miserably.

Charles cared deeply about the library, but he cared even more about Mattie. I'd found out on the night of her injury that Charles had sent me to Hanover to help verify her find . . . perhaps he felt I might not go unless he provided additional motivation. If I needed to redeem myself in the board's eyes because of the money missing on my watch, I would certainly follow through with my plan to go to Hanover. It gave me the heebie-jeebies to think Charles might have known I was getting married, and thought I might change my reunion plans unless he intervened. Mattie might have told him about the reunion, and he could have known I was attending by checking the list of attendees on the reunion website.

People would go to extraordinary lengths for their children, as Ryan had. It was not unthinkable that Charles would do the same for Mattie. But he'd told Ryan he'd make it right in the end. This, together with my naive optimism and Mattingley's recent flurry of attempts to contact the hapless banker, gave me hope.

I sat a bit straighter in my chair. "Ryan, can you log into the account right now and see how it stands?"

"Yes, of course." Apparently shocked that I was still speaking to him, he clattered away on the keys with shaking hands. We waited as the information appeared on the screen in front of him. With a yelp of surprise, he swivelled the screen so I could see it. "Look!" He pointed at one of a jumble of numbers that I'd have had trouble wading through. "It's *back*—every penny!" He tapped away on the keys again. "And it came from the account of one 'Alex Plumtree,' with the same number as the one it disappeared into." Ryan swore in disbelief and glanced at me to gauge my reaction.

One look at his face told me he would never compromise himself again.

"A piece of luck—for both of us," I told him. "If you could give me printouts of the two screens you showed me, I think we'll be done."

He set the printer in motion immediately. "Are you planning to . . . I mean, should I expect that you will—"

"I see no reason to tell anyone else about this bizarre game of Charles's. If you want to thank me, don't blot your copybook again."

He appeared to be weak with relief. A sweat broke on his face, and his voice quavered as he said, "I don't know what to say, Alex."

I rose to leave, took the papers from him, and offered a smile as I shook his hand. "Good-bye, Ryan. I'll see myself out."

Apparently incapable of further speech, he sat down heavily behind his desk.

Good heavens. As Pepys might have said, Lord! but what strange behaviour there is amongst men where money is concerned. Not that Ryan's behaviour had been unusual in the least, but *Mattingley's* . . .

I felt utterly exhausted. It was only two o'clock; I'd lived three lifetimes in one day . . . yet again. Before I could seek refuge at the Orchard, there was a special editorial meeting at the Press, scheduled specifically so I could attend. As it was raining, I descended into the bowels of the City once again and rode the tube back to Tottenham Court Road station. Riding in silence, rocked gently to and fro by the train on the rails, I reflected on how fortunate I was to have the staff at the Press. It was almost magical the way, among them, they possessed all the necessary talents to run a stellar publishing operation. I hardly dared to hope that this golden moment in Plumtree Press's history could go on for long.

It was still raining as I climbed out of the tube station and headed towards Bedford Square. Before the meeting, I wanted to call Urchfont and Mattingley and tell them that the money had reappeared; I wouldn't mention what I'd learned at First City Bank. The day was grim and dark, not at all what I thought of as a summer's day. And although I always looked forward to editorial meetings, today I felt the bleakest I had in a long time. I felt tricked and used many times over in the Pepys affair, discouraged by Ryan's and Mattingley's deceit. Even the joy of marriage to Sarah was dimmed by the barrier—a temporary one, I hoped—between us.

But as I drew near the Press, I saw the warm lights shining from the windows. I stood for a moment in front of the building and gazed at my second home, the site of so much hard work, happiness, danger, despair, and mirth. In spite of all I'd been through, I wouldn't change my occupation for the world.

"Is that you, *mon Capitain*?" The silky French accent penetrated the gloom.

"Hello, Lisette."

"What on earth are you doing, standing out 'ere in the rain? You look like a little lost boy. Well, perhaps a very big lost boy."

"Just ruminating. And what, may I ask, are you doing out and about? Tired of the grind? Bored with your job?"

She swore good-humouredly at me, but with enough creativity to make me laugh. "Come on, let's go in. I went to get some biscuits to 'ave with our tea."

She hooked her arm through mine, and we went up the steps together and into the Press.

The meeting was, as I had expected, rejuvenating. Plumtree Press was still going from strength to strength, and we were all enthusiastic about the Duke of York's project. Claire had drafted the press release and sent it to the Duke's staff; Nicola had learned from production that we would have the bound books within two weeks. The final edited draft was being checked as we spoke so it could be couriered to the typesetter.

It was Timothy who brought up Pepys. "What's this I hear about a Pepys discovery in Hanover, New Hampshire?"

I told him the bits I deemed of interest.

"Really! That's particularly fascinating in light of the fact that the manuscript I mentioned a couple of weeks ago came in—the one written from the viewpoint of Pepys's maid. And you'll *never* believe from whence it came."

He was forever keeping us in suspense like this. "Okay, I'll bite," I answered. "Where?"

He cracked a smile. "Where else? Hanover, New Hampshire. I had a quick look at it—very well written. It's a dead cert, particularly with Pepys in the news. Look at the article in the *Times* today: Pepys's maid's descendants emigrated to New Hampshire in the late eighteenth century. She must have kept some of his papers, and her family after her. Thus the Pepys treasure trove in the vicinity of Dartmouth College."

Tell me about it, I wanted to say. "Sadly, some of those discoveries appear to be forgeries. But yes, at least one appears to be legitimate . . . and there could be more. But Timothy, who's the author?"

He shuffled through the papers on his lap and came up with the packet in question. "I mistook a 'he' for a 'she'—his Christian name's *'Pettifer',* for heaven's sake. Pettifer Bartlett."

One more surprise, and I feared my colleagues would find me in a corner babbling nonsense. "Ah," I said. "He's written for us before, you know. As Ian will tell you, he was a contributor to the famous Plumtree Press Anthology of Seventeenth-Century Prose. May I see the letter?" My voice sounded surprisingly calm.

"Of course." Timothy handed it to me and I scanned it, noting that Pettifer had made no mention of knowing me or Ian. He had addressed it to Timothy, which meant that he'd checked into who was who at the Press. Curiouser and curiouser.

"Is there anything wrong?" Timothy asked.

"No. It's just that Bartlett was the Dartmouth College professor who got me interested in Pepys, that's all. I suppose I'm a bit curious why he didn't send the manuscript to me in the first place, and why he didn't mention it while I was in Hanover. I even saw him while I was there—Sarah and I had tea in his home."

"Authors can be very sensitive about being published on their own merit," Nicola painted out. "Maybe he wanted to be certain it was his book, and not his relationship to you, that won his contract."

"Mmm." We went on to other projects then, but I simply couldn't work it out. If Pettifer had made the discovery, why not simply ring me—and Mattingley—and tell us so? In fact, why hadn't he made it public to the world immediately? In order to put together an entire book from the material, he must have had it for some months, perhaps even years.

The rest of the editorial meeting passed in a blur. When Ian and I left the building at six o'clock, early for us, I was knackered. Jet lag was asserting itself. My mind flew ahead to retiring with Sarah in the big four-poster at the Orchard for the first time.

Ever considerate, Ian asked, "Would you like me to drive?"

"Yes, very much. Thanks." No doubt he sensed my reticence; I was very uncomfortable knowing that he and Sarah shared secrets. For a moment, exhausted as I was, I doubted the wisdom of having Ian live with us.

I fell asleep not ten minutes into the drive, something I could only have allowed to happen in the presence of family. But as we turned off the motorway in rural Hertfordshire, the car's noise diminished to a dull roar and I found myself fully awake. It was still light, a moist but clearing summer evening. I saw that we might well have a clear day tomorrow. Years of sailing in the Aegean before joining Plumtree Press had given me an eye for weather patterns that would be instinctive for the rest of my life.

Like a father, Ian didn't try to make conversation immediately I'd awakened. It wasn't until we were both inside greeting Sarah that we spoke. Ian, stepping through the door first, murmured a "hello, sweetheart" to her as I surveyed the worktop in wonder. I could scarcely believe my eyes and nose: Sarah had made one of my favourite dinners, a Chinese dish of poached chicken breasts, with a sauce of pureed ginger and spring onions. I'd hardly expected her to be home, let alone to have prepared a feast.

"Darling! How did you manage all this today?"

After giving Ian a hug and a peck on the cheek, during which time I noticed the figure-hugging skirt she wore, she wrapped her arms round me. "I was lucky. Things are going well." I breathed deeply of her perfume. How could I be angry with Sarah?

She poured us each a glass of white wine and raised hers in a toast. "Did you hear? The Queen is herself again. Come on," she said. "Let's relax for a while before dinner." As she led us into the library, I saw that the dining room was prepared for dinner—places laid, candles ready.

"What have you heard about Her Majesty?" Ian asked eagerly. As if bowing to a new order that was being established that evening, he lingered near the door as Sarah and I seated ourselves in the chairs my mother and father had always used. Only then did he come in and find his own place.

"It was on the radio as I was making dinner. This morning she sat up, looked around her bedroom, and said, 'Good heavens! Look at the time. I'll be late for my engagements.' Her doctor says she's right as rain."

"Thank God," Ian breathed, looking in his relief like a balloon that had partially deflated.

"There's more news, though nothing as dramatic as the Queen's recovery. Sarah, you'll never believe who's submitted a fictionalisation of the diary of Pepys's maid to Plumtree Press."

I watched carefully as Ian flashed Sarah another of their secret glances.

"Oh-oh . . . more Pepys," Sarah said, arranging her

pretty features into an expression of exaggerated fear. "Who?"

"Pettifer Bartlett."

"But—why didn't he talk to us about it when we were there?"

I shrugged. "Odd, isn't it," I agreed.

"But Nicola offered a reasonable explanation," Ian said. "Perhaps Bartlett thought you'd feel used if he told you. After all, you hadn't seen him in years, and when you finally do, he proposes a book deal? I can understand that, though I agree it looks strange now." Ian appeared to think of something that prompted him to consult his watch. "Excuse me for a moment; I need to make a phone call upstairs."

Ian disappearing to make phone calls was an unheard-of phenomenon. He was the quintessential introvert loner. Sarah and I looked at each other quizzically as we heard his footsteps climb the staircase.

Quietly, she asked, "Do you know what this is about?"

"No. I suppose it could be something from work . . ."

The chime of the doorbell interrupted us. It's unusual to have surprise visitors at the Orchard; secluded as we are, we rarely receive solicitations or unscheduled arrivals. I rose and went to the front door, turning on the front light and peering out cautiously. Two delivery men in a black suits held an enormous floral arrangement that was almost more than they could manage. I hurried to unlock and fling open the door. "Blimey!" I exclaimed.

"Where would you like it, sir?"

"Just over here, thank you . . ." I said, indicating the front hall table. Birds of paradise and four-foot-tall branches of gnarled grape vine warred with lilies, anthurium, iris, orchids, and exotic glossy green leaves. The spectacular array, held in a basket nearly three feet in diameter, dominated the entire entryway.

I panicked: had I missed Sarah's birthday? Couldn't be an anniversary yet . . . Ian's birthday?

But no . . . it was no special occasion that I could think of.

"Thank you very much," I said to the young men.

"My pleasure, sir," one of them said with a nod of deference, and went off down the steps to an unmarked black van.

Sarah and I looked at each other. "What floral delivery firm uses unmarked black vans?" I asked, and removed the envelope from a tall plastic cardholder stuck in the heart of the arrangement. I ripped open the envelope and was stunned to see Her Majesty Queen Elizabeth's crest at the top of the tiny piece of elegant card:

> *You remain a knight in shining armor.*
> *Our plans ran away with themselves, but*
> *in the end you and yours saved the day.*
> *Yours with warmest thanks and affection always.*

Sarah seemed uncharacteristically quiet at this remarkable arrival. I knew as well as I knew my wife that she understood why the Queen had sent flowers . . . and I also knew that she wasn't going to tell me.

I heard Ian coming down the staircase and understood as I looked at him that the flowers and extraordinary message were for him. He took in the scene, including the opened card in my hand and Sarah's look, and smiled. "My! What a stunning bouquet."

"Ian, I'm sorry. I—"

"Not to worry, Alex, not to worry." He took the card nonchalantly, without reading it, and tucked it into his trousers pocket. "Good heavens . . . such exotic varieties. Shall we move it into the dining room? Perhaps you'd help me, Alex."

My mother had always insisted that what she called "troubling matters" not be discussed over meals. In the force of long habit, stronger somehow in her dining room, I pretended that there was nothing extraordinary about the flowers on the long table—placed at one end so we could see one another. But all through dinner, as Ian enquired about our plans to continue the honeymoon and where we would take the *Carpe Diem*, my mind worked away on what I knew and what it might mean. By the end of the hour I was convinced I had it nearly sorted out . . . and it was a whopper. Now all that remained was to find a way to confirm that I'd got it right.

After dinner and the strawberry tarts Sarah had hidden away in the fridge, I offered to serve coffee—tea for Ian—in the library. The interlude gave me a chance to plot my strategy while the kettle boiled for the cafetière. I would ask them to listen to a story I'd invented—only listen, not confirm or deny. But I would know from their faces, no matter how artfully they dissimulated, and they would not have breached any trust.

"Here we are," I said cheerfully, reentering the library with a tray of cups and coffee. I busied myself serving the brew as I announced my intentions. "Now. I propose to tell you a little story . . . the perfect end to a busy day. The entertainment, if you will."

Both looked a bit taken aback—this was not my usual

behaviour. But they seemed willing enough to indulge me.

"Once upon a time," I began, settling into my chair, "there was a noble queen, perhaps the most conscientious and hardworking monarch in all history, who was beset with a nasty problem. In addition to whatever crises there might be in the nation, or with her family, there was a horrible rumour about the diary of a famous seventeenth-century court figure. Supposedly a yet undiscovered part of this diary contained information that would be extremely damaging to the royals: the story of how King Charles II, during the plague of 1665, kept a certain store of herbs from Tangier for the use of himself and his friends, his own use, while letting his people die by the thousands.

"From time to time over the years an article in a scholarly journal, or a new book about Pepys, would bring up the matter. It was all right as long as it wasn't a bad time for the royals, because after all it was only a rumour. But should the document ever be found, especially during a time when the people were rising up against royalty—not to mention a time when royals were accused of having access to medicines not available to others—it could be the final nail in their coffin. If this document were found, the Windsors hoped to acquire it before it could ever be made public. For decades they'd had their experts' ears to the ground in Pepysian circles. And one day, in the summer of 2002, it happened: an Internet posting suggested that the document had been found in a small New England town in America.

"Now, it so happened that in the Summer of 2002 the Queen was rather concerned about succession issues. Her son, who coincidentally would be King Charles (like Pepys's king), had been known to anger his mother from time to time with insensitive public statements. The press jumped on this practice years ago, speculating that perhaps she would abdicate to Prince William instead of Prince Charles.

"So when Prince Charles made a casual comment about the Church of England perhaps being a thing of the past, and the need to look at its potential abolition, a rising tide of nationalists and traditional Christians were upset by the remarks. The Queen decided to enlist a trusted friend"—Ian went rigid—"to conduct a test of the public's mood. She would find a week during which her engagements were slight, and slip out of the public eye. Some slight accident, or perhaps surgery, would be cited as the reason for the Prince of Wales to temporarily take charge. This would stimulate discussion of who the best heir to the throne would be, and the public could get a taste of 'King' Charles in action.

"But before the plan could be set in motion, the Queen really *did* have an accident. It was more serious than any she or her friend might have plotted. The friend was on tenterhooks as he watched television announcements from Buckingham Palace minimising her condition; privately he felt certain she had been seriously injured. The media went wild creating hypothetical situations: what would happen if the Queen were incapacitated and unable to fulfill her duties? Would the Prince of Wales be accepted by the people, or would that be the end of the House of Windsor? Perhaps even the end of popular support for royalty in Britain?

"When the Prince of Wales *did* step in to take on her official duties, everyone was in a tizzy. The loyal masses who loved the Queen and went to church every Sunday didn't want Prince Charles—perhaps soon to be King Charles—to do away with their beloved C of E. Those who had long sought to do away with monarchs and national religion saw this as their moment to make a move. Both sides expressed profound displeasure, and extremists chose the time to stick their knife in the wound. With the royals weakened and the nation already in an uproar, it was surely the perfect moment to throw England into total economic and physical disorder.

"A fascinating aspect of this crisis is its remarkable similarity to Pepys's time. In fact, the leftists resemble nothing so much as the Roundheads of Pepys's day— nearly four hundred years later. And, as in Pepys's time, the City—one of England's greatest symbols of financial and national strength—burned. Rumours of plots filled the streets; plots against the monarch, plots of modern-day revolution, plots of financial gloom and doom.

"More coffee, dear? Tea, Ian?"

They both answered, "Yes, please," rather more hastily than seemed natural. I served them, enjoying myself, and returned to my chair.

"Well. Where was I . . . oh yes. With the Queen perhaps permanently incapacitated, and Prince Charles about as unpopular as anyone since Pepys's *King* Charles, the last thing they needed was for news of the plague herb story to whip the nation into further frenzy. So the royals's public relations people leapt into action. They contacted Dartmouth College officials, who in an effort to help, scurried about trying to find out about the mysterious Internet posting referring to the Pepys diary extension discovery.

"The College in turn contacted its Pepys and special collections experts. Happily, they had something of a Pepys expert on hand, a man named Pettifer Bartlett. Bartlett, unbeknownst to the College, had been contacted by the heirs to Robert Frost's farm to determine whether there was anything of importance amidst the unruly stacks of papers in the barn. Bartlett happened upon a remarkable cache of historical documents that had spent the last three hundred years or so utterly undiscovered.

"Amidst the farm records, he found the later-life diary of Samuel Pepys's maid. She'd had to write all of Pepys's diary entries for him because he was nearly blind. Even better, he found a letter from King James II, who'd been the Duke of York under his brother King Charles, thanking Pepys for teaching him Shelton's shorthand.

"Now it just so happened that there were no papers mentioning the herb disaster, as the royals feared. There was no Tangier diary extension. But Pettifer Bartlett, ever curious, wanted to find out if there really was any truth to the plague herb story. He was especially intrigued because an exhibit had opened at the Hood Museum in Hanover featuring the art of plague and famine. Lo and behold, when he went to see the exhibit the docent told him of records written by French tradesmen coming and going during the plague, of a mysterious herb grown in Tangier and used only by the royal family.

"So he created a forgery—indeed, in some circles it was thought that he'd perpetrated a hoax at Yale's Beinecke Library by forging a Shakespeare play the year before. In the new Pepys forgery he used everything he'd ever heard about the plague herb rumour, and more rumours about what Pepys had seen on his voyage to Tangier with Lord Dartmouth, to create several fascinating new diary pages. What a creative, and naughty, mind."

I sipped my cold coffee and took a reading of my audience. Sarah was smiling; Ian wore a satisfied look.

"You have a great capacity for telling stories, Alex," my dear friend said noncommittally. "I really do wish you'd try your hand at fiction! Please go on. I'm enjoying this immensely."

"Thank you. I'm nearly at the end. Of course the Queen's staff nearly went berserk when they heard that the Tangier diary extension had been found, last week of all weeks. They offered to purchase it from the College, but it had disappeared from the Frost Farm bequest boxes of uncatalogued material, where Bartlett had put it. The College knew there had been a break-in at Rauner that week, and was eager to track down who might be responsible. But only the Dean had been entrusted with the information—the Dean and the president of the College. So the Dean himself staked out Rauner, and caught Sarah and me red-handed in the middle of the night, sneaking round the Library. Sarah was able to bring out the papers under her clothing, and we hid them safely—we thought—elsewhere.

"This next bit's slightly complicated: Bartlett's *son's ex*-girlfriend, Mattingley Harding, just happened to have a tie to the Pepys Library through her uncle, Charles Mattingley. She herself was assistant archivist at Rauner Special Collections Library at Dartmouth College. Bartlett had told her confidentially about the find, and wanted to help her career by letting her announce the King James II letter, once the Frost Farm bequest was made to the College. She in turn called me, ostensibly to see if I'd come and verify that the letter is authentic.

"But in the meantime, someone decided Mattie had to disappear. Clearly this someone was not in the know, because Mattie was not the only one aware of the letter . . . the College knew, and so did Bartlett. When I came on the scene, I mistakenly believed that the College might want both Mattie and me out of the way—mysterious people came after me and my crew mates. Ultimately, Bartlett disappeared, too, so I became convinced that the College was trying to get rid of anyone who knew about the Tangier diary. The College had its own PR problems, and if it happened that the second Earl of Dartmouth helped found the College with dirty money, they'd have hell to pay all over again.

"One pesky problem kept popping up: all of the attackers involved were English. I know, of course, as a loyal British subject that the House of Windsor would never in a million years have hired assassins to do away with people who might know nasty secrets about them. Why would the College have had a covey of English thugs standing by to help them? It remains a mystery to this day.

"Meanwhile, I was called out to help persuade one Vivian Porter, who for some reason had in his possession papers pertaining to the founding of Dartmouth College, to make a donation. Porter no longer wanted the papers and was looking for the best place for them. But while he and I ventured together up Mount Washington on the railway, his man tried to kill me and very nearly succeeded.

At this point I began to suspect that Porter, Jonathan, and the College were in league. Later I came to believe that Porter and Jonathan worked for the Queen, and had been authorised to offer Lord Dartmouth's papers in exchange for the Tangier Diary extension.

"Meanwhile, things were going from bad to worse in England. The royals were begging for progress to be made. The Queen's close friend, who was intimately involved in putting things right for her family even during this *accidental* version of the disappearance they'd planned, decided it was time to call in one of the best operatives he knew. Unfortunately, she happened to be on her honeymoon."

I glanced at Sarah. She wore the same mildly amused expression she'd worn throughout.

"Although her speciality through the years was banking, and keeping tabs on foreign governments that might influence the world economy, the Queen's friend persuaded this woman to put her considerable skill to use. She managed to prove that the Tangier diary extension was a fraud and a hoax by a recognisable but unknown hand, that of the Shakespeare forger. She kept her husband, who was still a bit rickety after his night camping, out of danger in the Hanover jail while she announced this news to the world and had it posted on the same Pepysiana site that started all the trouble. This wonderwoman told the royal family that the document was safely destroyed. All the baddies, whatever their allegiance, went away: the diary extension was a hoax and now destroyed in any event. There appeared to be no truth to the story. Everyone went away and was happy, no more violence, no worries.

"But I still couldn't figure out why Vivian Porter and his 'man' had tried to kill me. So when I went to consult with the modern Duke of York about his book, which he was nobly trying to announce to take some heat off of his brother, you can imagine my shock at finding Porter in the Duke's offices! Had he been acting on behalf of the royals after all?

"He attempted to elude me, but eventually shocked me further by inviting me to his club. There he proceeded to tell me that he didn't know who Jonathan was working for; Vivian only knew he'd been hired as a sort of prop for his act of visiting gentleman. But I *had*, he said, discovered the *real* Tangier diary extension—he claimed that it did in fact exist and was overlooked by Pettifer, stuffed in the butter churn as it was. I did actually believe him, until tonight. Now that I'm home, and with you, Sarah, I know you wouldn't have deceived the world about a historical matter like Pepys's Tangier diary."

She shot me a satisfied smile.

"I should mention that twice, now, I have heard intimations that I am not the only one in my family involved in this affair. The Duke of York let slip that this was 'a family affair' for both of us, evidently unaware that I'd been kept entirely in the dark. And tonight, the Queen's card to you, Ian, referred to 'you and yours' having saved the day."

I drew a deep breath. "I think that's it."

In the pregnant silence that followed, Sarah seemed to consult Ian. He nodded ever so slightly.

"What a remarkable story, Alex!" she said. Cradling her cup and saucer, she looked up at the ceiling as if summoning another tale, then back at me. "I'm sure you've already thought of this. But let's pretend for just a moment that what you've said about Pettifer penning a fraud is true. Wouldn't it be amusing if a certain party, or parties, believed the fraudulent diary extension to be authentic—and believed that by possessing it they'd avoid their public relations hassles? There they all are, happy as clams because the meaningless sheets of paper in their possession will never see the light of day. Even if they did, Elizabeth Mullion and I told the world they were a fraud. Their problems are solved." She sighed and leaned back in her chair. "Now, what really intrigues me is the possibility that a *real* diary extension might have been discovered in the Frost bequest . . . say, in the cider press. Somewhere no one had looked or expected. Almost certainly, anyone who found the real McCoy—*certainly* anyone married to a Pepys scholar and rare book collector—would preserve the document for posterity. They'd hide it in a very safe place where it would never be discovered—and no one would be looking for it."

Could she mean it? Had she in fact found the *real* thing in Rauner on the night we'd broken in? Could she possibly have brought it back to England with her? Was it right here in this very house?

Yawning, she said, "Time for bed. What a day!" She went to Ian and kissed him on the forehead. "See you in a few minutes, Alex?"

"I'll be up soon. I'll just take care of the kitchen." *Right after I check the document safe, dear.*

Ian rose too. "Good night, Alex."

"Good night, Ian." I smiled.

When he'd left the room, I sat for a moment enjoying the still of the library as if it were any other night. After

I'd heard him climb the staircase, I went to the mantel. There, behind a section of the carving, was the fire-safe box I'd installed. As I reached for it, I thought that there were several places in this house for Sarah to have stored such a document—here in the mantel, or in a space behind one of the library shelves where my brother Max and I had once found a book, or in a false-fronted section of the library shelves that my father had designed.

I peered into the box and saw several sheets of the right size resting on the metal surface. I reached in and pulled them out, enjoying the feel of the paper and the delicate scrawls . . . but these were not at all the papers I had seen in Hanover, and had transcribed so carefully. The writing was in plain English, not Pepys's code . . . and in a hand not at all like his.

Of course! *His maid* had done the writing for him at that stage of his life . . . these were the *real* diary pages. Pettifer had made quite a foolish mistake in creating his forgery.

At once the ramifications of what I held in my hand flashed through my mind . . . this meant that there had been two supposed Tangier diary extensions floating around Hanover while Sarah and I had been there. It also meant that Sarah had been perfectly ethical in saying the pages had been stolen . . . the ones we all knew of *had* been stolen.

I feared I was no match for my wife; perhaps it was just as well she'd got me out of the way while tidying things up in Hanover.

I sat down to read the pages, amazed at their clarity and cleanliness after so many years.

As my life draws to a close, I find that certain matters nag at me to record them, as if history wills it done.

My new maid is taking this down for me; she seems trustworthy enough, and my eyes can no longer do such work. For many years I have kept the secrets of our voyage to Tangier, fearing that I would damage the reputations of my King and my travelling companions. They are all dead now, with the exception of the King, and I will in any case and at all costs prevent these pages from being seen by anyone.

An awful secret lies behind the execution of those natives of Tangier who had stolen from the crown or otherwise been dishonest in their dealings. His Majesty merely wanted to escape paying these men for their service over many years—indeed he had never paid them. But he certainly never intended killing them. Lord Dartmouth's assistant, thought by some to be a blood relative of my Lord's by the name of Pliny Turner, got together the hundred men and women who had served the English party faithfully over nearly a decade in Tangier. He killed them in the most brutal, cold-blooded way I have ever witnessed. I have witnessed many executions at the Temple Bar, but after the Tangier massacre I no longer have the will to observe them. All of those people died because Turner fulfilled the King's wishes not to pay them in a most evil fashion. It was a most misguided and shameful episode in our nation's history.

I turned the page.

It saddens me to reveal another episode that none but those of us who served His Majesty in Tangier know. When the plague struck London, the Tangier

*natives told the British occupants that there was an
herb known to save people from dread diseases. They
seemed most confident that it would stop the plague,
and a great deal of the herb was sent to London. People saw it arriving at the Palace of Whitehall and a
most foul story was put about, supposedly by Pliny
Turner: that the King and his family and all of his
good friends did take the herb, and were saved by it.
But in fact, though many partook of this herb, it was
soon discovered that it had nothing to do with curing
the devilish disease infesting London. It was all
burned when its worthlessness was discovered, but a
story persisted for years that the royal family kept the
herb from the people through selfishness and lack of
love, and so killed thousands of people.*

Good heavens! The plague herb story, a fabrication? I
thought that perhaps we would have to make this document public at the earliest opportunity.

*It is a great relief to me that my nephew John
Jackson has taken such an interest in my books, for I
feel that my library will be well looked after. My
specifications for the smaller and more precious
portion of my library, once known as the Plumtree
Collection . . .*

Plumtree Collection?! Amongst Pepys's books? There
wasn't a . . .
But what if there was, and something had happened to
prevent it being revealed? Parts of my family hailed from
near Brampton, where Pepys grew up. According to his

diary, he was forever taking trips there, even burying his money in his father's back yard when he felt England was in crisis and he might go down with the ship. It's possible that he acquired a portion of my family's collection at a time when they felt it was prudent to sell.

> . . . which I also plan to donate to Magdalene, shall be held in reserve for those visitors deemed by Jackson to be worthy enough and knowledgeable enough of books to handle them. Under no circumstances shall they be housed in the same room with the other books in my collection, but in a separate, private facility within the same building. I fear that one day part of the collection might be destroyed, and I want a remnant to survive for posterity. Young Jackson shall know nothing of these books until after my death; only Elizabeth knew of the sliding wall behind which I kept them.
>
> He has promised to do what I have asked by putting the Plumtree Collection in the same building as the library, but not revealing it until I should tell him. I want some portion of the library to lie in reserve, protected, lest the entire collection be destroyed.

Where would it be now? Only God knew. Perhaps it was buried behind Pepys's father's house in Brampton.

As I studied the astounding papers in my hands, I thought through the ramifications of making them public. On the positive side, it would help the royal family to dispel the disastrous plague herb story once and for all. And surely the secret of Pepys's library could be revealed now, and the books uncovered for the public's benefit.

But points weighing against publishing the papers were equally strong. The revelation of the deaths in Tangier would add fuel to the anti-royalty fire. True enough, the king hadn't ordered the natives' execution, but certain groups would still place the blame squarely on his shoulders. Perhaps more importantly, whoever had made off with the fake Tangier diary extension would now *know* that it was a fake. Would that open Pandora's box again?

I would need to ask Sarah her thoughts.

It struck me that if we did not make the papers public, I would be doing with my children what my father had done with me, and what Pepys had done with his nephew John Jackson. I would pass along closely held, centuries-old secrets to my heirs and ask them to carry on the tradition.

After a last look at the papers, I replaced them in the box, put the mantel back into place, and went to turn off the lights.

Ah, it was good to be home. Gazing fondly at the bookcases as I went, I glimpsed the heraldry book presented me by the Dibdin Club the summer before. I detoured to the handsome book, pulled it off the shelf and took it to the desk. Porter, Porter . . . ah. Here it was.

As I read the account of the Porter family's lineage, I saw something very curious indeed . . . he was closely related to Pliny Turner—the man I'd just read about in Pepys's diary.

This explained why Porter had possession of the papers to do with the Earl of Dartmouth's aid in founding Dartmouth College; it was possible that his ancestor, Pliny Turner, had kept them and they'd been passed down through the generations.

Pliny Turner may well have begun his service as nothing more than a porter for Lord Dartmouth, carrying and keeping the nobleman's papers as he travelled the world for his King. History circled round, generation after generation: the Porter family had once again come into the affairs of the Tangier voyage papers nearly three and a half centuries later through Vivian's service to the Windsors.

Wondering at the eerie connections of history with the present, and the power of literature to suddenly reemerge from dusty crates to change the fates of men, I replaced the volume with care. Full of awe, I took comfort in performing the pleasantly mundane task of washing up.

CHAPTER 23

. . . a cat will be a cat still, and some time or other out his humours must break again . . .

This put us all into a stound.

. . . but he is cracked a little in his head.

SAMUEL PEPYS

Oooh, this is nice," Sarah murmured sleepily as I brought her a cup of coffee in bed. She sat up against the headboard and took it in both hands. "Is this my thank-you present?"

"I can't imagine what you're talking about," I answered, feigning confusion. "But I did wonder . . . are you free to roam at will now? Free, for instance, to finish honeymoons?"

She laughed. "Absolutely." She was, if anything, more beautiful in the morning when her eyes were misty with sleep.

"Fancy a quick trip up to Cambridge, then, before we fly back to Nantucket?"

"Ah, Cambridge—home of the Pepys Library. I'd love to go with you."

It felt odd not to be going back to work. But being in Sarah's company, and listening to her make plans for our week aboard the *Carpe Diem*, quickly dispelled any latent thoughts of Plumtree Press.

We arrived in Cambridge just after noon. I took Sarah to a pub on the river for lunch, then treated her to a walk round my favourite second-hand book shop just outside the Magdalene College gates. We were then ready for our visit to the Library, though I hardly expected that John Jackson had managed to install his uncle's portion of the Plumtree Collection in this building.

"That's the Pepys Library through there," I said, giving Sarah my tour of the college. "Lovely, isn't it? But see how the building is just slightly asymmetrical? Charming, in a way, but—"

Sarah was looking at me oddly.

"What?" I demanded.

"Alex. My love. Have you ever considered *why* the building might have been built that way? Perhaps to accommodate some unusual structure inside? Perhaps as a little hint that it *does* accommodate that structure?"

"Good heavens." I put an arm around her shoulders as we gazed at the building. "You know, there's just enough insanity to that to make it true. I don't suppose you have X-ray vision, too?"

"Very funny."

"It's just that if you were any more brilliant or talented, I'd begin to think you weren't human."

She kissed me on the cheek and pulled me along after her. "Come on! I want to know!"

The quad looked like an advert for a gardening centre. Specimen trees and vivid blooms punctuated expanses of lush grass. Hardly daring to believe that I could be here with Sarah as my wife at last, I savoured the moment.

Many, many nights I'd pined away here while doing my Pepys work, guiltily wishing that Sarah were my wife instead of my friend Peter's. And now . . .

"Let's not let on that we're looking for anything," I said quietly as we approached the golden building. "Okay?"

She gave me a look of mock disparagement. "I was going to run inside and shout it to anyone who would listen, but . . ."

"All right, all right."

We climbed the stairs to the library and I sensed that Sarah was recalling the tragic death of a Beowulf scholar in the building the year before. It lent further weight to a building already heavy with history. We were quiet as we entered; no one else appeared to be there.

I led her through to the main room that contained Pepys's treasured "presses" filled with priceless books. She went to the glass-fronted cases and studied the volumes; I joined her, loving her appreciation of the fine old books. Then, her flats tapping on the wooden floor, she moved slowly to the middle of the front wall. The building was most obviously off-kilter here, as if someone had stuck in an extra two feet or so. Nonchalantly, Sarah studied the wall from floor to ceiling, then went round into the next room and inspected it.

Though we'd decided not to shout about it to anyone listening, I thought it might be safe to breathe a word in her ear. I moved close and stuck my nose into her hair, murmuring, "If it's here, there must be an opening." She nodded.

"Alex Plumtree!" a voice boomed just behind me. I must have jumped several feet in the air. Wheeling round, I saw Percival Urchfont, Charles Mattingley, and Vivian

Porter standing together. I wondered how they'd managed to creep in without us hearing them, and just how long they'd been there.

What was *Porter* doing with this crowd, anyway? I thought his family seat was somewhere farther north . . .

"Good heavens, you gave me a fright!" I reached for Sarah's hand; she seemed unruffled by the men's sudden appearance and smiled at them with her charm intact. "Percy, Charles, Vivian, this is my wife, Sarah." To Sarah, I said, "My friends from the Pepys Library board—Percival Urchfont and Charles Mattingley. And Vivian Porter joined me on the cog railway up Mount Washington."

Sarah nodded at them pleasantly, quite a feat considering what she'd told me she'd like to do to Vivian Porter.

"Delighted to meet you," Percy enthused, reaching out to shake her hand. Vivian followed suit. The more reserved Charles murmured hello and kept his hands to himself.

Percy went on, "I didn't know you knew Vivian, Alex—small world, isn't it? Vivian is my cousin, once removed. He's up for his summer visit."

"Ah, lovely. I brought Sarah up to show her the library that's solvent again," I said. "Jolly good news, wasn't it? Evidently some sort of confusion at the bank."

Neither of them let on that there'd been anything odd about the money reappearing—or disappearing in the first place.

"*Excellent* news," Percy replied. "As I said, we knew you'd put things right. Shame about the Tangier diary extension proving to be a hoax, though." He shook his head. "I really thought the old thing had shown up at last."

"I know it. Still, Mattie made her brilliant discovery."

"Yes indeed!" Percy enthused. "A marvellous find."

Mattingley gave me a mirthless little smile that seemed to say, *"I know that you know; it's our little secret."* Something about his manner—perhaps just slightly less arrogant than usual—suggested an apology. Heaven knows I deserved it!

Porter listened, smiling vaguely.

"Well, I do wish you'd rung ahead, Plumtree. We got together for another emergency meeting, but decided not to trouble you. Never dreamed you'd be here! I'm afraid we've another crisis—albeit a small one. Apparently Charles has found dry rot. He wanted to come over to get the repair firm started right away—he's hired them to shore up a bit of the wall."

It was true that Mattingley sensed things about the library building of which the rest of us were oblivious; sometimes I thought he must practically live there to be so intimately aware of its every nook and cranny.

"When we came in, I thought perhaps you and Sarah had discovered it too," Charles said in his raspy whisper. "Or were you looking for something you'd lost?"

Was that a touch of irony in his voice?

"No," Sarah said, "but I am interested in the building's architecture. It's a splendid structure."

"Ah," Charles said.

I bristled at his tone; I thought I detected a touch of the frostiness Britons can adopt when speaking to Americans.

"Well, let me show you while we're all here. Do you see this strip along the edge?" He moved around us and pointed out a strip along the edge of the wall that extended perpendicular to the front of the building and divided the main floor of the library into two rooms. Bits of the wall had crumbled like dust onto the floor, but I hadn't even noticed it. "This is what I was talking about. We must get rid of it before it spreads."

Percy moved closer to the wall to inspect. "By George, you're right, Charles. That's going to be a nasty spot to fix, right there against the front wall."

Charles consulted his watch. "I hope the construction firm are as good as their word. Normally they're very conscientious; they specialise in minimising the impact of repairs on old buildings, including dust. They said they'd make a start by two o'clock; it's nearly—"

As if they'd heard Charles from afar, three men entered the room, each of them carrying a tall stack of plastic dust sheets folded into neat squares, along with other assorted equipment.

"Ah, here you are." Charles looked at his watch once again to send his message of disapproval.

"Sorry we're late," the foreman replied, setting down his burden with encouraging delicacy. Mattingley had been right about their sensitivity to the old building and its books. "Bit of an accident on the road. Where's the problem, then?"

Charles led the workers to the area. To my surprise, the foreman took a screwdriver out of his pocket and jammed it into the crumbling bit of wall near the floor.

I saw Charles and Percy wince as I did. These men were supposed to be gentle to old buildings? But construction workers were always bold and confident with their tools . . . and the rotten bit had to go anyway, I suppose.

"Blimey!" he exclaimed.

"*What?*" we asked in unison.

"You've got . . . there seems to be a *space* back here." He stuck his hand through the rather large hole he'd made and said over his shoulder to the youngest of the workers, "Bring the vac, will you, Tony?"

While Tony set up the industrial Hoover, the foreman stood and walked along the wall to the door that joined the rotting room to its neighbour. "Funny, I'd not have noticed this—it's not much more than a foot. I'd have thought it nothing more than a thick wall. But it looks as though you have an extra room in here—a long, narrow room."

Percy gaped at the man as if he'd just told him Pepys had come back from the dead.

Charles looked angry; perhaps he felt his supremacy in knowing more than anyone else about the building had just been challenged. But there was also a greedy glint in his eye, as if now he would have more library to love.

Sarah, standing at the back of the small crowd with me, nudged me ever so slightly with her elbow. I looked at her and widened my eyes for just an instant to say, "*Eureka!*" She smiled and returned her attention to the foreman who was now breaking away chunks of the rotten wall as Tony sucked dust from around the area. Before I knew it, he'd cleared away remains of crumbling lath and plaster all the way from the floor to nearly the top of his head, and almost a foot wide. We all stood behind him, like children at the window of a toy shop, watching and waiting for our chance to see into the hole.

"There you are . . . more books for your library." The foreman stood aside, pleased at the treasure trove he'd unearthed.

Charles, first in line for a good look, was utterly silent. He stood for a moment with his head through the hole, then put a hand up on the front wall as if for support.

"Are you all right, Charles?"

"Yes, of course," Mattingley rasped, but was clearly shaken as he stepped aside.

Porter stepped up to take his turn, stared for a moment and urged his cousin forward.

"Good heavens!" Percy boomed in his country squire voice. Evidently silenced by the wonder of what he saw, he stood motionless for some moments.

"May I?" Putting a hand on his shoulder, I brought him back to reality.

"What? Oh, yes—sorry, Plumtree. Good Lord, what a shock."

At last Sarah and I peered through the hole. A solid wall of books faced us, presumably stretching the eight feet or so to the door, most of them hidden in gloom. Surprisingly little dust covered the visible spines, considering the years the books must have been in there—no construction had been done since the building had been slightly modified in the eighteenth century to accommodate the Pepys Library.

The only books we could see, directly opposite us, bore uniform spines in Pepys's own hand—clearly these had not been bound in his wealthy days, for they were made of ordinary leather and not gilded—with titles such as, *First Poem Collection, Songs for Deborah (Pepys, you old cad, you're supposed to write songs for your wife, not your maid*, I thought), and *My Days at Magdalene*. It was difficult to see more without removing a larger section of the wall.

The construction man spoke. "Do you want me to see if I can take this whole wall away—just to the door, of course—without damaging the structure? It'll take time, but I'm guessing you'd like to see what's in there."

Percy and I looked at Charles, who'd gone an odd shade of white. His tightly clamped jaw warned us against asking if he was all right. He nodded briskly, once, to the builder.

"Shall I just see if I can find out what else is in there first?" I offered. "I have a pocket light . . ."

The builder said, "We've a torch, of course," and handed it to me.

I stuck my arm and shoulder into the hole first this time, and got my head as close as I could. "*In Defence of Cromwell, A Non-Conformist's Plea*—some political volumes here." Percy and Charles would recall that Pepys had worried about the fact that he'd sympathised with the Roundheads as a schoolboy, and that his benefactor Mountagu had been firmly on Cromwell's side. As the diarist became involved in court politics and received ever higher appointments, attracting the attention of the King and the Duke of York, he lived in fear that his earlier sympathies would be discovered.

"And"—I strained to make out the faint printing on some of the spines, but nearly dropped the torch when I saw several volumes that looked familiar. "*Malconbury Chronicles . . .*" Privately, I rejoiced. The extent of my joy was so great, it was as if—well, almost as great as if heretofore unknown *children* had been born. *More Malconbury Chronicles!*

Hushed silence filled the room; all of us there, with the exception of the construction people, knew that the *Mal-*

conbury Chronicles were the most famous volumes in the Plumtree Collection currently residing at the Orchard. The monks at Malconbury Priory in East Anglia had used dye of a particularly brilliant blue hue to illuminate their otherwise mundane records. No one had been able to reproduce it. Scholars had visited my library at home on occasion to photograph the books for further study, or just to see them in person. None of us had dreamt that there were more.

"*Splendid!*" Percy sounded as though he might actually be salivating. "What else can you see?"

"Many more mediaeval volumes . . . a number of them bound in plain vellum . . . and that's all the farther I can reach. I'd know more if I could take them out, but I'm not sure it's wise," I said, backing out of the hole. In truth, I saw a number of volumes that were extensions of collections widely known to reside in the Orchard's library. Immediately recognisable by their small size and primitive binding was a series of priceless books of hours, all gloriously illuminated by the same anonymous monk in red and green and gold. The monk was known by his distinctive signature: a tiny red fox, hidden in every third drawing.

I needed time to think how I would explain an obvious Plumtree connexion with this newfound library.

"After the wall's been removed, we should catalogue them as they are, in case there was a reason for their order. It's going to be difficult to protect the books during the demolition," I said, worried.

"Not for us, sir," the construction foreman said. "If you don't mind my saying so, we've had more difficult jobs than this—museums, country houses—and they never found a speck of construction dust or debris anywhere near the valuables."

"That's encouraging," I said.

But I knew uncatalogued collections were invitations to trouble; Mattie, Phil, Sarah, and I had learned it the hard way. I wouldn't rest easy until I knew that this one had been carefully catalogued, and alarms put on the cases.

"We need to get security over here," Percy said gruffly. He'd arrived at the same conclusion at the same moment. "I'll see to it."

Our initial excitement had already given way to worry, a sad but inevitable pattern. But I knew these men would sooner die than let anything happen to the new discovery. I could find out about the other books after we returned from our *Carpe Diem* holiday . . . even the name of the yacht was a reminder not to procrastinate when it came to the really important things in life.

Charles, rasping acerbic warnings to the construction workers, followed them out as they went to retrieve gear from their van. Percy went to the porter's lodge to call security.

We were left alone with Vivian Porter. I couldn't think why, but as we faced him in the sudden calm and quiet of the library, it struck me that he looked bitter. Even as he turned to us and smiled, I felt that he was deeply distraught. It was all the more troubling that this was masked by a cold, smiling visage.

"I've never been here before, you know," he confided. "Somehow Percy's always been too busy to bring me. Don't suppose you'd be willing to give the tour . . ." He glanced from me to Sarah.

"Delighted," I said, and led the way towards Pepys's bookcases, ushering Sarah ahead of me. "In all the excitement, we've managed to ignore quite a spectacular *existing* library . . . right here."

Not six feet from the hole we'd been peering through were Pepys's famous presses, holding books organised by size rather than content. Sarah was just ahead of me, hearing the tour for the first time. "These books on the bottom row," I began, "include a number of Pepys's Royal Society volumes. The most valuable is probably Newton's *Principia,* published while Pepys was head of the Society." Intrigued, she turned, as if to ask a question. But even as I watched, her face became a mask of horror. Just as I turned to see what was the matter, she dived sideways in front of me.

Unable to imagine what might have prompted such behaviour, I turned, shocked, to see Vivian Porter bringing a sledgehammer down on Sarah's head.

My entire life's purpose was reduced to thwarting that blow. Propelled by instinct, palms splayed, I connected. A nasty crunch reverberated through my body as the hammer and I hit the ground. Pain exploded through my right hand and forearm.

Sarah was behind me on the floor . . . Porter was getting to his knees next to her.

"*Sarah!*" I bellowed. "*Run away!!*"

But this time it was Sarah who dived for Porter's body, neatly diverting him to the floor. They grappled there. In that moment I felt certain my wife would prevail.

Still, I could take no risks.

I tried to pick up the sledgehammer, but my right hand wasn't working. Before I knew it, as Porter struggled feebly on the floor, Sarah bound Porter's hands with some bungee cords the construction workers had left.

"Better this way," she said, subduing him in a most capable manner. She looked at me with worried eyes.

I fell to my knees on the hard wood floor, cradling the injured arm against my chest. Now that the danger was over, pain prevailed. Suddenly Sarah was at my side; then she was phoning for the police. She wrapped herself around me like a cocoon, her love better than a soothing bandage, better than anything I could imagine. "We'll get you to the hospital just as soon as the police come."

Percy Urchfont came back then, followed by the construction foreman and Charles. The other two workers trailed behind.

"What on earth?" Percy asked, indignant. "What have you done to *Vivian*?"

"It's what he tried to do to us, I'm afraid," Sarah answered grimly. She told him what had transpired as my mind raced through Vivian's possible motives. Jealousy? Greed? Hatred? Or perhaps there was *still* more to be learned about the Pepys papers. I said nothing, and noted that Urchfont and Mattingley's faces reflected my own stunned incredulity in almost comic proportions.

After the police came and caught the drift of things, Sarah took me off to hospital. The next few hours passed in a fog of misery. I didn't refuse what they gave me to mitigate the pain, which quite honestly was some of the worst I'd ever felt. My right hand and wrist were shattered, the doctor said, and they had a bit of difficulty deciding how to proceed.

I do remember Sarah speaking over the phone to the police. Later, after the worst was over, two of them came in to the room where the doctor was casting my hand and wrist and asked questions about the attack. Percy came in, too, to apologise and see how I was getting on. He made a point of telling me that he and Charles were personally cataloguing the collection that very afternoon, and for as long as it might take into the night, lest any item be lost. Mostly, however, he spoke in hushed tones to Sarah.

It wasn't until much later, when I found myself in the passenger seat of the Passat with a white fiberglass cast in a sling, that we talked about it. It might have been the pain medication, but as Sarah piloted us away from the hospital and towards the motorway, I began to laugh at the blinding-white monstrosity that encircled my hand.

Sarah glanced over at me, looking almost sick with worry. "Oh *Alex* . . ." She must have thought I was in hysterics. Perhaps I was, but better in any event to laugh than cry.

"Look!" I said, unable to control my mirth as I stared at the overstuffed mitten in front of me. I couldn't have explained why it seemed so desperately hilarious; at the time, it was.

She studied me for a moment, then glanced down at the rock-hard gauntlet and burst into laughter herself.

With the release of tension, I laughed so hard that tears coursed down my cheeks. Sarah must have seen me lift the cast out of habit, as if to wipe my eyes with my hand. This started her on a new round of laughter as she rummaged for a tissue in her handbag.

With great tenderness, she wiped my cheeks and nose. "I love you so much," she said, a quaver in her voice. I saw that her laughter had turned to tears that she was barely keeping in check by biting her lip. At the sight, my own laughter died immediately.

"I'm so sorry about all this, Sarah. Thank God it's over." We rode in silence for a moment; Sarah reached her left hand over and massaged the back of my neck. "The worst thing is that I should have seen it coming. I actually knew, after looking at that document the other night, that Porter's ancestor was the one responsible for the Tangier disaster." I shook my head. "I *knew* all along that neither the College nor the royal family would stoop to violence to achieve their ends. But I just couldn't piece it together."

"Of course you couldn't," she said soothingly. "*No* one could have. And Percy told me something at the hospital that completes the picture: for nearly a decade now, Vivian has been trying to rehabilitate his reputation. It seems he's been working his way out of the role of black sheep into a position of trust as an aide to the royal family. That's why you saw him that day at the Duke of York's offices; apparently they were going to try him out in a small role of public relations for the Duke.

"Percy says Vivian knew all hope was gone when he was hauled off to the police station; he opened up to his cousin. The entire idea of a donation to Dartmouth was a sham, an excuse to get near the real Tangier diary extension and either remove or destroy it. Then he decided you and Mattie had already seen it, and knew he had to destroy you too. Just imagine what the Queen would say when she found out that it was a Porter relation some generations back who disobeyed and then blackmailed the monarch of the day . . . not the ideal credential for gaining employment at Buckingham Palace."

We talked most of the way home, sorting out who had

done what and why. "At least now I understand why all the attackers were English," I said. "*And* why Jonathan never tried to force me to tell him where the papers were: Porter thought he already had them, since he'd stolen the fakes produced by Pettifer. Jonathan must be some sort of generic hired hand for violent, undesirable deeds—spooking the Queen's horse, and arranging my climbing accident on Dead Man's Ledge."

Sarah shivered. "What a nasty character. I'll be glad when they've got *him* locked up."

"You sent everyone away, didn't you—Mattie and Moose, Pettifer—and put me in jail. You were trying to protect us, right?"

"You're much too clever."

"I'm sure Mattie and Moose were thrilled. They've probably taken a premature wedding trip." I smiled at the thought.

At last we pulled into the Orchard. I felt much better just for being home. Sarah put the kettle on and then followed me into the library, where I again found Ian attached to the television. The Queen was standing in a room at Buckingham Palace, evidently just beginning a speech to the nation. "Good evening," I heard her enunciate.

"Hello, Alex, Sarah," Ian said hurriedly over his shoulder. "Sorry . . . just want to hear this . . ."

The camera zoomed in on our monarch's smiling face. "We have just come through a difficult time. There is much rebuilding to be done: rebuilding in the City of London, and rebuilding our trust in one another. But I come before you tonight to tell you that I have never felt stronger, more equal to the task of serving Britain in the twenty-first century than I do at this moment. It is my fervent hope, and my absolute certainty, that I shall have the privilege of serving as your Queen for many more years to come.

"I would ask all of us who share the benefits of our United Kingdom to come together now and put the violence, the unrest, and the division of these past weeks behind us. As we seek the way forward together, let us remember that the strength of Great Britain today lies in our diversity.

"Thank you for the many kind expressions of concern during my recovery. I would like to thank all those who were of assistance." She paused for a moment, and it seemed to me that she was looking directly at Ian. "Good night."

As the camera pulled back and showed the monarch sitting with a very straight spine on an overstuffed chair of royal blue, her legs neatly crossed at the ankles, there was silence. The patter of news commentators began as the screen was filled with a shot of Buckingham Palace, flags flapping in the breeze. It was enough to stir my own patriotism, but one commentator quickly diverted my attention with the words, "*. . . and another member of the royal family is in the news today: Prince Andrew is publishing a book about Dukes of York throughout history to benefit the Pharmaceutical Foundation. We'll air royal correspondent Jeanne Douglass's interview with him tomorrow, but advance reports indicate that the book is entertaining and packed with little-known tales about those who have held the title in the past.*"

Ian turned to exclaim over the excellent publicity for the book and caught sight of the cast on my arm. "Alex!

Oh *no*." I saw that aside from his kind concern for me, he was wondering if the injury would ruin our sailing plans. He knew how much we'd been looking forward to it.

Sarah threw herself into one of the leather chairs and said, "We found the bad apple at last; the source of all the trouble at Dartmouth—one Vivian Porter. Unfortunately, he was *still* trying to get rid of Alex, and me. But this time it wasn't because he thought Alex might know the dark family secrets that would ruin his budding career as a royal servant. Porter had already stolen the fake diary extension from our room in the Hanover Inn; he knew that he was safe on that score. No, Porter wanted to be left alone with Pepys's secret library, so he could see whether there were any more troubling diary extensions in it to ruin his chances."

Ian was speechless. He shook his head, gazing from Sarah to me and back again. Sarah gave him the rest of the details of our extraordinary afternoon, including the contents we'd seen of the hidden library.

"Remarkable," Ian said. "No newlyweds have ever deserved a holiday more."

I caught the meaning of his looks at Sarah; she was easily strong enough, and skilled enough, to sail the boat herself. I had a momentary fantasy of relaxing in the cockpit, legs outstretched, one foot automatically minding the tiller. The *Carpe Diem* gently bobbed and rolled under the brilliant Nantucket blue sky while Sarah unfurled the jib. Her muscles were firm and strong, curving beautifully in all the right places as she braced herself on the deck.

Then she smiled as she came to take the tiller, and. . . .

"I think Alex is already there," Ian said, smiling.

I flew back to reality and had to laugh at myself. This time it was the laughter of pure joy and relief and anticipation.

We'd come through another biblioadventure intact—well—very nearly. If the Head of Special Collections in the sky wasn't going to stop building his compendium of these astounding escapades now that I was a married man, at least I had the only woman in the world who could face them with me, calmly and capably, side by side.

I grabbed Sarah and hugged her tight. A line from Pepys's diary came to me: *"I think I may reckon myself as happy a man as any in the world, for which God be praised . . ."*

. . . and so to bed.

CHAPTER 24

But it seems like a victory . . .

SAMUEL PEPYS

The next day was like reading the last chapter of a book. I sat back and watched a series of events already set in motion unfold—to my great satisfaction.

We were eager to cast away on the *Carpe Diem,* but several essential tasks beckoned. We'd decided upon a one-day delay.

I'd talked with Sarah about making the *real* Tangier diary extension public. She thought perhaps we should, especially now that Porter was incarcerated. Would she mind, I asked, if when I saw the Duke of York about his book, I showed it to him? She thought it an excellent idea, and suggested that for everyone's good, now that the dust had settled, we identify Mattie as the discoverer of the document.

I prepared a fax and sent it to Moose's family's second home in Bermuda, whence Mattie and Moose had rung to say they'd eloped. I informed her that upon her return to Hanover, Mattie would find herself an international literary hero. She was, after all, responsible for finding Pepys's true Tangier Diary Extension.

Only several hours later, I sat across the desk from Prince Andrew, watching him absorb the import of the documents in his hands. "This is *brilliant!*" he exclaimed. The Duke of York had an extraordinary force to his personality that was contagious. "This removes all the stigma from James II—*and* discounts that blasted plague herb tale. I can use this in upcoming interviews, set the record straight at last. Can you think of a better promotional nudge for the book?! *Or* the Pharmaceutical Foundation?"

I had to agree that it seemed heaven-sent, particularly because the book focussed on James II, *and* its profits went to the Foundation.

"If you wouldn't mind, sir—I mean *Andrew*—when you speak to the Press, could you please mention that Ms. Mattingley Harding, Assistant Archivist at Dartmouth College, is responsible for the find?"

"Mind! Alex, I don't think you realise. I'd do anything on God's green earth to thank you for what you've done for us. *Is* there anything I can do for you? *Personally,* I mean—to say thank you?"

"Well, actually . . ." I described the one crisis yet to be resolved.

He picked up the phone immediately and rang his friend at the Royal Navy training centre, smiling as if he anticipated a pleasant challenge. "Duck! How are you? *Excellent,* excellent . . . yes, well, I'll tell you. This time I'm calling not to give, but to take. We've an urgent need for four of your best rowing shells. Eights, mm-hmm . . . no, on loan. An entire fleet's been temporarily incapacitated. Yes, I know it's rather a lot, but in the interest of vital international diplomacy . . . *Me*? Joke?!"

He beamed across his desk at me. "Yes, I *know* it's only weeks 'til Henley. That's why I called you. If anyone could, I knew you could. Look, Duck, I wouldn't *ask* if it weren't frightfully important."

He raised a fist in a small gesture of victory. "*Brilliant.* Right, you'll have to get them to the Dartmouth College Crew, Hanover, New Hampshire, by next week."

I heard the enthusiastic curse where I sat and chuckled.

"Of *course* I know that's in America! Is this the Royal Navy, or what?" He paused. "All right. If that's the best you can do. Thanks awfully, Duck. Good-bye."

He gave me a look of apology undergirded with satisfaction. "He says his men will mutiny if he takes the very *best* four boats just now; they've only received them in time for Henley. But he's sending the ones they've been using right up until last week. He says some of the men want to keep them, in fact, since they did so well with them over the last three years. Now they're yours until you get your fleet rebuilt."

"Thanks ever so much, Andrew. I do appreciate it."

"I haven't even *begun* to even the score. We all owe you a great deal, Alex."

Elated, I stopped outside the door to ring Blake, still clutching the papers I'd taken to show the Duke. It would be early morning in Hanover, but . . .

A sleepy voice mumbled, "Hello?"

"Blake! Got your boats, my friend."

"Alex? Is this a joke?" He sounded wide awake now.

"Absolutely not!"

"But, that's *great!* I can hardly believe it!! How'd you do it?"

"You'll never believe me. They're coming from the Royal Navy—four of them, as a loan 'til we get our own. But Blake. Tell me. How will you keep people from wrecking them?"

I wanted to hear *his* version; I'd been in touch with the alums we'd seen the day of the reunion row, and knew they'd taken action.

"Oh, man—you wouldn't believe it. The coach and the Friends of Rowing alums have been all *over* us. They're actually staying here in Hanover, holding *nightly* meetings with us until it's all worked out. They've assessed fines for the destroyed boats, and they've called in professional arbitrators to work out the issues between the different crews. I don't think anyone would *dare* damage another boat. Financially, even. If you know what I mean."

"Great. You know the offer still stands for Henley, right? Good. Let me know when your flight is, and I'll come pick you up. Right—bye."

In great high spirits I headed for Bedford Square and Plumtree Press, where we had an important visiting author. I had the feeling of watching the last in a line of dominos fall into place . . . and I could hardly wait for them to do so, so I could be off on the holiday of my life.

I greeted Dee and climbed the stairs to the conference room, and there he was.

"Hello, Pettifer."

He got to his feet almost nervously, as if afraid I might be angry with him. I shook his hand. Now that I studied him in a certain way, he did look a bit like Frankenstein.

"I'm delighted that Timothy could get you over here," I said. "We're all very pleased about your book."

Pettifer looked relieved, and quickly assumed his normal attitude of confidence, even superiority. Sticking out the Frankenstein jaw, he said, "Good, good. Happy to be here."

I'd told Timothy earlier that I would need to speak with Pettifer privately; would he mind if I stole his author for lunch? Always a good sport, Timothy had agreed. I took my old professor to Le Chateaubriand in Charlotte Street. When we were seated in the quiet, dark eatery, our orders taken, Pettifer smoothed the tablecloth with his hands and broached the subject, his eyes darting to and fro.

"I'm relieved you're not angry, Alex. There's quite a lot you *might* be angry about, from me producing the fake document in the first place, to including that bit about the plague herb . . . I just wanted to find out, once and for all. I won't live forever, you know—and I've spent years tracking down every last bit of information on the subject." He smoothed the tablecloth again. "Lane told me you came to the house. Thank you."

"Good heavens! Of *course* . . ."

"I apologise for causing everybody worry," he said. "Including my own son."

"Please—as far as I'm concerned, don't think of it again. Everything worked out beautifully, didn't it?" I pulled out the rigid folder containing the true Tangier diary extension and handed it to him. "Before the meal comes."

He looked puzzled, but took the folder, opened it and saw its contents. Gingerly, he pulled out the pages and read them. "The maid. The *maid* didn't know speedwriting," he said in wonder. "Of *course*! Good heavens, that was stupid of me." He was half-laughing; I admired him for being able to laugh at his own mistakes. He raced through the document, then read it once more, carefully, shaking his head. "The plague herb story *was* a farce, then. Unbelievable." He looked up at me. "What are you going to do with this?"

"We're going to make it public, through Mattie. I'm hoping you'll personally take it back to her, for storage at Rauner. That seems the best way. In a way, she was responsible for Sarah finding it."

"Sarah?"

I nodded. "In the cider press."

He closed his eyes briefly and sighed. "The cider press . . . All the days I spent in that barn, and I never looked inside the cider press. Ah, well."

Then he raised his glass of claret. "To Pepys!"

"To Pepys," I agreed. "And to the author of another *fine* diary destined for success, Pettifer Bartlett."

He smiled and drank.

I don't think I will soon forget having so pleased my own professor.

CHAPTER 25

*The truth is, I do indulge myself a little the more in
pleasure, knowing that this is the proper age of my life
to do it; and out of my observation that most men that
do thrive in the world, do forget to take pleasure during
the time that they are getting their estate, but reserve
that till they have got one, and then it is too late for
them to enjoy it.*

SAMUEL PEPYS

With a start, I realised I was living my fantasy.

I sat relaxed in the cockpit, one leg outstretched, foot
automatically minding the tiller. The *Carpe Diem* surged
forward, slicing through the waves under the brilliant
blue Nantucket sky. I'd watched Sarah walk nimbly to the
bow and begin to unfurl the jib . . . the muscles in her
long brown legs stood out as she braced herself on the
deck.

She saw me watching her as she came back to the cockpit. "I know that look . . . you're dreaming again."

Grinning, I shook my head. "No need to dream. I'm
just trying to believe that this is all real."

"Here. Let me convince you that *I'm* real." She brought
her lips close to mine, brushed them against my mouth,

and we settled in for a long, luscious, utterly convincing
kiss.

I turned the boat into the wind and the sails luffed,
flapping wildly. We slid down onto the teak latticework of
the cockpit floor as the boat gently, rhythmically, rocked.

No, I thought, this was no dream . . . this was much,
much better.

ABOUT THE AUTHOR

JULIE KAEWERT worked for book publishers in Boston and London before starting her writing career with a London magazine. Her series of mysteries for booklovers has topped the mystery bestseller list around the country. She is the author of *Unsigned, Untitled, Unbound, Unprintable, Unsolicited* and *Uncatalogued*.